I0552784

JOURNEY OF DARKNESS

Dragon of Eriden Book 2

SAMANTHA JACOBEY

Lavish Publishing LLC

Contents

Prologue

"EXPLAIN YOURSELF!" Gwirwen bellowed, his ghost white body tense with rage. Squaring off at the younger male, he waited.

Pardodan and Vaudien had returned to the cliffs ahead of Lamwen, professing his demise at the hands of the satyrs, making his return awkward at best. A group of dragons were gathered in a circle, surrounding them to witness the interrogation and to hear what their witness had to say.

The morning sun still some hours away, a fire burned in the center of their gathering, lit to hold the darkness at bay. It added shadows to the proceedings, which danced eerily off the colored scales and wings of those in attendance.

Standing on the rocks of Adiarwen, the captain of his king's guard appeared sedate; a tribute to his level-headedness and mental fortitude. His body ached, but he showed no sign of his fatigue, no outward hint at the pain he suffered.

Below them, the waves were calm as they lapped against the rocks, and the night seemed to be at peace around them. Listening to the rhythm of the surf, Lamwen considered his response, unhurried by the king's angry rant.

When he had left the glen, he had been determined to make it home despite the extent of his injuries. His green scales sleek against his slim form were streaked with gashes and blood, and yet he had been called before the council as soon as he had returned rather than sent to be mended by the elves.

1

Treated as a prisoner, like a traitor among them, he felt the tension in the air. He desired to share what he had learned, but the king's reception had given him cause to be less than forthcoming. Unsure as to the cause of the sudden distrust, he refused to let it break him.

Their captain had been among the most trusted in their company, so such a hasty turn had seemed unlikely. His eyes narrowed, he wondered if they had lost faith in him over this series of events, this altercation with Esterbrook. Or had something else brought his fall from grace?

The captain had earned his rank by guile. Strength and cunning were his weapons as surely as claws and flame. Whatever had the latest king squirming, Lamwen would discover the truth and remain careful of what he revealed in the same. Holding the pause, he waited, ready to answer what had been asked when *he* had decided to do so.

Curling his torn wing tightly to prevent further loss of his precious plasma, he lowered his head. "Are they not our allies?" he finally breathed.

"By the narrowest of margins," Gwirwen growled, his burning eyes shaded as he studied his captain intently through narrow slits. "And what of the humans?" Pacing, the large white dragon swished his tail, sweeping the earth and scattering the rocks deliberately in angst.

"They are with the nymphs," Lamwen declared evenly. "I was bound, nose to tail, and at their mercy. They inspected me after I was taken. Three males and a female from what I saw."

"A female," Ziewen huffed, flames dancing between her teeth. Seated in the circle of the council, she squirmed, and the light of the fire glistened on her orange scales as she fidgeted. "What sort of female?"

"The average sort, I would ponder," Lamwen replied with a hint of sass, his head tilting and illuminating the sharp tips of his massive horns. "Mortals are one and the same I should suppose." He did not like being questioned by the dragoness, and her being the king's mate was cause to appreciate it even less.

"Yes, but this one. Had she any features you can describe?" their queen insisted, her words clipped as her passion rose. "Do not hesitate in your reply," she insisted with a huff of dark smoke.

"You mean the flaxen mess atop her head and the paleness of her flesh?" Lamwen replied evenly, toying with her as he recalled the mortal who had stood bravely before him and prevented his murder. He could picture every element of her fearless form, but why should the council be concerned with her so? Until he knew more of their reasoning, he would hold the details as tightly as he was able.

Standing, Ziewen gasped, "Gwirwen, you do not think she could –"

"Be silent, my mate," the Supreme Dragon cut her off. "I am certain this female is of no consequence."

"No consequence!" she spewed. "If she is the one and has found a way –"

"I said be silent!" Gwirwen shouted. Glancing around at the others, only a handful knew the specifics of the night he had overthrown Ziradon, the prisoner who would stand watch for eternity atop their great cliffs.

Considering his course of action, the king paced in a large circle, then turned to his previously trusted captain, doubt rumbling in his gut. "Why did they free you? Do the nymphs wish to hold true to their word?"

"I believe they wish us to think so," Lamwen agreed; having seen their weapons, he knew they were armed to stand against the dragons. His wing ached, and he longed to visit the elves for his treatment, if his benefactor could be satisfied before he could no longer make the journey. "But the mortal female had a hand in the persuasion," he admitted in a subdued tone.

"Did she," Gwirwen replied with a twisted grin. "How so?"

"The human males desired my blood, but she prevented them from slitting my throat with their swords." He pictured the young woman who had placed her small hand on the tip of his bound nose. "My lord," he pushed, "I do not believe this girl to be unkind. She preserved my life and presented herself before me without fear."

Ziewen snorted a small puff of smoke, twitching as she listened. Cutting his eyes over at his mate, the king silently implored her obedience on the matter. Aloud, he prodded, "And?"

"And, I believe she is a wielder of magic," he added quietly, curious if the knowledge would seal Amicia's fate.

"A wielder of magic," Gwirwen repeated, returning to his idle pacing. A few hundred yards away, his predecessor slumbered in his stone prison. Pausing his step to glare in his direction, he scowled, then commanded, "We must know more of this mortal of the rim who is gifted with such talent, and yet we do not wish to endanger our peace with the glen. You will follow her, Lamwen."

"My lord," Vaudien intervened, displeased with the choice. Stepping out of the shadows, he groveled, "Perhaps I should be the one to tend this task."

"No," his master replied, leaning back on his haunches and stretching to

3

tower above him. "She has shown weakness in his favor. Should the time come, he might use that against her. For now, you will not harm any of the new mortals. Follow them and watch their actions. Report any that should be of particular interest," he instructed. "Especially if they should choose to leave the shelter of the meadows."

"Yes, my lord," Lamwen agreed. "I shall lie in wait for them. As soon as the elves have made me whole again."

Gwirwen glared at him, the source of his injuries requiring further investigation as well. "The satyrs have been armed," he observed.

"Yes, my lord," Lamwen growled, growing weary of their game. He needed to be gone, to fly to the sanctuary of the mountains, and the sooner the better.

Pausing again, their king sat and stared at him. "Were there any other creatures who could have been the source of their new weapons?"

"No, my lord. I only saw the humans there among them, and they could not have provided such devices," he testified, hoping to hurry his departure.

"Yes, then any news of the nymph's dealings with others should be shared as well," Gwirwen tacked on. "We shall need to know who our enemies are, as no friend to us would have done such a thing."

"Of course, my lord," the captain agreed, his wing clenched firmly against his body growing stiff. "May I go now?"

"You may go," his majesty agreed, turning to face his wife, unable to deal with her until the others had gone.

Leaping into the air, Lamwen left the council to their quarrel, as he felt certain the discussion was far from ended. Gwirwen was a secretive ruler, hiding what his servants attended from one another; even the council was often kept unenlightened. *A poor way to run a kingdom*, he surmised as he fought his exhaustion and flew to the mountainside that protected the city of Jerranyth.

There, he would be shown to one of their magnificent gardens, where the elven nurses would tend to his wounds. They were brilliant healers, and it was their station within the kingdom to shield the lives of the dragons who protected the whole of the land.

As his massive wings carried him over the stretches of water and land, he thought about the interrogation and the questions that had been asked. His curiosity over the female had been piqued the moment she spoke to him as no mortal of the rim would or could. He had chosen to keep that bit of information to himself, certain any response would be designed to hide the truth.

Whoever this girl proved to be, she had the king's mate frightened and the king himself anxious. Those two reasons alone were enough to warrant further investigation, and Gwirwen had unwittingly granted him permission to do exactly that.

ONE

Peace in the Valley

AMICIA WIPED at the sweat dripping from her brow with her bare arm. Bent over a rock, she pounded Rey's shirt with the side of her fist, then gave it a rinse in the clear flowing water of the brook that ran through their part of the woods. Twisting it, she removed the excess water and held it up, bright sunlight shining on it through the leafy limbs of the trees above her.

"That should do it," she mumbled happily, adding the garment to the pile of the morning's wash.

Giving them a fold into a tight bundle, she hoisted the wet lump to her shoulder, where she carried them across to the edge of a meadow. Looping around their shelter to the north side, she dropped the load on their long table, wiping at her perspiration as she inspected their latest home. Sturdier than the one they had occupied at Riran, it still did not qualify as a proper cabin, but it would do.

A line of twisted vines and bark ran from the corner of it to a tree about ten feet away and back again to create two levels. It served as her clothesline, and she draped all of the men's shirts across it, spreading them to dry in the breeze.

Tearing around the corner, a satyr ran past, with a bare chested Bally and Animir in close pursuit. "You boys!" she hollered, laughing quietly when they disappeared through the large trees that shaded their cottage and yard.

Hearing her call, Animir pivoted to return and watch her work, while his best friend continued the chase without him. Catching a branch from the tree

7

next to him, he leaned against it, his mind drifting over the days and weeks he had spent in her company.

Animir had met the girl as part of a group of mortals that were taken in by the elves of Jerranyth a few months prior. He had helped them to escape from Lady Cilithrand, queen of the city, earning himself a banishment from the land that had been his home. *Not that I minded*, he thought with a smile. He would do it again if the need arose, as he had come to love the humans as his family. He would be hard pressed if he ever had to leave them, or when the time came that they would leave him.

Appreciating her long hair that had been pulled up against the warmth of the day, he continued the memory, playing it through to the night the satyrs had taken down a dragon over in the next field. The following morning, it was gone; freed on the say so of Queen Preivia, who ruled the glen. Piers had been furious, but Amicia had calmed him, and the two women had come to an agreement. Or rather, the queen had insisted, and Amicia had given in. The group was allocated to a corner of a meadow adjacent to the one that held the sacred rings, and there they had built what they commonly referred to as home.

Leaving the play to the others, Animir exited the line of trees, approaching the girl cautiously. "Would you need a hand this day, Lady Amicia?"

"I wish you'd quit calling me that," she muttered loudly, shaking out Piers's top and adding it to the stretch of line. "I'm not a noble woman, here or anywhere."

"You will always be a princess to me," he grinned, edging closer.

Her frown crinkling her forehead, she recalled that they often referred to her as such; *princess*. They used the term to mock her, she felt sure, after Lady Cilithrand's manipulative offer. Glancing at him, she could see the ripple of muscle across his chest. Pointing at his pale skin, she teased, "At least you're getting a bit of color while I tend the wash."

"And I appreciate your generosity. It is beneath you to serve us," he insisted, closer still.

"Rubbish," she replied, turning and walking briskly away, knowing full well one of them must mind the necessities, and it might as well be her. "Shall we have another lesson this afternoon?" she called over her shoulder when she had put a fair distance between them. She sensed his attraction to her, and it bothered her, just as Rey's notions put her on edge. She seemed to be gaining in admirers but never the one she longed to attract.

"Yes, my lady," he replied with a small bow. "I will arrange the targets for us as the sun passes midday." Leaving her to her work, he returned to his search for Bally and the satyr, so that their play might continue until then.

"Very well," she agreed with a hidden smile, watching as the former crewman entered her line of sight at that particular moment.

Reynard carried his designated pail and followed the path their goats kept to most of the time. They had discovered the creatures lived in small herds scattered across the glen, and he had demonstrated his abilities to create creamy delights using their milk soon after their arrival. He would gather some of their warm lactation and ferment it into a delicious cheese, which they all enjoyed.

At least I'm not completely alone in caring for the group, she concluded with a satisfied smirk.

Leaving Rey to his chore, Amicia ducked into their cottage and tackled the beds that lined the walls. Shaking out the blankets, she freshened each one in turn. They had constructed a mattress from dried grass for each of them, two on the left wall for Animir and Bally, two on the right wall for Rey and Piers, and those on the back side for Ami and Oldrilin, when the siren wasn't with the nymphs.

Ami's end had also been given a curtain, which afforded her a certain degree of privacy in their shared quarters. Not so much as a second room would have done, but enough she felt content in their efforts to respect her as the woman of the house.

In the center of their cabin, a small basin had been dug in the dirt floor and lined with smooth stone. It housed a smoldering fire, which they stoked for cooking on the sturdy frame that hung over it. They could have also used it for warmth, but being on the southern tip of the continent, it was unlikely that would ever be necessary. Like Riran, Esterbrook enjoyed perpetually warm weather, and being off the shore, even more so.

In the front corners of the room stood other requirements. On the right, at the foot of Reynard's bed, Piers had added a small table with two chairs. On the left, a permanent closet for her chamber pot had been installed with thatch walls to separate it from the main room. The Mate had claimed it was for all of them, but she had seldom seen anyone else use it, as the men used an outhouse built in the woods at the end of their meadow. Lifting the pot, she carried it out for the daily dumping and cleaning that kept it fresh.

Returning it a few minutes later, she sat on a bench with the long table before her. She always chose the same seat closest to the cabin door on her right so she could see all that happened out in the meadow. The others respected her choice and never took her seat from her.

Leaning on the flat surface with her elbows, she rested her chin against her folded hands and sighed, admiring the beauty of their surroundings. Any place she could be with her friends would be home, but the glen brought an ease to their lives they all seemed to enjoy. Remembering the night that they had fled Riran, she shivered despite the sun and hoped they would never be forced to leave.

However, living there had been hard for her companions to accept, despite the comforts and ease of their lives. Things were vastly different in Eriden, and although she herself held no desire to return to the rim of mortals, the men had once had their hearts set upon it. When the queen had informed them that none of them ever would, she had felt a deep sadness for them.

Knowing their sorrow, Amicia had done all she could to help them adjust. They were her dearest friends, and she wanted them to be happy in their new life; to accept it as openly and willingly as she had. *I want them to see this is home,* she mentally soothed, confident that they finally did so.

Coming around the corner, Rey held up a large bird, which had been stripped of its feathers and no longer had a head. Dangling it before her by the feet, he grinned, "These wild chickens sure are tasty. I came upon this fellow while following the goats," he beamed. "Thought you might like to start us a stew."

"Aye, then he must have been eager to join us for dinner," she teased with a small laugh. Accepting the carcass, she carried it over to the standing work bench that occupied the other side of the door. Placing it upon it, she pulled out the blade Piers had fashioned for her for cooking and began separating the pieces for the cook pot.

"Shall I bring a few vegetables around?" he asked, eager to.

"Sure, and you can set water upon the flame," she agreed with a smile. "And a pail for my bath if you don't mind."

"I never mind," he agreed with a nod, more than willing to return all that she did for them.

Sauntering around back, Rey gathered a selection of his favorites and carried them to the brook for a wash. Then, placing them on her work bench, he tended to the kettle with a sigh. He would still like to see home one day, the farm he had left behind years ago, but for now, this place would have to do.

The water on to heat, he returned to her to share her time, which was his most favored activity.

"Will my shirt be ready soon?" he inquired, rubbing absently at the thin layer of hair that coated his chest.

"Soon, yes," she chuckled. "I swear, you men act as if clothing never needs washing."

"It doesn't," he teased. "That's what swimming is for."

Shaking her head, she didn't argue and instead chopped the vegetables. Adding them to the pot over the fire inside, she then used her pail to wash her face and neck, then each of her arms before tossing the soiled liquid on the side behind the clothesline.

Ready to depart, she picked up her bow and set the string, then tossed her quiver of arrows over her shoulder. Hiking across the green field, she arrived on the far side, where Animir busily placed colorful leaves and flowers on a large bale of dried brush. The soft material would catch her arrows without damaging them, and they used it for target practice almost every afternoon.

"Someday I'm going to be as good as you," she informed him with a broad smile.

"Indeed, you shall," he agreed, lifting an open palm to indicate where she should stand for the first volley.

Taking turns, they pierced his colorful arrangement, destroying them with their success. Following his instructions as he guided her, her proficiency with the weapon had improved significantly since they first arrived.

In the shadows, unbeknownst to them, a dark form watched the couple. Lying curled between large trees and boulders, his green scales glistened in the patches of sun that reached his rough skin. He had taken up residence in the small woods when construction on their dwelling began, and from his camouflaged space, he could observe all, or near all, that they did.

Their days a boring cycle, he had pondered what about the girl could possibly have frightened Gwirwen and Ziewen so. She arose every morning and prepared a meal for the group of men. She cleaned their cabin and tended their clothes, and every evening she cooked their dinner to eat before they went to bed.

Most afternoons, they ventured over, closer to his hiding place, but never into the woods that sheltered him. They seemed to enjoy the shade on his side of the meadow, and there they practiced their aim with their primitive weapons; it was the closest they ever got to behaving uncivilizedly that he could see.

There was peace in the valley, Lamwen could not deny, and he probably wasted his days spying on such unimportant creatures. However, the rest of the continent, or at least all of the regions to the north, had been coated with the winter's treatment of snow, so there was little else to hold his attention on the continent until spring.

At best, he might have found some sailors who had ventured too close to their shores. Sinking their ships, or in the least turning them away, had always been a favorite past time of his, and he considered almost daily if he dared abandon his post even if only for a few days to have a look around the western part of the mortal's rim.

Knowing he wouldn't risk leaving his charges unattended, he surmised he could also attribute the winter as a reason the group remained in the glen. Therefore, he deduced they would become more interesting once the frosty lands had awakened, and they might be enticed to explore more of Eriden.

Stretching his healed wing, he growled in quiet satisfaction as patches of sunlight danced across the scars. *At least the elves were able to mend me,* he mused. After the satyrs had torn his appendage with their upgraded armaments, that had made his watch over the glen more important as well; at least he hoped that it would. *And eventually I will discern what all of this means in the grand scheme of things.*

Before him, the laughing couple enjoyed their afternoon, but soon the sun had made its track and sank low on the horizon. Gathering their weapons, they trotted through the tall grass, each glowing with exhausted joy at their training success.

Arriving at the cabin, they discovered that Piers and the others had served the stew and were already seated to eat. Zaendra had joined them, as she did many nights, and Amicia decided to take advantage of her presence.

"Shall you share a story with us this evening?" the girl asked with a small smile. Getting any of the nymphs to divulge what they knew of Eriden had been difficult, but their new friend had finally been coming around, giving them details about the kingdoms to the north and northeast of the glen.

"Only a small one," Zae grinned, her dark skin accenting her beautifully white teeth.

"Perfect," Ami agreed, placing her bowl on the table and taking her favorite seat across from their guest.

"I shall tell you the story of the nymphs," Zaendra began, smiling at Bally as she did so.

"I'd rather hear about the dragons," the boy countered between slurps of the thick soup.

"What about them?" the nymph asked in surprise.

"Well, I've been thinking," he replied, dropping his spoon for a moment and using his hands to demonstrate his meaning. "When they fly in, they always bring that crazy storm. You know, flashes of light and the roll of thunder, and that wild rain that whips around and flies sideways," he explained, animating the scene with his fingers.

Gazing at him with wide eyes for a long moment, the girl shrugged. "The dragons do not always bring the storm," she informed him. "For the most part, they are welcome within the glen and visit here often without disruption."

"They do?" Rey asked in surprise.

"Yes," Zaendra nodded. "There is one enjoying the meadow and woods across the way, even this night. He has been stationed there for weeks, but I'm sure you have not noticed," she observed with a disapproving shake of her head, her chin pressing against her chest.

"Because he didn't bring the storm?" Ami perked up, curious as well. "So, what does the change in the weather mean?"

"Well, they are magical creatures," Zae laughed. "It could simply be to intimidate their enemies, unleashing fear into their hearts before the attack comes. Or it could be an extension of their power as they use it against their foe."

"And you say one is hanging out near here?" Piers interrupted, concerned that they might be watched from afar.

"Indeed," the nymph replied with a smile. Shaking her spoon at him, she observed, "I dare say you lot see little of the world around you. Many creatures come and go within the shadow of the forest. Even Uscan pays the occasional visit, but I'm confident you have not spoken a word to him since the night of your arrival."

"Uscan was here?" Amicia gasped in surprise.

"Yes, and has been a few times. Checking up on you, more like, while staying out of sight. I swear, if it's not something you would care to eat, you don't notice much of anything that lives or walks in the woods or glen," Zae finished with a loud laugh.

Her face flushed, Ami shook her head, shame staining her cheeks. It was true, she had not known of the large wolf's visits. If he cared enough to check on her, it would be only right that she welcomed him to their new home. "Next time that Uscan comes, please see that I am informed," she asked in a subdued tone.

"And what of the dragon?" Animir asked, speaking up for the first time.

His features pensive, Piers nodded, "Aye, I'm curious about that as well. Perhaps we should pay him a visit and find out what he's doing here."

"Do you think he will talk to you?" Bally asked with wide eyes. "If he will, I want to come."

"The one they captured the night we arrived wouldn't speak to me," Amicia informed them with a shake of her head. "I tried, but he just laid there, and then as you know, he had been freed the next day. I wonder if he's the same one," she mused, her attention also aroused.

"Well, we could just make one big party of it," Rey laughed, "all gather up and clomp across the field –"

"Don't be silly," Piers cut him off. "If he's here, you can bet it's to spy on us for one reason or another. And you can also bet he's not aware that the nymphs have noticed him."

Her laughter light, Zaendra shook her head. Making the humans understand anything had always been a difficult chore. When it came to something as complex as a dragon, she knew it would be near impossible for their mortal minds to comprehend.

"A dragon may languish wherever he likes," she informed them gently. "If he prefers the meadow while the rest of our kingdom is covered in winter, who are we to demand an explanation?"

The group stared at her, considering her observation. After the pause grew long, the Mate declared, "So, you believe his presence is purely innocent."

"They are the leaders and head of our kingdom," Zae sighed, stirring her bowl slowly. "I think it would offend him should you confront him. Best to let him be. As Bally has said, he would have brought the storm if his intentions had been to seek an altercation."

Nodding, Amicia agreed. "There's logic in that. We should give him a wide berth; stay clear of his side of the woods and the next meadow over, to the west. Perhaps my message of peace held some merit and has been accepted," she finished with a small smile, hoping the others would heed her warning and leave the fire breathing monster next door alone.

14

TWO

Eyes Opened

THE FOLLOWING MORNING, Bally awoke with excitement tingling in his gut. "These breakfast cakes are delicious," he complimented the girl, while sharing a furtive grin at his comrade.

Instantly stiff, Animir shushed him, knowing full well the pair would shortly do exactly what they had been instructed not to.

Grinning at him, Baldwin continued his compliments and chatter, earning him only an occasional glance from Amicia, who had grown accustomed to his tendency to talk a great deal about trivial matters. She had become quite adept at ignoring him.

The air of the cabin felt different to him, as if something in Zaendra's words had changed his perception of the world. His eyes had been opened to the possibilities around him, and this newness gave him a strong desire to know more about it. They dwelled in a magical kingdom, with a dragon taking up residence next door, and he intended to pay him a visit one way or another.

Disappearing as soon as they had eaten and washed, Bally and Animir took the long way around so they could hide within the trees. They typically explored and played behind and to the south of the cabin, but not this day.

"Do you think he'll still be there?" Bally babbled in an excited whisper when they were out of range of the others.

"I'm sure that he will be," Animir agreed. "Zae said he has been there for weeks, so it is likely he will remain until the spring."

15

"Good," Bally laughed, rubbing his hands together briskly. "We didn't get to see much of the one the satyrs took down, and I want to look at them up close for certain. Do you think he will speak with us?"

"Let's have a look before we decide if we are going to talk to him," Animir warned. "A dragon isn't a playmate," he added with a laugh, then warned, "If he takes offense to our presence, all they will find of us is a pair of charred corpses."

Bally laughed at the image anxiously, thinking of Rey's description of burned cows during his story on their raft. It felt like ages ago that the older man had shared the tale. "We won't get burned," he countered, his eagerness undaunted. Walking with a bounce to his gait, he discerned, "We are going to learn all about this dragon. If we make friends, we can visit him every day."

Shaking his head, Animir led the way through a tightly grouped section of trees. *Baldwin will always be a dreamer*, he feared with a chuckle, *but I'll be here to make sure my young friend doesn't do anything stupid with this dragon.* He knew the danger they could stir by merely being in the beast's domain, even if the boy did not.

Creeping through the wooded area on the southern end of their meadow, they continued on, towards the western woods that ran between their field and the next. Arriving on the far side, they pushed through the denser foliage, choosing their path carefully until they came out on the opposite side, where another expanse of tall grass and flowers spread before them.

In the center of it, a group of three large boulders stood, jutting out from the waves of plants that undulated under a gentle breeze. His back against the furthest rock, so that he faced away from them, a massive green form slept.

Frozen in place, Baldwin stared at the creature. Its spine lined with giant plates larger than his hand, they stuck out into a "V" and would impale anyone who attacked from that angle with their sharp points and edges.

His skin a pale green, it shimmered in the morning light. Its side rose and fell as the creature breathed, and for the moment, it appeared to sleep. It held one wing outstretched in a comfortable, haphazard position, a jagged scar accenting the injury he had suffered the night of their arrival in the glen. Listening to his heavy breaths, the two young men glanced at one another, questioning their hiding place and if they dared for more. Their breathing shallow, they pushed their heads up and around, straining for the best view.

"He's magnificent," the Bally declared, recognizing him as the one the satyrs had shot down and held captive. "We should get closer; I want to see all his scars."

"No!" Animir hissed loudly, seizing his arm to prevent his movement. "This is enough. If he picks up our scent, he will know we are here."

"You don't want to talk to him?" Bally laughed, mistaking his friends concern for fear. "I can't believe you're scared."

"I'm not." Animir's fair skin took on a pink hue. "I'm cautious, as we have been instructed not to be here. Come away," the elf insisted with a firm tug on the appendage. "We should at least be out of sight if we are going to observe him further."

Wearing a heavy pout, the smaller of the duo turned and chose a new location a few trees back, where he could still see the slumbering form. "I think we should try to talk to him," he insisted.

"And Amicia said we should leave him alone. Besides, if something goes wrong and he becomes angry, any attack would be our fault," Animir stated persuasively.

"What do you care? I know you don't really like the nymphs, the satyrs, or even the sirens for that matter," Bally teased.

"I like them well enough," he countered, his brow furrowed. "Elves are taught that we are above all such creatures, tis all. Only the dragons out rank us. Besides, I certainly wouldn't want to see our cabin burned to the ground." Craning his neck for a better view, the dragon rolled onto his belly and stretched. "He's going to get up. We should go." Turning, he marched the way they came, fully expecting the other man to follow.

Reluctantly, Baldwin did so, and a few minutes later, they had arrived on their own side of the woods. "We should practice with the swords today," he suggested when they were clear to speak normally. "We need to be ready in case we have to fight."

"Only if we use the sticks," Animir replied. "After your cut, I will never practice with an actual blade again."

Shaking his head, Bally laughed, "You are not as much fun as you used to be. You know my cut was an accident and not your fault."

"And you, my friend," Animir joined in the chuckle, "are a reckless boy who will never change. At least I hope you don't." Grabbing his companion, he half hugged, half wrestled him to the ground as they cackled.

Sitting in her seat at the cabin, Ami enjoyed a midmorning cup of tea and heard their laughter as it carried across the field. Watching the pair as they exited the trees, she knew immediately where they had been.

Biting her lip, she studied them, pondering if she should confront them or inform Piers of what they had done. Lately, their leader took her advice often, but he was still in charge of their group as a matter of principle. *It would probably be best to leave the matter in his hands.*

Before she could decide, a giant wolf padded into view on her right, stopping in front of her work bench and sitting to face her. "Uscan!" she screamed, leaping up to greet him.

Throwing her arms around his neck, she buried her face in his thick fur. The scent whisked her away, and for a moment, she sat on his back once more, Bally in front of her as he carried them to Esterbrook. Sighing, she succumbed to the memory and the joy of his return to see her.

"I've heard you desire an audience," the wolf stated with a formal air.

"Oh, Uscan," she sniffed, standing straight so she could look him in the eye while still clinging to him with one hand. Wiping at her tears, she laughed. "How silly of me. Can I get you anything? Water perhaps, or do you take tea?"

"I've just been to the brook, actually," he replied. Cocking his head slightly, he studied her, noting her changed appearance; older and perhaps wiser than when he saw her last. "Did you have a particular conversation in mind?"

Shaking off her astonishment, she smiled, "Do I need one? I heard you had been paying visits to the glen but had not presented yourself to me. I was quite offended," she teased, still gently stroking his mane as she refrained from hugging him again.

Glancing across the meadow, at the woods on the far side, he only hesitated for a moment, but it was enough.

"You know about the dragon," she said more quietly, her tone less jovial as she realized the real reason he visited the glen.

His gaze snapped to meet hers, and he growled, "The girl without fear. What do you know of the beast?"

"Nothing," she shrugged, releasing her grip on him and stepping back. "We only discovered his presence yesterday, and we have decided to let him be." *Decided, not that all have obeyed*, she lamented to herself.

Rising, he walked to the edge of their yard, staring harder at the line of trees. "I'm afraid my visits have not been of a social nature," he confessed. Pivoting slowly, he asked, "Walk with me?"

"Of course," she agreed, smoothing her flushed cheeks with her palms. Adjusting herself to carry on a serious conversation, she gathered her nerve. "I really am glad to see you," she stated more calmly as she fell into step beside him. "We are friends, after all."

"Yes, one in a strange collection of friends you keep," he observed. Leading her through the stand of trees behind their cabin, he held their pace slow and unhurried. "You have a kind heart, Amicia Spicer; that is for certain."

"Well, it's not like we have found an abundance of humans for us to settle down with," she defended flatly, "and why shouldn't I be kind to others?"

He nodded at her resolve, "There is nothing wrong with caring for those who share your world," he agreed. "And no, you haven't met any other mortals; not that you have been looking for them, either. There is still much of the kingdom left for you to explore."

"Are you saying there are other humans here?" she gasped, taken by surprise.

"A few," he informed her. "They live in small pockets, here and there."

"Because they can't leave," she snapped, angry for a moment that they had been trapped there. "You know, mortals of the rim know nothing of Eriden. If you really wanted to be rid of us, you should simply let us go home."

"And would you leave, my lady?"

Tightening her jaw, Ami considered her reply. True, the others in her company would jump at the chance to get back to their own world, but she would have a harder time making that decision.

"You have done well here," he praised, seeing her indecision.

"Well, I guess that we have," she accepted his compliment with a shrug. "We have the cottage to protect us from the elements. Food in plenty so that we do not starve. Yes, I think we live well here in the glen," she finished without committing herself to anything.

"And yet, you are uncertain," he challenged.

Inhaling deeply, she folded her hands before her. "I have enough," she insisted, not really wanting to discuss Piers or her feelings for him with the wolf.

Letting her hold the secret that was not really a secret, he observed, "I fear your days here will be short lived."

"Because of the dragon," she assumed aloud. "Why is he here?" she asked, stopping and turning to face him. "We really hadn't planned on leaving Esterbrook now that we've settled here; we do not wish for the beast to drive us away."

Pausing his step, Uscan sat on the dark earth, his eyes on the trees above them. "I cannot say as to the why," he confessed, "I only see the connections, not the cause, or his intent for that matter."

"And what connections do you see?" she insisted.

"A group of humans moves into the glen, and a dragon takes up residence one meadow over," he replied, cutting his eyes over at her slyly in a mocking fashion.

Laughing loudly, Ami agreed, "I can see that much for myself. What do you know of the dragons, anyway? Everyone treats them with such mystery. We ask questions, but we don't get many answers."

"They are mysterious," he approved with a nod of his giant head. "In the centuries past, they were the protectors of our lands. Even during the great war, when many stood against them, they treated the whole of Eriden with great care."

"Cilithrand said that some wanted to overthrow the Supreme Dragon, and that was the cause of the great war. Is that really what happened?"

"They tried, perhaps, but they did not succeed. It was only recently that Ziradon was removed from power. I hear he is housed in a great prison, but my eyes have never seen it."

"Ziradon," she repeated, the name feeling heavy on her tongue. "He's the Supreme Dragon?"

"He was," Uscan provided, turning to face her. "Some decades ago, he was taken down from within the ranks of his own house. The kingdom has suffered in his absence, as Gwirwen is less interested in the wellbeing of his realms. I fear dark times lay ahead without our protector."

Nodding, Amicia understood. "That's too bad," she sighed. "So, the dragon here is a spy. Should we try to run him off, or simply let him be?"

"Only a fool would disturb a dragon who has made no quarrel with him. If he is content to watch from afar, you should count yourself fortunate and go on about your days."

"If that's true, then why are you concerned about it?"

His eyes shining, he knew she had seen through the purpose of his visit. "Because four humans, an elf, and a siren are an odd lot, and the dragon only became interested in this meadow after they arrived."

Grinning, she deduced, "He really is here because of us."

"As it would seem," Uscan agreed, standing and continuing their walk. "Besides, you must know why the rim is unaware of our beloved kingdom. Any who have ever seen are not able to return and share the tale. Your friends may desire to go home, but the price for them to do so would be far greater than you can imagine. They may dream of it for a lifetime, but I am certain it will never be allowed."

Laying her hand on his coat as she followed, the girl sighed. "The perfect protection. A door that swings but one way." Her face somber, she paused when a few of their small kids ran towards her. Kneeling before them, she fished a few roots from a pouch she kept about her waist for the purpose and fed them, petting them as they butted against her.

Watching her care for the miniature goats, Uscan drew a deep breath. Her heart open to all creatures, great and small, he hated to say things he knew would bring her pain; it was exactly why he had avoided speaking to her on previous visits.

"Precisely," he agreed. "You will find a place here to live out your days, perhaps even remain here in the glen. Your company will as well, although you may not stay together."

Amicia heard his words but wondered at the depth of their meaning. Inhaling slowly, she released a long sigh as she stood, watching their herd scamper away. It would pain her greatly should any of her companions be lost.

"Uscan," she said softly, "I'm grateful for all that you have done for us. And you are right. I am a collector of odd friends, but none mean any less to me than another. Will you stay with us this evening and share more of what you know?"

"I'm afraid the Shadowlands awaits," he replied, ambling along in the direction he intended to leave by.

"But you will come again?" she persisted. "I have enjoyed our visit," she confessed, happy both for the company as well as his insight.

"I will come again," he promised, noting the sun had passed midday. "Stay away from the dragon," he warned, walking away to begin his journey back to his own kind. Stopping, he looked over his shoulder to find she stood watching his departure.

Seeing him peek, she waved, calling, "Thank you," as he turned and continued on his way.

THREE

Unfettered

"HAVE YOU LOST YOUR MINDS?" Piers shouted, towering over the two youngest males later that afternoon. "You were told not to disturb the dragon. Not even go near him, and yet you have!"

"He never knew we were there," Baldwin stammered, toying with his fingers sheepishly.

"He was asleep," Animir agreed, nodding vigorously. "We kept our distance and did not disturb, no."

Shaking his head, the Mate's blood boiled. They had been part of the glen for months, the last thing he wanted was to have the nymphs suffer for their presence. Glaring at each of them in turn, he snapped, "What exactly did you see?"

"He's the one that was captured," Bally offered eagerly. "He sleeps in the next meadow, near a pile of rocks."

"And?"

"And he woke up," the boy shrugged. "We were hiding in the woods, and we left as soon as he stirred," he gushed, cutting his eyes over at his friend. "He never saw us, I swear it."

"Is that true?" Piers demanded, poking Animir in the chest.

"Yes, absolutely," the elf agreed.

"Do not cross the midline of our meadow again," their leader instructed.

23

"You stay on this side of our field," he stated forcefully while pointing at the ground.

"Aye, sir," Bally agreed, stepping back and preparing to get out of the other man's sight.

"Get your supper and early to bed, both of you." the Mate instructed, then shouted, "Go!" sending them scampering with a wave of his hand.

"I'm sure they meant no harm," Zaendra soothed from her seat next to Rey, as she had also been present at their interrogation.

"I think they should have been punished," Reynard grumbled his opinion. "Going to bed early hardly qualifies."

"They're just boys," Piers observed in a calmer tone, his hand running over his stubble-coated face. "However, the fact that the dragon is here presents many problems for us." He glanced at the dark-skinned girl, and she smiled at him, which only deepened his frown. Turning to the other man, he nodded, "Next time their consequence will be more severe."

"There, you see," Amicia stated in a chipper voice as she prepared their stew. "The Mate has handled the situation, as he always does," she praised.

Rolling his eyes and cursing under his breath, Piers stomped away, leaving the cabin and marching across the field. Reaching the center, he sat down facing west so that the tall grass and flowers surrounded him. Barely able to see over the tops of them from his seated position, he sighed. Watching the dancing waves of green and patches of color, he did not move as the sun sank low in the sky and disappeared. Even as darkness covered the land, he did not leave.

Instead, he rummaged through his thoughts and evaluated his circumstances, and theirs. He had sat with his back purposefully to the cabin and its occupants, but he could hear their sounds as Ami served their meal. The younger males chattered as they still discussed the beast they had been instructed to ignore; *damn them.*

They all seemed happy in the glen, especially the blonde. He could sense the way she fawned over him; making his bed, washing his clothes and preparing his meals. Every choice he made, she applauded, seeing no fault ever in his actions. She did all that she could to instill herself as his wife, or even his lover, and yet he resisted. She was in love with him but only a glorified version of the man within. She would follow him to her death, he felt sure of it.

Covering his face with his hands, he breathed deeply, calming his nerves.

He knew there were words that must pass between them, and he doubted that this night was the best to share his thoughts. However, the dragon changed things; his very presence added an ominous realization to their existence. He had to speak to her, had to put her in her place before things had gone too far and he had no way to escape.

Once the full moon sat high in the sky, he stood and walked slowly back to their cabin. His face scrunched under a heavy frown, he helped himself to a drink from their supply that stood at the end of the work bench, noting that the girl had waited up for his return. "Are they in bed?" he asked.

"Yes," she replied, sitting up straight as she observed him. His back to her, Ami smiled at his knot of hair at the base of his neck, longing to pull it down and run her fingers through it. "Are you ready for your supper?" she asked softly. "Everyone else has eaten, but I saved you a serving."

"Aye," Piers replied, not turning to face her.

His disconnect disturbed her, but she did her best to hide the trepidation. Slipping inside, she quietly brought out the remainder of the stew and poured it into a bowl for him. Placing it before him, he sat facing the cabin, with his back to their confirmed intruder.

Instantly hungry the moment he tasted the broth, Piers scooped the bites rapidly with his right hand, while his left lay in a fist next to the bowl. Washing the kettle and tidying the work bench, the girl waited for him to speak, but he ate in silence. Taking her usual seat across from him, Amicia leaned across to lay her hand over his and squeezed him firmly.

"There there, love," she whispered. "I'm sure no harm will come of their foolishness," she soothed in a soft whisper.

"That's not what has me on edge," he replied, withdrawing himself from her grasp and cutting his eyes up at her without lifting his head. The fire inside the cabin burned, casting an eerie light upon his features through the door.

Swallowing, she studied him, then asked, "Would you like a lamp to eat by?"

"No," he grunted with a shake of his head. Resuming his consumption, he finished the bowl and pushed it towards her. "Has everyone else already turned in, including Rey and the siren?"

"Yes," she supplied as she stood. "Everyone else is asleep," she assured, smiling that he might want to have her completely alone. "Will we have words?" she asked meekly.

"Aye," he growled.

25

Hearing them from his bunk, Rey lay still and listened to their exchange. He always feared the times Piers and Amicia shared; it was no secret she wanted to be his bride, and the younger man felt certain at some point their leader would give in. Holding his breath, he waited to hear what his elder would say to her.

Outside, the couple carried on, unaware they were overheard and spied upon. Taking the bowl and giving it a wash, Amicia placed it with the others that had been cleaned after their meal. Turning to the bucket, she seized the handle and walked around the side of the cabin, presumably to fill it before she went to bed.

His stomach tight, the Mate rose from his seat and followed. "We need to talk," he informed her firmly once they were away from the cabin. "We have something to discuss, and I fear it would be better left between us."

"*Between us*," Rey mocked him, sticking to the shadows, having left his bed and not far behind. Guilt burned in his gut, but he had to know if his chances to have the girl had finally been spent.

Amicia's heart pounded as she paused her step, allowing Piers to catch up. They had been in the glen for months, and they had known each other half a year; could he at last have decided to court her? Her face flushed at the very notion of such a thing. But, as much as she desired it, she doubted that would be his reason to converse.

The woods dark around them, he stopped before her and she smiled up at him. "Walk with me then, while I fetch our nightly pail," she cooed, plying him with her best smile.

Falling into step beside her, the Mate grumbled, "Yes, by all means, fetch your nightly pail. Every day is the same in this despicable place. Almost worse than being trapped on the flat for all those weeks."

"Piers, what is the trouble?" she asked gently, hearing the anger in his voice. "We have a routine. Is that such a terrible thing?" she sighed, slowing her pace as they approached the brook. Her heart heavy, she knew that he had not followed to give her a proposal.

Stopping when they reached the edge, he faced her and glared down at her pale green eyes. "You know I will never touch you, love."

"What?" she gasped loudly. "What makes you think that I desire for you to?"

"You want something that can never be, Amicia," he sighed, grasping her

26

shoulders firmly as if to shake her. "Here, this place, this cabin..." His voice trailed away.

"Yes, this is our home," she supplied, her voice trembling as tears filled her eyes. Thankfully, the darkness would help her to hide them.

"No, it isn't," he insisted with a wobble of his head. Releasing her, he turned his back to collect his thoughts.

"*I'm sorry, Amicia. I cannot be the man you wish me to be,*" the older man's voice floated through the trees on the night air, and Rey inched ever closer, a hint of joy lifting his spirits at the Mate's confession, and the unmistakable sound of a quarrel.

"This is punishment, isn't it," Ami replied stiffly. "Fate dealing me this hand for Rupert's sake," she bit tartly, taking a scoop at the brook with her bucket.

"I don't know any Rupert," Piers spat, turning to face her and leaning against a tree with his right shoulder.

"He was the man you remind me of," Amicia confessed. "Every day he courted me, proposing our betrothal, but I refused him, as you have refused me so callously despite all my efforts to make you a proper wife." If he only knew how deeply she despised the notion of being *proper*.

"There is nothing callous about the truth. I'm an old man, Ami. My days for taking wives and having young are behind me," he shouted, then realized the woods slumbered, and finished more quietly, "and I will not stay here."

"You're leaving?" she gasped. Her eyes wide with horror, her chest ached as if she had been punched.

"Aye, on the morrow," he nodded firmly.

"But why?" she pleaded, no longer holding back the drops of sadness as they stained her flushed cheeks. "We have everything we need here. We should stay the rest of our days and be happy in the ease of our lives." Her thoughts turned, and she remembered the dragon. "And what about our safety? You would leave us to that beast?"

"The ease is exactly why I must go," he insisted, running his hand over his hair and pulling at the knot to free it. His shiny locks falling about his shoulders, he shook them, enjoying the feel of the night air and longing for the sea. "I didn't fight my whole life to end up here, in this wretched place. I don't care what the nymphs say; there is a way off of this rock, and I intend to find it."

"What's so wretched about it!" she bit through clenched teeth, anger seething inside her. "Tell me that, will you?"

"Gah," he fumed. "Stubborn woman. Where's the challenge of the glen? To build a shanty? To wander through green meadows and fields of flowers? There's no thrill in the hunt; the food practically falls upon our table. No enemies to fight, as peace floats about us as if this were a dream."

"The dragon!" she supplied, stepping towards him and shoving her finger in his face. "That's the challenge! You must stay and protect us, as you always have," she finished as a small plea.

"The dragon," he scoffed. "He is no threat to us. He could torch the entire valley with a few simple passes should he desire it," he informed her, waving his hand in the direction of the monster's field. "I'm certain he isn't here for that, and what he is here for is of no consequence to me."

Raking his jaw side to side for a moment, he grunted, "I'm leaving, and that's final. If you wish to go, pack your things. If not, I bid you happiness in the life you have chosen."

Staring at his back as he stomped towards their cabin, Amicia whined, then cried more loudly. She had no desire to leave Esterbrook, but her heart ached with the idea of living without Piers Massheby to share in whatever lay ahead. "And to think this very afternoon, Uscan had warned me our paths might part," she sighed to herself as she hauled the bucket towards their home, such as it was.

Still observing from his hiding place, Rey grinned to himself. Sure, he respected the Mate, but the other man had always stood in his way with the girl. *After he leaves, I can stop standing in his shadow,* he determined to himself; *I'll have a real chance to move up in her estimation. I'll get my turn to court her at last.*

Following behind a few minutes later, the air felt heavy when he arrived back at the cottage. Pretending he had been out for a piss, he exaggerated a yawn and flopped back onto his bed. Staring at the light of the dying fire as it danced on the ceiling, he remained still until he had fallen asleep while dreaming of the days to come in the glen.

FOUR

Long Goodbyes

THE FOLLOWING MORNING, chaos reigned in the meadow. Piers had risen early and had his things packed to leave when Baldwin and Animir joined him.

"But why must you go?" the former cabin boy sulked. "Is it because we disobeyed?" he asked, his heart filled with remorse as he watched the other man prepare to leave.

"No," the Mate clipped. "It's no one's fault. I simply can't stay here any longer. Winter will break soon, and I wish to go north and explore options for getting out of this kingdom."

Animir gaped at him, "You know it is not possible to leave Eriden. Queen Prcivia has even vouched it is so."

"Well, I don't believe you have exhausted every possibility," the older man replied calmly, looking over his pack.

Joining them, Amicia announced, "I'm going with you."

All three of the males turned their heads to gape at her simultaneously, but it was Rey who spoke up, coming through the door from outside. "Have you gone mad?"

"No, I just think it would be best, that's all," she bit harshly. The depth of her devotion to the man who had saved her on more than one occasion could never be doubted.

"Then we're all going," Bally agreed, almost eagerly.

Glaring at the girl, Piers growled, "Don't be silly. The rest of you will

29

remain here in the comfort of the glen. Trust me, if I find a way to get us home, I will return for you."

"Nonsense," Ami replied, turning her back and locating her bag. "I'll pack the food," she announced, her voice filled with excitement she did not feel.

"Amicia, listen to me," the Mate spat, taking her arm and turning her to face him. "It will be dangerous. You've heard enough from the natives. You know I have to cross the desert to get to the north, and even then, there are no guarantees."

"I don't care," she replied sharply, pulling herself free and marching towards the exit. "You said I could come."

"I," he stammered, recalling their conversation. "I didn't think that you would," he confessed. "And certainly not drag everyone else along. Look at what we have here," he said, raising his hands to indicate the shelter and the surrounding lands.

"Exactly," she said quietly as she left the room.

Instant rage filled Reynard's heart, and he turned on the older man, screaming, "How could you do this?"

"I haven't done anything," Piers informed him, throwing his pack over his shoulder and marching out after her. "Ami, you can't come."

Ignoring him, she layered their dried meats that Piers had prepared over the months on the bottom, followed by Rey's cheeses in the middle, saving room for a few loaves of bread on top. "I'm not taking the vegetables," she announced. "We'll eat off the land for as long as we can and keep all of this for when we need it the most, out in the sand."

Glancing up at the men, who stared at her rather than pack, she sniffed, "Bally, you'll carry the weapons again?"

"Aye," he agreed, spurred into action. Locating the swords and bows, he placed everything in a bundle atop the table and bound them with a line to hang on his back.

"Rey Daye go?" Oldrilin said softly, looking up at her friend with sorrow-stained cheeks.

"Aye," he replied, grinding his teeth. Turning to Animir, he declared, "You should return to Jerranyth."

"There is no place for me with the elves," he replied. "I have failed to report our whereabouts since the night we left, and I am certain there is a price on my head. If I go back, the queen will see to it that my fate is complete."

"He's going with us," Baldwin interjected, tossing his bedroll out onto the ground in front of the door. Making the round, he rolled one of the quilts for each of them and tied it into a small bundle.

"All right," Rey agreed, cutting the Mate an angry glare. "Lin, I'll carry you in the pack we made to flee the elf city, or you can walk whenever you like, unless you want to remain here with the nymphs."

Her smile brief, she nodded. "Thank you, Rey Daye. Good friend you always be."

Pausing to lay his hand affectionately atop her head, he nodded his agreement. "Yes, my little siren. Always will we be."

The cabin abuzz with preparations, Zaendra could tell something wasn't right as soon as she arrived. "What's happened?" she asked in a surprised tone.

"The Mate has decided it's time to go," Bally informed her.

Crossing her arms in an angry pout, the nymph stamped her bare foot against the dirt floor of their cabin. "Why would he ever want to go?" she huffed.

"I have no idea," Bally replied, still locating items they might need and seeing to it they were packed. "But the Mate's in charge; when he says we go, we go."

"I never invited you on this journey," Piers shouted over his shoulder. Standing in front of the cabin, he glared at the woods on the far side, pondering if their newest neighbor was aware of their pending departure. "Damn folly, if you ask me," he muttered. One man might slip by unnoticed, but with the whole group, they would find out rather quickly if the dragon were actually after them.

Lining up outside, Amicia had finished selecting their stores. Standing next to him, she asked, "Have you brought the bottles for the water?"

"Aye," he clipped, not looking at her.

She could tell his mood was foul, but at the moment she didn't care. "Look, Piers," she snapped, "You said I could come, and you're not leaving without me, and that's final."

"I'm waiting, aren't I?" he held up a hand to indicate the magnitude of his evidence.

"Right," she spat. "I want to say goodbye to the queen, so you'll all need to wait here."

Emitting a disgusted sigh, he cut his eyes over at her and declared, "Well, we don't have time for any long goodbyes. Go tell her we're off and thank her for the use of their lands. Then get straight back here so we can leave."

Not bothering to argue, Ami left her pack on the table, brushing away tears as she marched through the woods behind the cabin. Coming out on the far side, the sacred rings lay before her, and to her surprise, Preivia stood in the center of them.

The long gossamer material of her dress floating around her on the breeze, the smaller woman waited for Ami to join her. When she had, she announced, "The time has come for your departure, Amicia Spicer."

"Yes," the girl breathed, "but how did you know? It was only decided just this morning!"

Her smile faint, the nymph gazed up at her with her crystal blue orbs, the morning sun glinting off her silver hair. "So special you are," she whispered. "But you have not realized yet what lies before you... or behind."

Confused, Amicia stammered, "No, I suppose not. We wanted to thank you for taking us in. The cabin was lovely, and the meadow, and the brook..." Her voice trailed away and her shoulders shook as she began to cry in earnest. "Damn it," she fumed, clenching a fist and wiping at her eyes.

"You could let him go without you," the queen quietly advised.

Coughing, Ami sputtered, "Never could I do such a thing. Piers Massheby may be a scoundrel, but he has stood toe to toe with danger in our favor. He had our backs when no other was there for us. We could never allow him to make this journey alone."

"Then cry not for what is left," Preivia advised. Offering her hand, she waited for the girl to take it, then gave her a firm squeeze.

Filled with the strength of the smaller woman, Ami closed her eyes and drank in the connection between them. "I may never see you again," she sniffed, her tears subsiding. "I've lost so much," she sighed, thinking of her parents, the ship, and Riran in turn.

"But think of all you have gained."

Peeking through a half-opened eye, Ami studied her. "Do you have a response for everything I could say?"

Laughing quietly, Preivia nodded, "It would seem that I do. Zaendra will be with you; her future does not lie within the glen. Take care of her and know that a special bond is grown between you."

Frowning, Amicia gasped, "I cannot take your maid from you."

"She is not my servant, though she has served me well," the queen informed her, giving her a final squeeze and dropping the connection. "Return to your friends and resume your journey, sweet princess."

Puckering her lips, Amicia agreed with a small nod. Her steps back through the forest slow, she considered the words that had passed between them carefully; for if she had learned anything about the queens of the southern realms, they seldom said exactly what they meant.

As soon as Amicia had disappeared into the trees, Reynard turned on the Mate, pouring out his anger full-force. "Why didn't you just leave?" he demanded. "You told her last night you were going to go. You should have left while she slept and saved her the trouble of trying to follow!"

"How would you know what I told her?" Piers countered coolly.

His fury only heightened, the younger man stammered, "I heard you... I was awake you know, taking a piss," he lied.

"Awake, for certain," the Mate agreed, "listening to words not meant for your ears, more like. I fully believed she would remain behind with the rest of you. How was I to know this would be her choice?"

Glaring at him, Rey faltered, "How could she not?" The air caught in his lungs, he felt as if he'd been kicked. "She loves you, Mate." Blinking a few times, his face crinkled as if he might scream or cry. "She does! She would never let you leave without her, and she will *never* be mine!" he shouted, unleashing his pain.

Shaking his head, Piers remained calm. "She may love me, but she loves you as well. She doesn't see it; my star has blinded her to all other light. But it will pass, and one day she will realize what has been hers all along."

Wiping at his tears, Rey glanced at the others who stood around him, gaping at his display. "What's everyone staring at?" he bellowed. "Haven't you ever seen anyone mourn before?"

"She's just a girl," Bally replied, shaking his head in disbelief.

"She isn't *just a girl*," the older man mocked his words while clenching his fist and displaying it for him. "She's the woman I wish to make my bride. To have for all my life and to hold through all the nights."

"If that's true, then you must be patient," the Mate stated with a smirk. "Now, look around and make sure we have everything. We'll leave as soon as our girl returns."

Holding the scowl, Rey hated the way Amicia had been referred to as *our girl*, but he had to admit, it was an accurate description. She cared for them all, and they all cared for her. "Don't tell her I cried," he requested meekly as he used what remained in the pail to wash his face.

Grinning at him, Animir agreed, "We will keep it to ourselves."

Making another pass through the cabin to calm himself, Rey gathered Amicia's personal items, slipping her brush and mirror, dagger, and what remained of the writing items into his bag. Then, presenting himself out front, he dropped the full pack on the ground and toyed with the empty one that would carry the siren when the time came.

Taking her place beside him, Zaendra placed a smaller bag at her feet and leaned on a long stick formed from the limb of a tree.

"What are you doing?" Rey demanded, glaring down at her.

"Waiting to leave," she replied smugly, her dark button nose raised into the air as she stared straight ahead.

"You can't come with us," he countered, looking to the Mate for support.

"Don't look at me," the other man replied with an upturned hand.

At that moment, Ami rejoined them, oddly cheerful as she hoisted her pack. "Is everyone ready?" she inquired. "Zaendra, you have your things?"

"How did you know she was going?" Bally demanded in surprise.

"The queen told me," Amicia replied with a full smile. "She helped me gain a little perspective," she informed him, and she patted the shorter girl on the shoulder.

"Good, then I guess we can be on our way," Piers observed, still half expecting to be attacked by the flying demon before they ever cleared the glen.

FIVE

Circle of Friends

LYING in the woods across the way, Lamwen watched as the group gathered their gear and left the cabin, walking in single file just inside the line of the trees. They were headed north, towards the open end of the valley, and it wasn't hard to decipher where they would go from there.

The morning sun warming his scales, he had been awoken early by the heated discussion that preceded their departure. If they had intended to sneak away, they had failed completely in that respect, and he had been aware of their movements since daybreak.

"Silly mortals," he chided, exiting his hiding place and returning to his meadow for a nap.

He would have no need to watch their every move; he knew exactly where he would locate them, when he was ready. The question was, would he alert Gwirwen to the new development?

As far as the king knew, Lamwen kept an eye on the humans for him and would inform him if and when they left the glen. However, after having lain in the sun observing them over three moons, he had developed a few theories about the Supreme Dragon's fear of the girl; theories he would like to test before he informed his leader of anything.

Stretching out next to his favorite rock, he blew bits of fire into the air and watched the rings of smoke that formed float into the blue sky. *The girl is special,* he surmised. *That's why Ziewen had been so concerned about her but not the males.*

With Amicia being a wielder of magic, her bloodline could not be too distantly removed from Eriden. It would be impossible for a true mortal to use the shell. *Unless she were a wizard,* the thought occurred to him. *But female wizards who can use magic are extremely rare,* he turned in his mind once more, still searching for the right clue.

Rolling onto his side, he drew a deep breath and growled loudly as he released the air. *So, what else could she be? She had certainly smelled of mortal flesh and blood,* he acquiesced. *Perhaps she has been forced into the form of a human.* He toyed with the idea for several minutes before finally falling asleep, the answers still beyond his reach.

Awakening with a start hours later, the sun had moved far west and hung low in the sky. On his feet, Lamwen's heart raced with excitement. Leaping into the air, he followed the path he felt certain the humans would have taken, as there were only a few that led to the desert but avoided the mountain of the elves. After several miles, he spotted them, as they were making camp near a small pond.

Laughing to himself, he contemplated his next move. During his sleep, the answer to his conundrum had come to him, and he felt certain he knew exactly who the young maid was, or once had been.

For now, she was a delicate, mortal flower, with wild blond hair and a warm heart for lesser creatures. *Yes, her devotion to others gives her away even if she is unaware of her past life,* he assured himself as he settled into a nearby forest and hunted down a meal. *But soon, she will be enlightened, which is only fitting that she should know her name before she dies.*

"Everyone gather round," Piers called. He had started the fire and placed the kettle of water atop the embers. "I still can't believe you brought the cookpot," he chuckled, shaking his head at Baldwin.

"I thought it might be nice to –" he tried to explain before his leader cut him off with a raised hand.

"I'm joking," the Mate informed him. "It was good thinking, and for once we had a bit of time to plan. Thank you for the addition," he praised, glancing at Rey, who had saved the day when they had left the sinking ship. "If I were

36

ever to choose who I wanted to be stranded with, this group right here is exactly who I would pick," he said more quietly.

Smiling covertly, Ami added the wild herbs and vegetables she had gathered to the stew, as the water containing the cleaned rabbit meat had begun to boil. Dusting off her hands, she found a seat on one of the rocks they had rolled into a circle around their fire and observed, "It is better to travel when we're not on the run."

Looking up anxiously at the sky, Rey and the Mate shared a knowing glance and then laughed in unison. They had both been expecting to be overtaken by their nemesis at any moment, but so far, they had not seen or heard from the beast.

"Perhaps it will remain so," Rey observed, giving the other man a nod before he pushed. "So, old man. Where do we go from here?"

"North," Piers informed him with a bob of his head. "We have that desert we must cross, since we can't go through elf lands, and that will take some effort. I figure if we gather as much food and water as we can before we get there, we should make it ok."

"Many miles will it be before we reach the oasis," Zaendra informed him while warming her hands before the flames.

"Have you ever seen the desert?" Baldwin inquired. "I've never seen one."

"No," the nymph shook her head but smiled. "I have only heard of it, but I have longed to see it. The glen is a beautiful place, but there is so much more of Eriden to be seen."

"Is that how Preivia knew you would want to come with us?" Amicia asked quietly. "Have you always dreamed of traveling?"

"I thought the nymphs and satyrs never left Esterbrook," Rey observed with a shrug.

"Most do not," Zae nodded. "But for some of us, the wilderness calls. I have known since I was young that I desired to see faraway lands. But to have companions for travel, that is more difficult to come by," she informed them, her dark brown orbs dancing mysteriously in the fire's glow.

Dropping her arm across the smaller girl's shoulders, Ami grinned, "Well, I'm happy you have chosen to join us."

Rolling his eyes, Piers held his tongue, as any words he shared at that moment would more than likely start a fight. Instead, he stood and gave the pot a stir. The water boiling, he knew it would still be a while before the meal was ready to eat. Clapping his hands together as he reclaimed his seat, he announced, "I guess we have arrived at story time."

Laughing, his three mortal companions looked at one another, then pointed back and forth as they decided who would go first. Watching them, an odd sense of correctness stirred within their leader. He had not felt at peace since they began building their cabin at Esterbrook. However, getting underway had set things right, and having the others with him had made it only more so, no matter how much he complained.

Seeing none was eager to begin, the Mate waved his hands to cut them off, "It's ok. I'll tell one, and then one of you can take tomorrow night."

Agreeing with a smile firmly painted on her lips, Amicia studied the older man. Somehow, with the darkness folding in around them, she felt grateful that they no longer cowered in the glen. His eyes meeting hers, he nodded at her, and then he began.

"Once, there was this unbelievably wealthy young man," he said confidently, earning groans from Bally and Rey, as they knew exactly who he was talking about. However, out of respect, they held their tongues.

"And this young man had never spent much time around people his own age," he continued, a bit more quietly. "He never had any friends, and his parents always thought he had to be and act a certain way. But he didn't care what they thought," he laughed.

"He made his own rules and insisted that he didn't need the life they had always wanted for him. So, he sailed away on a ship and spent his time managing cargo," he used his hands to imitate the shape of a large box, "and entertaining the ladies." He again wafted them in the air, outlining the curves of a woman, causing his male companions to snicker. "And he was very lonely," he confessed. "For more than twenty years, that's all his life consisted of."

"And then on one particular trip, one such young lady snuck on board his ship, and she turned out to be… one of the most amazing women he had ever met." He stared straight at Amicia as he confessed how deeply she had moved him. "Then, of course, a dragon noticed she was on board and ripped the ship apart, sending it and the crew plummeting to the bottom of the sea."

The two crewmen groaned, but Zaendra, Animir, and Oldrilin all leaned forward, hanging on every word. Shaking her head, Ami giggled to see how caught up they were in his telling.

"What happened then?" Animir finally prodded when his pause became long.

"Well, they built a raft to escape. The rich boy had become the first mate on that ship, and he stayed behind to fight the dragon while two of his crew rescued the girl. After the fight, he joined them on the flat, and they got away," he replied, holding up his hands as if to end the tale.

"But then what happened?" Zae insisted, certain that wasn't all to be heard.

"Well, after weeks of floating on the sea, they had no food and only water to drink, which they had collected from the rain," he said somberly. "It was hot when the sun shined, cold when the rains came, and the three sailors were very afraid their princess was going to die."

Grinning deviously, the Mate lowered his voice and growled, "But at the last minute, they saw land off in the distance. They leapt into the water and swam hard, pushing their raft towards it. By some miracle, they were able to reach the shore and crashed on a beach, where a group of sirens saved them," he informed her with a wide-eyed stare.

Lin giggled loudly, realizing then who the lost shipmates were. "So scary," she squealed.

"Aye," the Mate agreed with a wink. "They hid in the woods for a few moons, but the dragons soon found them and burned the mermaid lagoon. Running away, they took one of the tiny creatures and fled into the woods, where they met the elves."

Catching on, Animir moaned, "You are speaking of yourself."

"Aye," Piers said again, only this time even more quietly. "But now the boy who never had any friends, has enough to fill his table... and his heart with love," he whispered. "I'm sorry that I threw such a tantrum this morning," he coughed. "I should have known none of you would have allowed me to face this journey alone."

Beaming at him, Amicia shook her head slowly. "Oh, Piers."

"I meant what I said," he declared more loudly. "I'm too old and set in my ways to think about starting a family," he chirped, pointing at her with a stiff digit, "so you can forget about us ever making babies. But, when it comes to friends as good as brothers and sisters, or me ever being an uncle," he paused, gazing at each in turn, "then this is the family for me."

Blinking back tears, Ami couldn't hold her emotions any longer. "Is it that obvious?" she asked quietly.

"Of course, it is," Rey snapped, smacking her gently on the arm with the back of his hand. "But it's ok, we understand," he said with a smile. "Now, do we get to eat?"

"It might be ready," the Mate agreed, rising to give the pot another stir.

On his feet, Bally left the circle in search of his pack, calling over his shoulder, "Well, since I thought of the kettle for stew, I have another surprise." Turning around, he presented the goblets, bowls and spoons that he had also brought along.

"Oh, now we have everything," Piers said with a laugh. "See, I wouldn't have thought of half this stuff if I had been left to my own devices!" Glancing at Rey, he could see the other man's face almost glowed, and he hoped it meant he had been forgiven for dragging them away from the easy life of the glen.

SIX

Matter of Survival

AMI AWOKE EARLY the following morning. The air still, a light fog hung over the ground, but only a few inches high. Holding her head, she pressed on her right temple firmly, where a sharp ache had settled behind her eye. "Shit," she muttered, managing to sit up.

Thin clouds masked the rise of the sun, and the day seemed at odds with the tranquility they had each felt the night before. Enjoying the fire and each other's company, perhaps deeper than they ever had before, they had not slept as much as they should have. In light of this, she easily blamed her foolishness and the late hour for her pain.

Rising next, Piers joined her. "You look as if you enjoyed too many spirits," he teased when she blinked at him.

"My head hurts," she confessed, "but I doubt spirits were involved."

Nodding, he stoked the fire. "Warm the leftover stew and have a big drink of water; see if it helps," he suggested, then set about waking the others.

Soon, the camp was alive with giggling girls and eager young men. The ease of their departure had bolstered their nerve, and they felt confident in their ability to reach the desert, which would be their next conquest in the Kingdom of Eriden.

Scowling at them, the noise seemed to vibrate within Amicia's skull, and she winced with pain.

Rey seconded the Mates opinion. "You look ill, love."

41

Her features drawn, she sighed, "Please don't speak of it. I would not wish to bring everyone else down in our moment of triumph," she suggested with a hint of sarcasm.

Taking pity on her, he fished her hairbrush out of his pack and announced, "I'll help you with your hair."

Staring at the device, her eyes grew wide. "I had forgotten it. I was so upset about the departure, I left it behind," she recalled, growing anxious, "And –"

"And the dagger and the mirror. I know. I gathered them all for you," he informed her while turning her so he could reach her tacky braid. Pulling at it, he freed the tie and brought it down. Running the brush over it, starting at the ends and working his way up, he admired her golden waves. "Remember when I did this for you when we were lost on the raft?"

"Aye," she agreed. Tears in her eyes, she didn't know if they were wrought by the pain or by the tenderness with which he cared for her. When her new bun had been secured, she faced him, catching his hands between hers.

Staring into his hazel orbs, she smiled. "Thank you. I would have been lost without the brush for sure," she joked, making light of her weakness.

"Don't mention it," he returned the grin, only pausing for a moment before he pulled himself away.

Rolling up the quilts, Piers made note of the tender moment between them and tamped down his moment of jealousy. He would remain true to his word, and the other man would have her if he could manage it.

Feeling better, Amicia ate her bowl of stew along with the others, and the pain had been reduced to a dull ache by the time they were packed and ready to depart. Hoisting her bag, she smiled at her lanky comrade who had come to her rescue as he helped the siren into the pouch on his chest.

She had been surprised that Oldrilin had managed to walk the entire day before. Noting that she faced him, resting her head on his shoulder, she knew the mermaid would sleep. "Do you need any help?" she offered.

"No, we've got it," he replied, adjusting his pack and ready to go.

Looking around, Piers waved his hand, calming the group and getting their attention. "Well, this was much easier when there were only four of us," he laughed. "I'm a bit concerned about this fog. We can't see the ground, and we all need to watch our step. We stick together, so no wandering off. If anyone needs to stop, give a shout. We're in no hurry, so everyone just keep your heads and stay safe," he instructed.

Amicia grinned approvingly at his speech. "You make a wonderful captain, Mate."

"Aye," he replied with less conviction than he felt. Taking the lead, he entered the undergrowth on the north side of their abandoned camp with Zaendra, then Animir behind. Bally followed his best friend, with Amicia only a few steps behind him, while Reynard brought up the tail, plus one siren strapped to his chest.

Keeping the pace down, Piers picked their way through easily enough, while hoping the fog would burn off when the sun found its way to the top of the sky. Catching glimpses of him as they moved, Amicia felt better as the day wore on, and her mind turned to other things to ponder.

It had been a relief that Rey had thought to collect her things for her. He had always been there to look out for her, she recalled of him fondly, even the first day he had sat with her and then presented her with her meal in the evening. Always kind, she hated to use the word decent to describe him, as she had seen the characteristic as weak when she had applied it to Rupert.

Thinking of the older man, her memories from further into the past floated to the surface, and she was back in Nalen when Zae screamed in front of her. Closing the distance with a few quick strides, the group huddled on the path as the girl struck out at an unseen enemy with her staff.

"What is it?" Ami demanded as she stood back to back with Rey, turning in a slow circle.

Dropping their load of weapons to the ground, Bally handed them out, shoving Amicia's bow into her hand. "Take it," he grunted.

Closing her fingers around the shaft, she pushed against it and set the string. Then she knelt to retrieve her quiver. "Are they elves?" she asked with a shaky voice.

"No," Piers whispered, "it looked like a small dog or a very large rat. I really can't be sure."

A hissing noise rose from one of the trees, and the group looked up to find an oversized rodent on the limb, searching for a way to get out over their heads. Having claimed his sword, Piers held it up, ready to deal with the beast.

"Wait!" Ami commanded. "Let me try to talk to them," she suggested, recalling her success with the wolves.

"Well, make it quick," he agreed. "They don't appear to be in the mood for conversation."

Using the silver ribbon that held the device, she freed the shell from her cleavage. Pulling her merdoe out through the neck of her shirt, she gripped it tightly and closed her eyes, reaching out with her mind. Finding nothing, she scowled. "I can't get to them," she confessed a moment before one of them leapt upon her back, clearly trying to separate her pack from her shoulders.

Dropping the bag, she used her bow to whack the giant mouse, noting its red eyes that seemed to burn with flame. "It is a rat!" she exclaimed when it had run away.

"Everything's bigger in Eriden," Bally teased. "Remember the wolves?"

"Absolutely," Rey agreed, adjusting his sword in his hands. "It seemed to be after our food. Perhaps we should spill it on the ground and make a run for it while they are gathering our scraps."

"Out of the question," Amicia retorted, setting the nock of an arrow and gripping the string. "We need this food; it will be a matter of survival once we reach the desert."

The group still held the circle around the bag, and Rey gently lowered the siren to the ground, where she claimed one of the fallen quilts and used it to cover her head in fear. "Good girl," he praised, "just hide. Zae, you ok?"

Brandishing her staff like a club, the dark skin of the nymph hid her flush. "Fine time to ask," she growled. They had only seen a glimpse of her anger, but a moment later they witnessed the extent of her rage; a fat brown body darted through the low-lying fog, and she bashed at it with the limb while screaming, "AAAAyaaaa!"

An instant later, a swarm of the creatures seemed to pour in from every side. Arrows flew and swords sang as they twirled through the air, catching the tiny carcasses and filling them with holes.

"Keep them away from you!" Piers shouted after receiving a nasty scratch to the back of his hand.

"Too late," Bally replied, sporting toothmarks across his old scar.

"Kill them all!" Animir rallied, his arrows catching one after another.

Accurate, but slower on the draw, Ami managed to get a few, and the ground was littered with bodies by the time they had cleared the hoard. "Oh my God," she panted, wiping at the blood that coated her face. "Did that just happen?"

"Aye," Piers replied, his sword still high as he turned in a slow circle, waiting for the next wave.

Looking around at the carnage, Bally laughed, "Do you think they're edible?"

"You're kidding me," Rey replied, smacking the smaller man playfully on the back of his head. "We're damn near killed by these things, and you're worried about dinner."

"Well, a man's gotta eat," he laughed, then held up his bite. "Ok, seriously, I almost lost this hand once already."

"Let me see," Zae took charge, leaning her staff against her shoulder and grasping his hand. Squeezing the punctures, she caused them to bleed. "You must be treated," she announced, glancing around at the others. "All of us."

"Treated with what," Piers demanded, standing still at no further sign of the aggressive rodents.

"I know a medicine," she said with a nod. "We must make camp. We need fresh water, and I must hunt for the vine."

Falling silent to listen, they could hear the run of a brook in the distance, and their leader sighed, "Well, then we go that way," he commanded, pointing with his sword. "Pick up our gear and bring a few of their bodies. If Zae thinks they won't poison us, at least we'll have dinner."

Ami wrinkled her nose at the thought of consuming the creatures, but she did not voice her doubts. She could remember a time when she would have gladly eaten the smelliest, filthiest of vermin, and she had no desire to ever be that hungry again.

"So sorry, Rey Daye," Lin's small voice cut through their chatter as she offered him the cover she had hidden beneath, which was now splattered with blood.

"It's all right, love," he soothed, accepting the article and rolling it into a loose ball. "We'll wash it if we can. At least you were safe." Scooping her up, he carried her as they followed the Mate through the thicker greenery.

It took the better part of an hour to reach the sound of the running water, but when they did, the sight of it stole their breaths away.

"Oh my," Amicia whispered, taken in by the small water fall that spilled over about four feet above the ground, which gathered into a pool. Fifteen feet long, it then fell away onto a steep slope, cascading into a frothy torrent as it was swept away into the brook. "This is magnificent!"

"Aye, and we never would have noticed it if we hadn't been attacked," Piers agreed. Locating the axe, he began clearing away the area around the edge so they could gain access.

"You don't suppose animals use this pond," Rey suggested in a concerned tone.

"Doesn't look like it," the Mate replied, still stripping away what he could. "The foliage is too thick. Let's get the drinking water from up top, and we'll use this in the lower pool for the baths. The rocks down below will be good for the wash."

"I can climb it," Animir offered, locating a few handholds he could use for the task and making it up to the next level with minimal effort. Pivoting, he accepted the elvish wine bottles and their cook pot to be filled.

Below, Zaendra wandered around, in and out in a slow circle. Her eyes sharp, she gave a happy shout when she had located their cure. "Bally, come come!"

Following the sound of her voice, he joined her, then grunted, "This one?"

"Yes," she confirmed with a nod. "Cut it down and bring it to the camp."

Thick juices coated his fingers as he separated the dense strand from the limb of the tree. "Oh, dear God, this thing smells horrid!" he announced at the top of his lungs. Carrying the long strip, folded so both loose ends were up, he used his free hand to pinch his nose.

"Oh," Ami agreed with a small belch, "I'm going to be sick." With quick steps, she darted out of the camp the Mate had been clearing.

"Oh, no," the elder intervened, "we'll have to cut that up outside of camp. Are you going to cook it? Maybe that will remove some of the smell," he offered.

"No, we crush it," the nymph informed him, grinding a fist into her palm to demonstrate.

Holding up his hand, he stopped her. "Ok, I don't want to know. Just... make the medicine and be sure all the wounds get treated, no matter how small. We can't afford for anyone to get sick, even if we have to spend a day or two here... dealing with this," he finished with a small scowl.

Returning to the group, Ami suppressed her urge to gag. "Everyone, peel off your clothes, and I'll get on with the wash. Zae can whip up that remedy, and one of you guys can get a fire going while the other makes dinner," she suggested.

"Sounds like a plan," the Mate agreed, only marginally pleased with it, but what else could they do?

"I need a knife," Zae requested meekly.

"Here, use Ami's dagger," Rey offered as he slipped off his shirt and pants, presenting them to the blonde and the blade to the nymph. Standing in his undergarments, he shivered. "Hey Bally, how's the fire coming?"

46

"I'm on it," his best friend replied, blowing the sparks into a small flame. He had gathered a small stack of loose wood, and announced, "Ok, I have enough to get us going but we're going to need..." His voice trailed away as Piers added a few more logs to his reserve. "Ok, fire's good."

By the time the sun had set, the group had managed to remove the blood from their clothes the best they could, and the outfits all hung from vines stretched between the trees. Wearing only their undergarments and wrapped in their blankets, they had washed and sat waiting for their nurse to apply her salve.

"Eww," Bally observed when the girl dipped her finger to taste the mixture she had been crushing in one of their bowls with a rock.

Giggling, she stepped towards him, offering the creamed vine. "It's ready," she announced. "Hold out your hand." Wiping the pale jade-colored goo over his scar, she coated the new wounds carefully. "Any more?"

Presenting a few other scrapes and cuts, he made his best effort not to vomit as she treated him. "So, are we eating them?"

"Aye," the Mate laughed, presenting himself next for coating. "Think of it as justice served for attacking us," he mused as he handed Bally a bowl.

Making the rounds, each member of the group received their ration of vine ointment followed by a fresh bowl of vermin stew. However, their pleasant mood was gone, as they had come face to face with the danger that had awaited them outside the peaceful glen.

"Do you think we should go back?" Bally asked when they had settled into semi-comfortable positions for sleeping.

"Go back?" Ami repeated, as if the thought had not even occurred to her. Glancing around at the others, she could see that Baldwin was not the only one with doubts. "What do you think, Mate?" she asked when her gaze fell upon their leader.

Taking his time, he stoked the fire, then relaxed into a reclined position. "I think we need to be careful," he stated firmly with a nod. "But, we won't ever get out of here if we go back."

The correctness of his observation sinking in, the group fell into a few minutes of deeper thought before Bally agreed, "Ok, so we don't go back. I just hope we don't have to fight off any more giant rats," he sighed, turning his back on the fire and closing his eyes to get some sleep.

Watching the Mate, Amicia shivered. "Is everyone going to sleep, or is someone going to keep watch?"

"I'm keeping first watch," Rey advised, giving her a small wave. "When the moon sets, I'll wake the Mate, and he'll take second."

Smiling at their plan, she snuggled deeper under her blanket. She hated the thought they weren't safe when they slept, but it would have been folly to try and do so without a guard.

SEVEN

Foreboding Forest

SITTING ALONE in the darkness while the others slept, Rey selected a thin strip of vine to toy with. Picking off bits from one end, he tossed them at the fire, enjoying the small pop that each one made as it was incinerated. Peering through the dancing flames, he stared at the girl who slumbered straight across from him.

His heart skipped a beat when he recalled they had shared a moment that morning, albeit brief. She had seemed deeply happy that he had remembered her things, and brushing out her hair had been a true labor of love. Fond of many of Amicia's attributes, her golden mess of frizz had to be his favorite.

Restless, he climbed out of his bedding and stretched, then carefully stepped between their bodies and scaled the rocks to fetch himself a drink. Peering upstream, he could see the water glisten at each level as it cascaded down the mountain, forming small pools between sections of rocks where the water tumbled to the next level below. The waterfall amazing, he grinned at their luck at finding it before the memory of the rodents wiped the smile away. They were no longer on the rim of mortals, and forgetting that fact could at some point cost them their lives.

Pushing his way through the brush, he found a spot to take a piss before he made his way back to the fire. Stoking the flames, he checked the moon and then gave the Mate a shove. "Hey," he whispered, "your turn."

49

"Umph," the older man grunted, pushing himself up to sit. "Anything going on?"

"Nope." Rey reclaimed his seat and pulled the blanket up to cover his bare legs. "You think our clothes will dry? It's not exactly warm here."

"They'll dry," Piers assured, stretching and searching for his bowl to fetch water. "Get some sleep, son."

Leaning back against the tree behind him, Rey didn't argue. Closing his eyes, the next thing he knew, Lin was bouncing on his chest.

"Happy Rey Daye," she sang.

"Yes, happy day," he laughed. Sitting up, he looked around, finding that they had let him sleep longer than everyone else, and he was the last one awake. Standing, he located his clothes and felt them tentatively. *What do you know, they are dry,* he mused, pulling them from the line and shoving his legs in the stiff bottoms. Tugging the shirt on, he asked, "What's for breakfast? More vermin stew?"

"Bally caught some small fish upstream," Ami replied. "I saved a few strips for you if you would rather have them," she offered.

"Thanks, I'd definitely go with the fish," he laughed, then countered, "not that the stew was bad."

"Yeah, I know. Desperation dinner," she agreed, presenting the thin slivers of meat. Looking up at him with her large green eyes, she smiled as he took them, then turned away to continue her packing.

An hour later, they had regrouped, with all their gear stowed once again, only this time Bally didn't carry all of the weapons. Instead, he carried the bedrolls, which had been folded into one large bundle, and each group member brandished a weapon. That way, if they met any more undesirables, they would be ready for the fight.

Leading them out, Piers didn't bother with any speeches; they all knew what was expected. They didn't need reminding what would be at stake if anyone got careless. Behind him, each reclaimed his or her position, and they trod along through the thick brush well into the afternoon, when they came upon a wide clearing that resembled the meadow they had left behind.

"Well, this is an odd place," Rey observed once they had gathered on the edge, with the open expanse before them.

"Indeed," Piers agreed, staring at the woods on the far side. "Is it just me, or does that remind anyone of the Shadowlands?" he asked, only half joking.

"It doesn't look pleasant," Ami agreed, fishing out her magical trinket. "If we can have a break, I just realized I have left the glen, but Uscan might expect to see me there."

Scowling, the Mate asked, "Can you reach him at this distance?"

"I won't know until I try," she replied with a grin.

"All right," he approved. "Let's spread out and see if we can find some water. If so, we'll make camp here tonight and take on the next foreboding forest on the morrow."

"Foreboding forest," Bally parroted, laughing as he did. "Come on Mate, it's not that bad. Just a bunch of trees, you know."

"Aye, and giant rats," Rey corrected, also disturbed by the woods they would enter next.

Choosing a large rock, Ami climbed up and sat, pulling her knees to her chest. Holding her merdoe within her right fist, she squeezed the left around it and closed her eyes.

"Uscan," she called, her thoughts echoing his name.

"Amicia," a voice replied, causing her heart to beat faster.

"Is that you?"

"Who else would it be?" She could hear his deep laugh.

"I'm so glad I could reach you," she confessed. *"We've left the glen,"* she informed him hesitantly. *"A couple of days ago, in fact, in case you wanted to pay me a visit."*

After a long pause, his voice asked, *"Have you reached the desert?"*

"No, we ran into trouble with some large vermin. We handled it though and have put another day in of walking."

"So, you are safe."

"Yes," she agreed with a nod, forgetting he could not see the gesture. *"We are spending the night in a clearing, I think, and will enter another forest tomorrow. It looks like the Shadowlands from here,"* she informed him with a laugh.

"Dark?"

"Yes."

"Dense?"

"Very," she agreed.

"Be careful, Ami," he warned.

Her breath growing shallow, she opened her eyes and stared at the trees across the way. *"Do you know this place, Uscan?"*

"Perhaps. There are places in Eriden that have been cursed, like the Shad-

owlands, and others where the trees trap the light and steal it from the ground below. Nothing grows there, save the haunted trees."

"Oh my," she gasped. *"Is it safe for us to enter?"*

"Carry a light," he instructed her.

"I wish you were here," she whispered, fear causing her to tremble.

"You must ask," he replied.

"I must ask?" she repeated. When he didn't answer, she pushed, *"If I ask, you will come and travel with us?"* she clarified.

"Yes."

The others had searched the clearing and discerned that no water could be found. Gathering around her, they were watching her come out of her trance and return to them.

"Wait," she requested, softening her grip on her shell. Locating Piers, she stared at him with wide eyes. "I think the forest is cursed. Uscan says he will come and travel with us but only if I ask him to do so."

"Did you?" Rey intervened.

"No, not yet. I wanted to discover your thoughts before I did."

"And what difference will it make if he comes?" Piers questioned.

Blinking, the girl's mind raced. "He's strong, and he knows this land," she tallied. "He could fight for us and carry us if he needed to."

"He would be our servant," the Mate clarified.

"No, of course not," she denied. Closing her eyes, she pictured him there with them. "Yes, I think he would. We have to do this for ourselves, don't we," she sniffed, looking up at their leader with emerald pools of sadness.

"I think it's better if we do," Piers quietly agreed.

Lowering her lids, she lifted her chin; *"Uscan."*

"Yes?"

"I cannot ask this of you. We will carry a light, as you have instructed."

"Very well," he agreed.

Her eyes fluttered, *"Goodbye, my friend."*

"Ami," he called.

"Yes?"

"Be sure to seek out our cousins, the great white wolves of the north. Once you have crossed the desert, they will help you on your quest."

"Thank you," she sighed, smiling as she rejoined those around her.

"Ok," Piers said in a loud voice, clamping his hands together and giving them a good rub, "the only water is that in the wine bottles. So, we either go back until we find some or go forward until we do."

"There's no water in the forest," she informed him. "Uscan says the trees here are haunted, and that they devour the sunlight, so nothing else grows."

"Oh, brother," he groaned, catching his head with his hands to squeeze it.

"He also said we need to carry a light."

That gave him pause. "What kind of light?"

"He didn't specify. Torches, or lamps, would be my guess."

Sighing loudly, Piers turned and sat against the rock next to her. "Well, that makes two things we don't have. Ok, we make camp here tonight. We'll divvy up the water from the flasks and decide which way to go from here in the morning; probably the way we came to find another way around."

None voiced their disappointment, but they all felt it. Without water, there would be no stew, and they would be forced to dip into their desert stores. Seeing the discontent on Ami's face was almost more than Rey could bear. "Hey, while you set up camp here, let Bally and me back track. I bet we could find some kind of water back the way we came," he suggested.

Glaring at him, Piers was still considering the option when Ami sighed, "You might as well let them try."

At her approval, their leader gave a single nod, stipulating, "But not too far. If you don't find anything within half a mile or so, just come back and we'll dig into the pack for tonight."

Each eager to go on the errand, the two quickly disappeared down the trail they had just come off of with the pot for stew in hand. The rest gathered their packs and carried them over to a decent spot to lay out the camp.

Arranging a circle of stones, Piers prepared to build the fire while Amicia and Zaendra spread out the blankets to make the beds. Each night since they had left the glen had been a bit colder than the last, and they would certainly need both if the pattern held.

While they were doing that, Animir gathered the weapons and placed them against a tree. He then set out to stock the wood for the fire to keep it burning through the night.

Following him, Oldrilin skipped along, singing his name in a silly song. The third time through, he stopped, turning to face her. "Can you not bother someone else?"

Looking up at him with sad blue eyes, her bottom lip quivered. "Animir is not a friend of Lin?"

53

"Honestly, no; why would you think that I would be?" he asked grumpily as he started to walk away. He could see the hurt on her small features, and it occurred to him that Rey might be upset if he made his siren cry. "Wait, you know I didn't mean that," he teased as he knelt before her and offered her his hand.

Grasping it, she gave him a shake and returned to her singing while she hopped in circles around him. Sighing, the elf went about gathering the wood and doing his best to ignore her. Reminding himself that Rey looked after her most of the time, he guessed he could do it until the other man returned with their water.

Once their chores had been completed and camp was in order, they formed a small circle around the fire to wait. Noticing the sun had all but set, Amicia pondered, "Do you think they have gotten lost?"

Noise echoing from the trees behind, Piers shrugged, "I believe I hear them, actually." Standing, he met them as they cleared the line of trees. "Well, it took you long enough," he berated them mildly.

"We stopped to catch a rabbit," Bally bragged, holding up the carcass while Rey carried the kettle filled with the water.

"Well, you're forgiven," Amicia pronounced with a giggle. "But you caught it, so you get to clean it. I'll get the vegetables ready while I still have a bit of daylight."

Making a quick scavenge, she located some mushrooms and a few tubers that would make a nice addition to the meal. Deciding to throw in some of the spices she had saved from a few nights before, she added them as soon as the rabbit had begun to boil and then took her seat.

"Well," Piers managed a tired smile, looking around at the circle of friends, "It appears we have a bit of a wait, so who will be entertaining us with a tale?"

Leaping to her feet, Oldrilin claimed the honor, "Me, me, me!"

"You want to tell a story?" Rey asked in surprise. The siren had never made the attempt before, save the time Ami had translated for her back in their spire in Jerranyth. "All right, tell us your tale."

"Elf friends," she began with a small laugh. "For hundreds and thousands of moons, the sirens and the elfs have lived in Eriden," she proclaimed, swinging her hand in an arc before her to emphasize that fact. "Then, the great war came, and the elf king was lost." She threw up her palms and wriggled her fingers in the air.

"After that, the elfs and sirens were no more friends. Until Lady Cilithrand gave us the gift," she ended. She pulled the crystal that had been presented from her pocket and held it up in the air. Offering it to Animir, she beamed, "Elf friends."

Staring at the enormous crystal, Animir gasped, "The queen gave you that?"

Seeing his surprised expression, Oldrilin withdrew the oversized gem, her face once again forming a small pout. "Elf gift," she insisted, patting it a few times.

Placing his hand over his mouth, Animir hid his shocked expression, his mind racing. Once he had his emotions under control, he said more calmly, "May I see it, Lin?" Holding out his hand, he waited for her to place it in his grasp.

Frowning, Amicia inquired, "Is there something wrong with her being given the gift?"

"No, I don't suppose," the elf replied, accepting the gem when she placed it in his hand. Testing the weight of it with a few bounces, he cut his eyes over at her. "Have you held it, Ami?"

"No, why would I," she clipped, still disturbed by his reaction. "Lady Cilithrand gave it to her. She made a special trip to our suite to present it as well."

Flicking his gaze between the large stone and Amicia, Animir licked his lips, then confessed, "I think you should hold it." Extending it out to her, he waited for her to take it.

Pursing her lips, she considered doing so for a long moment before she leaned forward and reached for the gem, but the instant her fingers touched the smooth surface, it began to glow. Yanking her digits away, as if they had been burned, she gasped, "How'd you do that?"

"I didn't do that," the elf replied in a hushed voice. "You did."

Her mouth hanging open, the girl still leaned towards him, frozen with fear. No one spoke, and time seemed to pause, until she reached out again, this time poking it with a single trembling tip. Again, the stone took on a dim glow.

"Fuck me," Piers swore, glancing between them. "Ami, how are you doing that?"

"I don't know," she whispered, lifting the stone from his grasp and sinking back into her seat. Focusing on it, she willed it to grow brighter, and it lit up her face with a strong white light. Then she thought of snuffing it, and it grew faint, almost to the point of disappearing. "This gem is enchanted, isn't it?" she demanded, closing her fist around it firmly and glaring at the elf.

"Yes," he breathed. "That is a sacred gem of hamar; from our temple. There is only one reason our queen would have given it to the mermaid, and I'm afraid it has nothing to do with friendship."

"A magical stone," Reynard stated with a frown, cutting his gaze over at Amicia. "You can control it, like the merdoe."

"Apparently, yes," she replied, flipping her hand and opening it with the gem on top. Focusing, she caused it to glow brightly, then changed the color of the light, making it green and then a deep blue. "I don't understand," she sighed. Presenting it to Oldrilin, she commanded, "Can you not make it glow?"

"I have not tried," the siren replied, holding it up and putting obvious effort into the endeavor. Her face scrunched, she grunted, but nothing happened.

"Why would Lady Cilithrand give the siren a magical stone she can't even use?" Bally put the question into words.

An extended silence followed, as if there had been a good reason, but no one dared to speak it. Glancing over at the forest they would attempt to pass on the morrow, Ami frowned. "Well, I guess we don't need any torches."

"What do you mean?" the Mate growled.

Indicating the gem with a flattened palm, she quipped, "It's a light."

"Surely, he didn't mean this," he replied tartly.

"He said *carry a light*," she replied. "Light, not lights. And he was talking to me, so I am fairly certain that he meant this one."

"But how could he have known that she had it?" Rey asked in confusion. "Honestly, love; it doesn't make sense."

"What in this place ever does," she replied wryly with a shake of her head. "Put it away Oldrilin, and let's have our dinner. We can talk about it on the morrow, before we head into the next haunted woods."

EIGHT

Haunted Passage

GATHERED NEXT to the stand of trees, the motley group waited. Removing the magical stone from her hidden pocket, Oldrilin offered it to Amicia; "Here."

"Thank you, Lin," the girl replied, accepting the rock and closing her hand around it. Not completely shielded, white light glowed about the appendage.

Breathing deeply and exhaling slowly, Ami worked to calm herself. Flicking her gaze around at the others, she admitted quietly, "Gosh, I'm really scared."

"Are you sure you want to do this?" Piers asked, placing his hand on her shoulder. "We can find another way if you've changed your mind."

"No, no," she whispered, shaking her head. Swallowing hard, she gave him a faint smile and stated more confidently, "The desert is through there. Uscan said –"

"Aye, we know what Uscan said," Rey interrupted her, claiming her other side, "but the wolf isn't here. We're here. If you're not sure you can do this, then we shouldn't try."

"Yes, we should," she replied more forcefully. "He knew about the stone; he had to. And that means he has faith in me. He trusts me to get us through."

Not sure about her logic, Reynard shook his head and dropped her arm. "All right. Lead the way, princess," he joked.

Giving him a quick frown, Ami turned slowly to face the wall of trees with

57

the rest of the group behind her. The trunks and branches of this forest grew tightly together, so close that scarcely an opening could be seen. Sliding her foot forward, she entered through the widest gap they had found; the one they had voted unanimously must be the trail.

"Hold on to me," she commanded, her voice trembling.

"I've got you," Piers replied.

They formed a chain, each holding the hand or arm of the person before them, with Amicia in the front. The Mate followed, his hand still on her shoulder, with Zaendra holding his other elbow, as his left hand held his sword. From there, Animir and then Bally followed, with Rey bringing up the rear, only today Bally carried the siren so Rey could also wield his blade.

As soon as the company entered the tree line, the path seemed to close in around them, cutting them off from behind. No light made it in from the world outside, and they were plunged into total darkness, save the soft luminosity of Amicia's stone. Inhaling sharply, she froze, bringing the procession to a halt at only fifteen feet in. "There's something ahead of us," she breathed.

"How do you know?" Piers required.

"I see eyes…" she dared so speak quietly, gazing unblinking at the yellow glow of paired orbs.

Brandishing his blade, he pushed up behind her. Seeing nothing, he hissed in her ear, "Be brave, love."

Stepping forward, they inched along, but as the light fell upon the small creature, it turned and ran away into the darkness. "Oh, shit," she panted. "It's gone."

"What's gone?" Rey asked, not having seen it.

"I don't know, some kind of goblin. It ran away just when I could see it."

"Good," Bally snorted, "they're scared of your light."

"Aye," Piers agreed. "You're doing good, love. We can do this."

"Yes," she agreed. "We can do this."

Tree limbs groaned above them. Cutting their eyes up, her light shone onto the lowest branches, but higher up… anything could have been there.

Shuffling their feet, the group pushed forward, weaving between the narrow spaces in the trees. In the shadows created by her glow, they could hear the movement, with an occasional glimpse of a foot or hand, but never anything concrete.

Placing her free hand on each trunk as they approached, Amicia could feel the smoothness of the bark; slick and unlike any she had ever encountered. The trees themselves were dark, almost black, hard and slippery, but reflected the light with a glossiness that added luster, as if they had been polished. Her fingers rested against the bark, detecting cool clamminess that prompted her to wipe them against her shirt or pants as she moved to the next.

"You're doing fine," the Mate praised, encouraging her to stay calm.

"Aye," Ami panted, sliding to the left when a larger obstacle presented itself. "I think this is a rock," she observed, noticing the different texture, with roughness and sharp points. Shuffling further around the left side, they cleared it, and she breathed a small smile. "Whew."

Spurred on by their success, she increased her speed. "Stay close," she whispered.

"Yeah, no problem there," Bally agreed, causing Animir to chuckle.

"Easy," Piers warned. "We don't want to spook them."

"Spook them," Rey laughed. "How about they don't spook us."

A loud thump sounded just beyond the light to their right.

"Is something really out there?" Zaendra asked in a shaky voice, craning her neck as if to hunt for the source.

"Eyes on Ami, nymph," Animir commanded. "Do not worry about the shadow and focus on the light."

"I can't believe we're doing this," Rey observed, glancing quickly to the sides before returning his attention to the glowing stone Amicia held slightly above her head.

"We're doing it —" Piers started, but a loud scream to the left cut him off.

In panic, the whole group gathered into a single lump. Clinging to the girl as their feet scuffed the ground, they shredded the silence with the noise of their fear and the grating of boots and bare feet against the powdery dust-covered stones of the path. A ripple effect sounded through the trees as the creatures reacted to them in a flutter of adjustment before returning to their still, silent existence.

"Shit," Ami croaked, panting loudly. Gasping for air, she huffed, "Everyone breathe." Cutting her eyes over, she inspected the direction of the squall without turning her head. She could make out the shape of a naked being the size of a small child. "I see it," she informed them. "It's about the size of Oldrilin, maybe a little more. It looks sick, like it's starving, and its skin is the color of the trees, almost black."

"Like me," Zae said with a funny smile in her voice.

"Aye, almost as dark as you, love," Amicia informed her, "but not like you." She swallowed, her mouth hot and dry. She did not want to get anywhere near the creature and hoped it continued to respect her glowing stone. The sight of it had locked her in place, and the blood rushed in her ears as she forced her lungs to work more slowly. She wasn't sure she could go on, but what choice did she have?

"What's it doing?" Rey hissed when many seconds had ticked by; at the back of the pile and furthest from the light, he glared at it, blinking against the urge to look away. If anything approached, he didn't want to know.

"It's just standing there," she shrugged. "Watching. Waiting."

"Let's keep moving," the Mate suggested. "We've calmed and gathered our nerve enough," he added, squeezing Ami's shoulder to nudge her forward once again.

"Ok," Amicia agreed, pushing her foot ahead. The group still clung to her, and they moved as if they were a giant blob of water rolling down the side of a goblet. Slow, painful progress, they inched their way.

"How deep do you think these woods are?" Baldwin suddenly asked.

"It doesn't matter," the girl informed him. "We're going all the way."

"Oh yeah?" he panted. "I'm going to wet myself if another one screams out like that."

"Another one?" Rey teased, "I thought you probably already had."

Snickering, Ami lost herself for a moment before she gave in to the laugh and they paused again as the giggle rippled through them before it ebbed away. The sound of their feet scraping on the bare earth surrounded them in the silence that followed, and Amicia froze.

"Now what?" Piers prodded.

"It's too quiet," she replied. "I don't see them... or hear them, anymore."

"You think they're up to something?"

"I can't tell," she admitted, taking another half step. Ahead of her, she could see a light that wasn't hers. "Oh my God. That may be the exit," she breathed, her voice rising in pitch with excitement.

"Let's move that way, then," he suggested, gripping his sword tighter.

"Ok," she agreed, making the adjustment. The air had felt cold when they first entered the line of trees, but at that moment, beads of sweat formed on her brow and ran down her temples. "Anyone else getting warm?" she asked, mostly as a distraction from the silence.

"Aye," three voices replied at once.

"It'll be cooler when we get out of here," Piers assured. "There's no air moving in this place," he explained.

"Yeah, there isn't," Baldwin agreed.

"Ten feet," Ami announced. "I almost want to run for it," she laughed.

"Well, don't," the Mate instructed sharply. "We're doing fine. We should stay with what's working."

A loud bang sounded at their heels, followed by a snap of a limb as it gave way, dropping a large body to the ground behind Rey. Without hesitation, Ami spun, pushing her way through her friends and shining the light behind them while commanding, "Kneel down!" and pumping extra energy into the glow, pushing the light out farther than she ever had.

Only Piers, Rey, and Animir obeyed, but it was enough, and the strength of her radiant stone illuminated the full area around them, sending dozens of bare feet scampering across the dusty earth, their tiny, dark bodies writhing to get out of view.

"Wow," Bally observed quietly, meeting her wide green eyes. On his chest, Oldrilin buried her face against him, not daring to view their would-be attackers.

"Yeah, wow," she replied, smacking his arm. "Do you not know what get down means?" Resting her free hand against the siren's back, she comforted the smallest of their group.

"Sorry," he replied, rubbing the spot and still turning slowly, taking in the myriad of trees. "We're not going to get lost in here, are we?"

"Not a chance," Ami replied confidently, returning to the front of the line. "Everyone up. It's less than ten feet, and I can see the sun from here."

"I don't see any sun," the Mate replied, reclaiming her shoulder.

"Well, I do," she insisted. "Everyone ready?" Hearing muffled agreement, she pushed forward. "Eight feet."

"We're going to make it," Zae whispered.

"Six feet."

Oldrilin whimpered, and Bally squealed, "Easy with the claws, Lin!"

"Four feet," Amicia called, pivoting to check the left and right before she turned around. "I'm standing here. You go forward." Holding the light straight above her head, it shone down in a white cascade of brilliant comfort.

Parting around her like a rock in a stream, they formed up on the other side, and a moment later, they stepped out into bright sun.

Bringing up the rear, she pushed at them, moving them away from the line of trees before she started to cry and squealed, "We are never going through there again!"

Moved by her tears, Rey pulled her to him with his right arm, catching her by the back of her head as he comforted her. His sword hanging from the left, he squeezed the handle as he called, "Let's get up this hill a bit."

Before them, the incline grew steep after about ten yards, and they dug in, not stopping until they had reached the top. Another field opened before them at the crest, covered with tall grass that stretched as far as they could see.

Lamwen circled slow and high as he observed the party that had fled the glen. He had kept his distance, watching as their path unfolded, fairly certain that eventually the natural obstacles in their way would overcome them, at which point he would simply return to Adiarwen and pronounce that she was dead.

Somewhat impressed with their tenacity and how they had overcome the swarm of rodents, he had been tempted to draw the line, swooping down and finishing them himself. However, he hated to deny them the chance to make it to the desert, which he felt confident would be their greatest challenge; if they survived the tree-crawlers of the dark forest in between.

Watching as they formed a small group and moved as one to enter the south side of the trees, his keen eye spotted the hamar gem within her grasp. "Perhaps," he grumbled, the fire burning hot inside his belly. The light disappeared the moment they entered, and the forest swallowed them as if devouring a meal.

Continuing the unhurried turns, he waited, unable to see anything through the canopy of the trees. If the group perished within, his only evidence would be their failure to appear on the other side.

At the moment he began to suspect they had met their demise, the nymph pushed out of the line of trees and stumbled towards the hill on the north side. The males quickly followed, and the girl brought up the rear, still holding the glowing stone above her head.

He could hear her cries, and the fire smoldered, leaving a dull ache within his chest. "So, it is true." She had passed the challenge and proven herself worthy of her name. His mind turning, he knew he would not notify anyone of his discovery and further would do his best to hide what he had come to know.

It was not time yet to make his introduction, but soon he would separate her from the others, and they would get to know each other better. He had watched for two decades as Gwirwen ruled, or failed to rule, their kingdom. Lamwen had never seen himself as a traitor, either to the old regime or the new one, but he could hear the whisper of change upon the wind.

Soon, a choice would have to be made, and a side would have to be taken. He did not yet fully understand this delicate creature, this mortal female who instilled fear in the heart of his master, but if she were strong enough...

No, if he were strong enough. Yes, if he were capable of walking the path of an outcast, perhaps an ancient wrong could be set right, and the Kingdom of Eriden would live in fear no more.

Or he would kill her and be done with it. Making a final turn, he searched for a place to make his bed for the night, confident the fate of many rested within his grasp.

NINE

A Lesser Man

MARCHING THROUGH THE GRASS, it caught and pulled at their calves, and the ground felt soft beneath their feet. His brow furrowed, Piers led them on, guiding them to the north east rather than due north.

"I thought we were crossing the desert," Rey observed, still holding Ami lightly by the shoulder.

"We are, but we need to make a few preparations. I didn't expect it to begin so abruptly this side of that last area of woods," the Mate explained.

"You mean this is it?" Bally asked, a hint of excitement in his voice.

"No, but we're close." Stopping, the first mate knelt to lift a hand full of the soil. Squeezing it, he opened his palm to show them the sample. "See how it acts? No clumps, just loose grains."

"Aye," Reynard agreed. "Like a beach."

"Yes," Piers concurred, "much like that, only no ocean to wet it. That's why this is all grass and not too tall. If we stay to the right here, we may catch a stream coming down the mountain from the thaw if we're not too early in the season."

"And what good does that do us?" Ami asked, having recovered from her fright.

"We'll need water to carry," the Mate explained, his palms growing moist with apprehension. "The oasis is three days walk; we'll make camp and rest until nightfall. We'll be cooler if we travel by moonlight and need less water."

"Water," Rey repeated, not having thought of that. "Three days is a long time to go without a drink. And we can't eat the food," he sighed, glancing at Amicia's bag.

"We'll have water," Piers informed him, "that is we will if we find a source before we begin the crossing."

"How?" Ami pushed, finding it odd he hadn't mentioned this part of his plan before.

"I have some receptacles to hold it," the older man growled. "Not a lot, but enough to get us a few days if we're careful."

"How?" she asked again, this time, an edge to her voice.

Licking his lips, the Mate swore under his breath. Dropping his bag, he searched to the bottom and pulled out a waterskin. Offering it to her, he set his jaw firmly, ready for her reaction.

"Where did you get it?" she demanded as she accepted the leather pouch.

"I made it," he replied stiffly. "I have four."

"Four," she gasped, turning it to inspect before she passed it to Rey. "Exactly how long have you been planning this little trip?"

Looking past her to the horizon, his lips moved a few times, but no sound came from them. Inhaling sharply, he spat, "Since we finished the cabin and I knew you would be cared for."

"Basically, right after we arrived in the glen," she shouted in dismay.

"Aye." He still didn't look at her; he had known she would be upset, which is precisely why he had avoided telling her... until he had to. Turning on his heel, he hoisted his bag and marched on, bearing right and watching for signs of a stream or water collection of any kind.

"Ami," Rey called as he grasped her arm, preventing her from chasing after him. "Please don't, love," he whispered, pulling her to face him.

Looking back and forth between the couple and their leader, Bally appeared confused. Taking charge, Animir observed, "We should keep up."

"You guys go on; me and Ami will be there in a few minutes," Rey suggested. His eyes meeting hers, he didn't break the connection as he spoke.

"Did you know about this?" she hissed when they were alone.

"No, but I'm not surprised," he confessed. "Piers hasn't been happy since we got here. Not in Riran, or the glen, or really even in Jerranyth, although I think he tolerated the elves the best."

Rolling her eyes, the girl didn't have to guess why. "I'm such a fool," she breathed, closing her eyes and fighting the tears.

66

"You're not," he countered. His hand raised to caress her, his thumb traced the bone of her cheek. "He didn't want to hurt you."

"No, I did that for myself," she confessed. Pulling herself free, she followed the group, tears stinging her eyes and blurring her vision as she stomped along.

Letting her go, Rey trailed a few feet behind. He felt helpless, as if he would give or do anything to make her feel better; but he couldn't. He didn't have that kind of power.

Ahead of them, Piers could see green in the distance. Stopping, he turned to discern if the others were coming and felt relieved that everyone was moving in his direction. Resuming his march, he didn't stop again until he had reached the patch of woods and grass that were fed by a small spring.

Not pausing to rest, he began the preparations for a camp. Dropping his bag, he walked up and down along the green until he found a good spot to reach the water. Giving it a taste, he sighed; *it'll do.*

By then, most of the others had arrived, and Piers gave out orders. "Bally, we're going to need the fire pit set up. Animir, we're going to want a good meal this evening, so fish or rabbit; whatever you can scare up for us."

The two youngest males didn't argue and set about their chores. "Zae, can you and Lin take care of the bedding? Get us all comfortable spots so we can have a nap in the shade until the sun sets," he suggested.

"Yes, sir," Zaendra replied, not sure what to make of the disagreement that had obviously upset Amicia quite severely.

Drawing a deep breath, the Mate prepared to face the blonde but hoped the hike had stolen some of her anger. To his surprise, she ignored him, setting to work on preparing the kettle for a stew.

Walking along the edge of the trees, she hunted for tubers, mushrooms, or any other items that could be added to the pot. When she had found a few, she gave them a good wash and returned to the camp.

The air felt electrified with the unspoken quarrel. Each member of their party completed their chore in silence, and dinner was on to cook well before the sun was ready to set. However, instead of sitting with the others, Amicia strutted down the soft bank of the stream. Locating a long stick, a thick dried reed of some kind, she used it to smack the water, enjoying the crack that it made when it hit.

"That looks fun," Piers informed her as he approached.

"I don't wish to speak to you," she replied, swinging the staff angrily.

"Well, good, then you can listen." He walked right up to her and waited, but she continued to abuse the dead limb, so he pushed on. "I understand you being upset. I fully expected it. But tonight, we are going to walk out into the desert, and we all need to have our wits about us."

He paused to see if she had some retort to make, but she remained silent, still swinging the club. "You know," he said more quietly, "I really am sorry. I tried to tell you that the other night. I meant what I said about coming back for you if I found a way off. It's not like I was going to leave you here forever."

Her arms frozen in mid swing, she cut her eyes over at him and growled, "I'm not going with you when you go back to the rim of the mortals. Obviously, I don't belong there."

"What do you mean you don't belong there?" he faltered, as that was not the path he expected their discussion to take.

"I'm a wielder of magic," she hissed. "The merdoe was only the beginning. You saw what I did with the elf gem."

His mouth forming a pucker, he couldn't argue with that. "And what do you think it means?" he asked calmly, folding his arms across his chest.

"It means I was right; this is the place I was supposed to come to. The place where I belong. You guys may go home, by all means, but I'm not leaving if or when we find a way out," she bit tartly, resuming her whacking.

Grasping her arms, he prevented her swing. "Could you stop that and talk with me, please."

"Why? Obviously, you don't really consider me much of a friend. If you did, you wouldn't have kept your secret all this time."

"That isn't fair. Friends come in many forms, and truth be known you are one of the closest I have ever had. It scares me to death to think of you staying here after we've gone, alone."

"Scares you what I may be capable of, more like," she accused, stepping up to him and giving him a cold glare.

Not backing down, he replied coolly, "My, my. You do have spirit, I'll give you that. But I don't scare easily, princess. So, if that's a threat, you better think long and hard before you cross irons with me. So far, you've used a seashell to talk to the natives and made a rock glow to scare away a few goblins. Next time we get attacked by a dragon, maybe I'll let you handle it. See how you fair then."

Turning, he left her to her thrashing, heading back to the camp and his bed for a nap before dinner.

Watching him go, Amici's seethed. Tossing her stick, she wanted to tear at her hair and scream, but she couldn't let him see he had gotten to her. Instead, she located a bit of shade to sit under and pulled Lin's gem from her pocket. She felt like she should return it; Cilithrand had given it to the siren after all. But for the moment, it wouldn't hurt to see if there was anything else she could make it do.

Gazing onto the facets, she admired the intricate detail it had been given. Even beneath the tree, it caught beams of light and reflected them. Thinking about how she had made it glow in the woods, it lit up, and she went through a few color options, then let it fade back to the plain clear version.

"It will take practice," Animir informed her, taking a few more steps closer.

"I didn't hear your approach," she apologized, feeling as if he had caught her or judged her behavior in some way.

"Hmm. We elves are sneaky, or haven't you heard," he laughed.

She smiled up at him. "Yes, I've been warned. Sit with me?"

"Of course," he agreed, gingerly taking a seat. "You know, trust can be a very valuable thing. Sometimes the only thing of worth that we have."

"What do you mean?" She cut her eyes over at him, wondering if he were sticking up for the Mate in his own way.

"I simply mean, it is important to me that I have your trust. I did not bring you from Jerranyth under good circumstances, and it was a hard decision to make, disobeying the queen."

"Would she really punish you if you went back?"

"I would be tortured, most likely, and put to death if I were lucky," he replied, his eyes filled with sorrow.

"I don't understand," she clipped, shaking her head. "How could you give up your home for us? I mean, you didn't even know about Lin's crystal or that there was anything special about me... did you?"

Appearing thoughtful, he blinked a few times, then confessed, "I knew you were special the moment I first laid eyes upon you, Amicia Spicer. A fire burns within you; I fear all you meet in Eriden may see it."

The air caught in her lungs, she gasped, "What do you mean by that?" Piers had said the same thing to her the night he had wooed her in his cabin, unsuccessfully she might add.

"It's just an expression," he said with a chuckle. "It means that you have an air about you. A confidence that commands the respect of all who are around you."

"Oh," she laughed, never having really thought about it. "Well, apparently, that doesn't include Piers Massheby," she accused.

"To the contrary, my lady," he denied, "I should think his respect for you must be greatest of all of us."

"And what makes you think that?" Her eyes narrowed.

"The Mate knows you are fond of him. If he were a lesser man, he could have what he likes of you, without regard for your feelings or what it might cost you. He cares for you quite deeply, of this I am certain."

Her lips forming a small pout, she didn't know what to say. Since she had met him, she had thought of little else, always formulating how she could convince Piers that the two of them should settle down together. Had her ambitions been flawed?

"You're saying it's because he cares about me that he keeps himself at bay," she surmised.

"Exactly," the elf replied, preparing to stand. On his feet, he continued, "It hurts us all to see this fight between you. This struggle for something that can never be. Once you accept that, you will be ready to see the possibilities that are hidden by your desire."

"I can't see them because I'm blinded... " Her voice trailed away, and her lip quivered.

"I'll leave you to think," he offered, turning to walk away.

"Animir," she called after him.

"Yes, my lady?"

"Thank you. For the advice and for being such a good friend. And don't worry; we aren't going to let Lady Cilithrand do anything to you if we can help it."

"You are a good friend, Amicia Spicer. I am very fortunate to be a part of this group and to share with you this journey." Leaving her, he walked back to the camp.

Alone, Ami leaned her head back against the tree. Watching the blue sky in the distance, she turned over the elf's words. She knew both he and Rey were attracted to her; she certainly wasn't blind to it by any means.

Closing her eyes, she considered what it would be like to form a deeper relationship with either of them. Almost instantly, she rejected the idea. No, she needed to learn more about herself before she became entangled in any long-term relationships.

As soon as she made the realization, it felt as if a weight had been lifted from her. She needn't worry about Piers, Rey, Animir, or anyone else; at least not until she had worked out how and why she felt connected to Eriden. Only then would she be free to offer her hand, for doing so was something she knew she could never take back, and a decision with such finality should never be taken lightly.

TEN

Desert Moon

SITTING BENEATH HER TREE, Amicia could feel the heat pressing in on her. Small bugs swarmed around the water and were attracted by the sweat that formed on her arms and neck. Swatting at them, her hands felt heavy, and she licked at her dry lips with a swollen tongue.

She would have remained in her solitude until they were ready to eat before they left, but thirst drove her to seek out a few swallows of water. "We haven't even started, and I can already feel the dryness in the air," she grumbled as she stood and walked calmly back to their camp.

Gathered in their small circle, the others had stretched out on their blankets, as even the shade was too warm for covers. Pouring a goblet of water for herself from one of their elvish wine bottles, she thought again how their resources would be limited out on the sand, and a small wave of fear tickled the back of her mind. The time they had spent on the sea had nearly been the end of them, and this would surely be another test of their ability to survive.

It's only three days walk, she reminded herself firmly. *Besides, we'll be in the Mate's care, and he has never let us down.*

Checking the stew, which boiled lightly, she gave it a stir, approving of the aroma rising from the bubbling pot. They would be on dried meat and goat cheese once they left the small patch of green, so tonight's dinner held special importance.

Finding everything in order, she stood for a moment, shading her eyes as

73

she glared off into the distance. She couldn't see the line where the dried yellow grass ended and the actual desert began, but she knew it was close. She wanted to be relaxed about the journey and breathed deeply as she examined the horizon, her anxiety slowly being released.

Calmer, she turned to her bed, which Zae and Lin had placed next to their leader. Glancing at him, his eyes were closed, and he slept soundly. His peaceful expression brought a faint smile to her lips as she recalled the first time she had seen him; bare chested and sorting cargo. He was a good man, hardworking and dedicated to a fault. The image warmed her heart, and she sighed, ready to get her nap.

Curling up on her quilt, she watched the sun slowly inch across the sky as her lids grew heavy. Hours later, she awakened to find that Piers had begun serving the bowls. They would eat and pack their things before the darkness completely covered the land. Accepting hers, she could see the tenderness in his eyes, and guilt roiled in her gut. "Thank you," she mumbled, cutting her eyes away and blinking rapidly to hide the emotion behind them.

"I hope everyone had a decent nap," he announced, sitting down on his pallet next to hers with his serving in hand. "We'll be night walkers until we reach the oasis," he laughed.

"Will we need anything besides the waterskins filled?" Rey inquired. "I'm sure there won't be any resources once we head out."

"No, we'll be totally on our own, so be sure the bottles are full as well," the Mate suggested with a nod. "And, I had an idea. I hunted down a few more staffs like the one Zae has been carrying," he informed them, giving her a broad smile. "I think they'll come in handy in the morning, when we're ready to bed down and rest during the heat of the day. We can use them to construct at least a patch of shade to keep the sun off us in case there isn't any, which I doubt there will be."

Finishing his stew first, Baldwin took the receptacles and dutifully went to fill them, with Animir close behind. Rey and Zae set about rolling up the packs, while Ami stirred her bowl, not really eating it.

"Is something wrong with your dinner?" Piers asked, shifting to sit beside her.

Looking up at him with a doleful expression, she said softly, "I'm really sorry... for the way that I've behaved. I can see that it would have been wrong for us to consummate any kind of relationship as husband and wife. I need to

74

know more about who I am before I can be a part of a marriage, to you or anyone else."

"Oh," he more or less agreed, pulling his knees to his chest and holding them there with his arms wrapped around. "So, I am forgiven for keeping you at bay?"

"Yes," she nodded, then sniffed, "I won't pester you about it any longer. You've been a good friend to me, Piers," she said more strongly, raising her clear green orbs to meet his. "I do love you; all of you. It pains me to think we may one day go our separate ways."

Placing his arm over her shoulders, he gave her a squeeze. "Me too. We have been through the worst of times together and seen each other through."

Leaning into him, she sighed, "Do you forgive me?"

"Aw, love; you know that I do. Finish your meal, and we'll get everything washed and packed for the journey."

"Aye," she agreed with a giggle, spooning her bites in earnest.

Gathering their supplies, Piers whistled merrily. He felt at peace with the girl, a peace he hoped would last. He knew it had not been easy for her to speak those words to him and to accept responsibility for the tension that had been almost constant between them. He mused that if she were able to maintain it, the change would thankfully make things easier for them.

Feeling better, Amicia washed the last of their dishes and packed them. Then, grouping with the others, they planned who would carry what, as their amount of supplies had grown significantly. Peering at the long poles that the Mate had selected, she held one up and suggested, "Let's carry them on these, in pairs. You know, like a sling."

"You mean a litter?" the Mate asked, stroking his beard thoughtfully.

"Can it be done?" she asked with expectant wide eyes.

"Hey, that's actually a great idea," Rey agreed, taking the staff from her and balancing it to test the weight. "It will take a few minutes to set them up, but we'll be able to walk a bit easier. I'm sure of it."

Setting to work, they spread one of the blankets out flat, then laid two of the poles across it side by side about two feet apart. Watching as they folded the blanket over each staff into the middle as layers, Zae pondered, "How will it stay and not fall through?"

"Friction," the Mate explained, feeling a bit of pride at her curiosity. "The two pieces of cloth will be pressed against each other by the weight of the load. That will hold them in place," he stated with a firm nod.

Stacking half their gear evenly across it, he and Rey hoisted it up to their shoulders to give it a test. "See? The blanket is as solid as if it were made of planks."

"This feels nice," Reynard observed. "We'll be able to keep a good pace, don't you think?" he asked as they strode back and forth a few times, with Piers in front and Rey following behind, then trading to try the other way around.

"Aye," the Mate agreed. "Let's set it down and build one for Animir and Bally."

Using a second set of poles, they constructed the next and let the two younger males give it a test. Walking along for a minute, they were less smooth, but they quickly got better. Bouncing it a few times, the boys laughed.

"This isn't a game," the Mate reminded them sternly. Stroking his chin, he suggested aloud, "Do you think we should tie everything down?"

Her eyes wide, all the perils they could face leapt into Ami's mind simultaneously. "Is the journey going to be dangerous?"

Glancing at her alarmed expression, Rey sidled closer to pull her into a hug. "Are you still upset about the goblins?"

"No," she replied with a tremor in her voice. "But it was hard being on the raft. So many things happened we couldn't control..." she trailed away.

"We're way better prepared this time," Bally intervened, pulling out the ropes. "Let's tie it down. We would rather be safe than sorry," he suggested, smiling up at the girl as he knelt to begin the job.

The sun had set by the time they finished, and they headed out in their typical single file. Piers and Rey leading, Animir and Baldwin trailing, and the girls marching along in the center. Their mood was light, almost as jovial as the first night they had spent together after departing the glen, and their laughter carried through the darkness as they strutted along in rhythm.

Before long, they had cleared the grass, and only sand remained. Her mind turning, Ami became lost in her thoughts as the group fell silent. The sliver of moon above lit their path and she could see far into the distance all around them, with no trees or structures of any kind to obscure their view. Looking up at the cloudless sky, the bright stars twinkled above, and she found herself contemplating a wide range of fleeting topics.

"Ami," Oldrilin coaxed, tugging at her sweater.

"What is it, Lin?" the girl snapped to attention, afraid she had been ignoring her tiny friend.

"I've had my fill of walking," the siren confessed. "Would you carry me now?"

Smiling, she called, "May we take a small rest?"

When the procession had come to a halt, Rey helped get the mermaid positioned on her back. Recalling the first time he had carried her on his shoulders, he laughed. "Watch out for her hair, Lin," he reminded the mermaid gently.

"It's in the braid," Amicia observed. "I doubt she could pull much."

"Oh, you'd be surprised," Rey countered with a snort.

Bally chuckled as well, running his hand over his chest, tenderly observing the bruises she had given him when Ami had led them through the haunted woods filled with goblins. "I'm sure she's going to be fine," he agreed with more confidence than he felt.

Passing one of the elf bottles, they used the stop to have a refreshing drink. Looking around at the wide-open expanse of nothing, Amicia sighed, "I guess taking a piss would be out of the question."

"You can," Piers informed her with a shake of his head, "but it's not going to be the most private. We'll turn our backs if you want," he offered.

"Hey, let's just leave the gear here in the middle and each take a side," Rey suggested, helping Lin out of her pouch and placing her on the ground. "Boys go left, and girls go right," he chanted with a laugh.

In silent agreement, the group parted and marched out into the soft sand for about fifty yards, putting nearly a hundred yards between them. Returning to their packs when all were refreshed, they took up their loads and reformed the line.

After a short distance, Amicia dropped back a few paces so that she could walk beside Animir instead of in front of him. "I was hoping we could have a small chat," she offered, noticing that he seemed focused on balancing his end of the litter, as he followed while Bally led.

"Of course, my lady," he agreed readily with a grin. His white teeth shone brightly in the moon lit night, but he had been worn down by the journey, as they all had been; a conversation would help distract him from his exhaustion.

"I've been thinking about the stone, the hamar you called it. I had been so angry, I didn't really ask what you meant, but I'm curious. What sort of practice?" she asked anxiously. "Is it something I should be worried about?"

"Practice?"

"Yes, I was making it glow and adding colors when you joined me, and you said it would take practice," she recalled aloud.

"Oh, that," he laughed. "You have the ability to draw the power within the stone, but only on the surface. In time, and with a bit of training, you would be better at it; stronger, I guess you might say."

"Will I be able to use it to do other things?"

"Perhaps," he gave a firm nod. "You would be able to use more power and do more impressive things if you were properly trained and focused. When we make camp, I would be most pleased to show you what I know."

"You're a wielder of magic?" she gasped.

"Well," he hesitated, "elves are considered magical people. Only about ten percent of us are truly powerful, though."

"The ruling elves, like Lady Cilithrand," Bally interjected, having been listening as usual.

"Correct," Animir confirmed. "Even though not all of our class can readily use magic. It is more difficult than one might think. But I would be willing to help in any way that I can."

Her heart beating faster, Amicia grinned, "That would be lovely, Animir. Yes, when we have settled to rest, I would love to hear more about it." A spring in her step, Ami hurried ahead to retake her place in their line as they marched on.

The sand beneath her boots had tired her, and the added weight of the siren had only added to the issue. Her legs ached, but she pushed herself for every step. Piers had asked them to keep a positive attitude when they first set out on their journey on The Bobber, months ago, and she would do her best to fulfill his mandate. Besides, she didn't want to be the one bringing everyone down by complaining. Raising her chin, she focused on her breathing and putting one foot in front of the other.

Pulling them up for another break as the moon sank low on the horizon, Piers could see the exhaustion on their faces. Passing around the bottle again for another swig, he hesitated to let them sit for long.

"We need to keep moving," he informed them when Bally dropped down onto the sand.

Squatting next to him, Amicia giggled, "This is a lot harder than the raft."

"Aye," he agreed, stretching out flat and staring up at the star filled heavens. The ground had been warmed by the sun all day, and it still held a small amount of heat. However, the air around them had cooled drastically. "Tell me again why we're walking at night?" he demanded quietly.

"To conserve our water," the Mate replied, longing to join his young friend. Resisting the urge, he shifted from one foot to the other, placing his arms across his chest. "This place will be an oven by midday tomorrow, so we need to push as far as we can tonight and set up our camp once the sun comes up."

Glancing between them, Amicia sighed. They needed something to lift their spirits. Her gaze falling on Animir as he had his share of the water, she grinned brightly, "Can you show us your magic?"

His eyes darting around the members of their group, the elf drew an anxious breath before he agreed. Closing the flask, he placed it on the sand and took a few steps back. Then, holding out his hands in a stopping motion, he focused on the container for a long minute before Bally gasped, "Oh my God, it's floating!"

It had only risen about six inches from the ground, but it was enough. Giving it an imaginary push, Animir sent it over to him as it silently levitated over the sand.

"That's impressive," Piers observed as he knelt down to check the level of clearance he had achieved. "Can you make it go higher?"

"Yes," the younger man replied, "but I don't want to risk the bottle, should I drop it."

"Is your control not that good?" Rey asked, also on all fours to look beneath it.

"I don't practice it much," the elf confessed. "I was forbidden to use magic as part of my banishment. I've always feared being caught and punished even worse than being made to serve."

"Aww," Ami comforted as she stood, picking up the pouch and preparing to take on her passenger. "Maybe you can practice now," she consoled.

"I guess so," he shrugged. "It has not meant that much to me."

"Hasn't meant that much," Bally chortled, also getting to his feet. "Man, if I could make stuff float, I would practice it every day. Imagine how much work you could save if you sit in a chair and just think it into being."

"It's not that simple," the elf replied with a laugh while watching the girl. "It requires a bit of effort and skill to do anything useful," he confessed.

Falling into line, the group pushed on, but their pace had dropped off significantly. Trudging through the dunes, they met a patch of ripples, which gave the landscape odd shadows. The moon had set, and although the stars still burned above, the darkness pressed in on them.

The night seemed endless, and the air around them continued to drop in temperature. If they had not been moving, it would have become more than Ami could stand even with the warmth of her passenger. Wrapping her sweater around herself more tightly, she kept going, but she wore a heavy frown from the effort.

Catching the first streaks of sunrise to the east, Piers announced, "We'll stop as soon as the sun breaks into the sky. We want to get our shelter assembled before it starts getting warm."

He wouldn't have to tell the group twice, as they were all ready to pull out their blankets and lie down. Pushing for every foot, he finally made the call, and the two youngest males nearly dropped their litter getting it off their shoulders.

"Easy with it," the Mate directed. "We need to unload them. We're going to use the poles to construct a shelter."

Doing as he instructed, all their gear was stacked to the side and the blankets unwrapped. Taking the poles, they leaned the four of them into a point that met at about six feet in height. Using three of the blankets, they covered three of the sides, but left a gap of about a foot at the bottoms.

"This is an odd shelter," Ami observed.

"Well, it's just to keep the sun off," Piers explained while making sure their ties were all secure. "The opening is to let the air move through," he explained while pointing at the feature with an open palm.

"We're going to be cozy," Rey observed, as two blankets spread side by side covered the floor of their make-shift dwelling.

"Who cares, as long as we get to sleep," Bally whined, dropping their gear on the four corners of the mat to hold it down.

Quick to agree, Ami announced, "We should eat before we sleep, don't you think?"

"Aye," the Mate seconded. "Pull out the rations; let's eat, drink, and get down for our rest."

ELEVEN

The Desert of Peaswan

SITTING in the shade of their tent, the group parceled out portions of meat and cheese and each enjoyed a goblet of water. With the four waterskins and two bottles, they would have one container per meal if they ate twice a day, which should see them to the oasis.

Stretching out across the blanket, Ami wiped the perspiration forming upon her lip. "I'm not sure I can stay under this," she mumbled as she squirmed.

All taking a section of the accommodations, they drifted off to sleep, but their comfort did not last as a blast of hot air sometime later stung their skin with flying grains of sand. Squealing loudly, Zae covered her face with her arms to hold the blast at bay.

"I think we've left too much space," Bally observed, squinting at the bright light shining on the ground on the other side of the wall. Lying on the edge, closest to the gap, he had the perfect view of the sand storm, as well as the waves of heat that floated in through the gap.

"Everyone up!" the Mate ordered, then seized one of the blankets to roll it, tucking it around one of the sides and changing the size of the hole between the earth and the wall. "Get the other side," he instructed Rey as he adjusted the height.

Ami knelt as he did so, pushing her hands into the soft grains they had

81

been lying upon. Her fingers wriggling, she could feel the coolness of the layer below. "I think we should pull out some of the sand," she observed.

Pressing his hand in as well, the Mate agreed. "Aye, the heat of the day has not reached so far below. Let's use the bowls to scoop it away and pack it against the blankets for support."

Each using their dinner dish, they removed and shaped the sand, arriving at a cool, damp layer several inches down. Stretching out upon it, Amicia sighed at the small amount of comfort the change provided. Closing her eyes, she breathed deeply, and a few minutes later, she had drifted into exhausted slumber.

When she awoke, the sun hung low in the sky. Lying still and staring at the point where their poles came together, she could hear Rey, Animir, and Bally talking quietly in front of the opening to their manmade cave. Lifting her head, she could see the backs of their heads as they laughed, using sticks to draw pictures in the sand. "Silly boys," she muttered, laying her head back and running her hand across her forehead.

"Another headache?" Piers asked, observing her movements.

"No, just tired," she replied, sitting up for a better look around. "Looks like we survived the first day," she attested with a chuckle.

"Aye," he agreed, pulling out their second bottle. "Let's have our dinner before the sun sets, then we can tear down the camp with what's left of the light and be on our way."

"I can make us light if we need it," the girl reminded him with a small grin as she portioned out their meal into each of their bowls.

"True," Rey agreed, accepting his and crossing his legs to sit beside her. "That will be a handy trick for us again at some point, I'm sure."

"She will become much more useful with it in time," Animir assured.

"Well," Piers directed, "I believe Lin and I have both told a tale, so who will be sharing this evening's entertainment?" His eyes darting around at the others, he waited for one to volunteer before he made the call.

"I should share," their elf spoke up. Sitting in the entrance to the tent, but not completely inside as the shadow on that side had grown long, the wind caught his long hair, and he squinted against the gust.

"Are you ready for that?" Ami asked, eyeing him doubtfully. He had dropped enough clues about his past, she knew this would be another sad story in a long line of them, as each member of their group had seemed to endure his or her own brand of suffering.

"Yes," he agreed confidently, offering a weak smile. "I am among friends," he informed her, placing his hand firmly against his chest, over his heart. "My past should not be held a secret from such individuals as I have found."

Nodding, the Mate agreed, "Let's hear it then," raising his goblet of water in a mock toast to their elven companion.

"My story begins with my father," Animir stated quietly. "He was an advisor to Lord Galiodien, Lady Cilithrand's father."

"Wow," Ami breathed. "That makes him very old."

"Yes," the elf nodded. "I am not so young as you think," he admitted with a small nod.

"How old are you," Baldwin pushed with a scowl. He had always assumed the pair were near the same age.

"I will be fifty-seven on the quarter waxing crescent of this year's eighth moon," he supplied.

"Fifty-seven!" Rey gasped. "But you look so young!"

Chuckling, Animir cut his eyes over at the man across from him. "Did you see any old elves in Jerranyth?"

Curling his tongue, Rey glanced around at the others, who all held pensive appearances. "No, I don't guess that I did," he admitted quietly. "Are you saying that you never get old... or do you get rid of them before they get that way?" he asked cautiously, causing the elf to choke on his drink of water.

"No, we don't do anything to them," Animir spat. "Lady Cilithrand is over three centuries, and her father was close to seven when he died."

"That's insane," Piers breathed. "How have you not run out of room if you are so long lived?"

"We don't over populate," the elf supplied with a shrug. "Each elf can expect to have only three to five children in their lifetime, and we do die you know."

"From what?" Rey clipped, in shock at the numbers their newest male member had been throwing around. "People who live in the centuries – no wonder you call us mortals of the rim!" he observed.

"Precisely," Animir nodded, rubbing his hands together to remove the crumbs as he finished his meal. "We can expect to live a millennium, or more in some cases. Not really immortal, but with such a long life to contemplate," he shrugged, "who's counting?"

"And you appear young the entire time?" Amicia gasped, considering how beautiful the queen had appeared.

"Only a few attain their end naturally," he grinned, seeing the wheels turning. "We have our issues and often meet our doom by more abrupt and final means."

"Is that what happened to your father?" the Mate clipped, returning them to his story.

"Yes," the elf agreed. "As I said, he was an advisor to the king, who was killed in the great war. He knew all his secrets and was a faithful servant. Lady Cilithrand came to power at his passing, a young queen of barely a century."

Amicia grinned at the thought of a hundred years being young but did not interrupt.

Adjusting himself in the soft sand, Animir leaned forward, toying with the grains as he gathered his thoughts. "Our new queen did not have such use for him, but he remained in the service of the crown until shortly after I was born."

Her chest growing tight, Amicia could tell this history bothered him. Of course, it ends with him being banished from the upper class and being treated as a mongrel; how could he be pleased with such a tale?

"He took his leave of the palace, but he still held his rank until near two decades ago. I do not know the details. I only know that he was accused of treason, oddly enough very near the time that Gwirwen became the Supreme Dragon of Eriden," he smirked. "He was put to death, and I was censured as his heir; demoted within the ranks to servant and stripped of all titles and rights of the ruling house."

"And yet you did nothing wrong?" Zaendra gasped, her eyes wide as he spoke.

"Nothing that I am aware of," he sighed. "I was still very young then, and I had no idea what the ruling would cost me. I had been in the armory for a few years before I realized how truly alone I had become. None of the lower classes have anything to do with me, as I'm not one of them, and of course, the upper stations hardly acknowledge my existence, as I have been branded a traitor by name."

"And yet Lady Cilithrand saw fit to see you as our caretaker," Piers observed. "She had to know you would help us escape when we were ready to leave."

"Yeah, about that," Bally observed. "You told her the night we left. You didn't help us, she let us go."

"I have nothing to say in my defense," the elf admitted with a shrug. "I

84

have thought of this many times since, and I can only assume it was her plan for you to leave, and I therefore acted in accordance with her schemes."

"Why?" Ami asked warily, uncrossing her legs to stretch them out in front of her. "What did she gain by our leaving, especially after she offered to make me her heir?"

"I do not know," Animir admitted quietly, lowering his gaze.

"And then there's the hamar," Piers coughed. "Mustn't forget that. She gave it to the siren, but I have my doubts that it was actually for her."

"True," the girl agreed, studying the mermaid.

"There is also the matter of the weapons," the elf observed. "The satyrs could not have forged such massive arrows to stand against the rulers of our kingdom."

"And you think Lady Cilithrand had a hand in this as well?" Amicia exclaimed. "She armed them to stand against the dragons?"

"The possibility is strong," he agreed.

A heavy silence settled over the group as they considered the last bit of news. Having finished their meal, Piers instructed, "Everyone drink up, and let's get packed. We'll want to be on our way as soon as the light is gone so that we may cover as much ground as possible before time to break again."

Moving to comply, the walls of their shelter were removed and the litters reformed. Placing their gear atop them and tying it down, their mood remained somber as they each considered what the elf's tale could mean and what Lady Cilithrand might have in store for their unsuspecting crew.

TWELVE

March of the Dead

DESERT MARCH – Day 1

The night was uneventful. The litters are perfect, and everyone maintained their pace, so we covered our allotted distance with ease. We made camp as the sun came up and discovered removing a layer of sand helped keep us cool as the day progressed. Water will be tight, but we are sticking to one ration shared per meal. The walk is three days, so it should get us there if we are careful.

Piers Massheby, First Mate
Desert March – Day 2

The group is restless. We survived our second night, but the temperature has soared this morning. The canopy feels like an oven with us as loaves of bread baking inside. We have made a second dig, and the sand is cooler, but the swirling air is stifling. The siren looks pitiful, but she still breathes. I fear Rey won't take it well if she passes.

. . .

87

Piers Massheby, First Mate

Desert March – Day 3

Our third night was slower on the pace. Exhaustion has ravaged our ranks, but we manage to maintain our rations of the water. We will drink the last of it tonight with the meal and should reach the oasis before the next sun rises.

Piers, First Mate

Desert March – Day 4

I fear there has been a miscalculation in the distance to the oasis or in our direction of travel. We walked for the fourth night but have seen no change in the landscape, nor met any walking to or from this supposed city. With no water, no meal was taken, but camp is made and the others sleep from what I can tell. The siren's condition has deteriorated further, and I fear she will not last another evening.

Piers, First Mate

Desert March – Day 5

The elf swears that the oasis does exist. Zaendra, the nymph, is equally confident, but I see no sign of such a place. The group has been slowed to a crawl as it was our second night without food or water. We have had sightings; the others have all seen things out in the distance. Mirages that get no closer, yet do not leave us. Death is now our companion.

First Mate

Desert March – Day 6

The siren breathes, only faint. Her eyes do not open, so Amicia has carried her the whole night. We will not last another.

Mate

Staring at the page, Piers read what he had written. The words blurred, they danced before his eyes. A gust of wind cut under the edge of their shelter, rippling the sheaf of paper as he gripped it tightly, as if it were his last hold on reality.

"Mate," Ami called to him softly, placing her hand over his.

Looking up at her, his dark eyes swam. "Ami," he breathed, recognizing her and her wild strands of hair that had escaped her braid.

Taking the log from him, she rolled it around the pen, then returned it and the small bottle of ink to her bag. Still half full of food, they had not eaten since the last of the water had been spent.

"Lie with me," she commanded, stretching out between Animir and Bally the best she could.

"There's hardly room," he slurred. Slinking across her form, his hand slid down, then gripped as he moved in case he lost his balance.

She wanted to laugh at his silliness when he had found his position, which was opposite of the direction she lay, his boots next to her head. Instead, she grasped them firmly and wept against the smell of their leather.

His head close to the door, Piers struggled to free himself and then rested on his right arm, which he had pinned beneath him as he crawled. Panting from the effort, he stared at Rey. Slumped against one of the back poles, he held the mermaid to his chest, rocking her gently side to side.

Cutting his eyes up, he watched the horizon. The clear blue sky met the earth in the distance, as it had for six days. They had walked as far as they could, and this is where their corpses would be found; or covered by the blowing sand.

Closing his deep brown orbs, he listened to the ragged breaths of his friends. The wind tore at their canopy, bits of the blanket flapping noisily. He had no tears to cry as his mind drifted, floating over the memories as he slipped quietly into his last sleep.

Watching his companions lying before him, Rey held Oldrilin's limp form. His eyes glazed, staring through the opening at the waves of heat coming off the sand. His mind lost, he could feel the gentle sway of the flat, and lightning flashed in a distant cloud.

Caught by a spastic laugh, he chuckled. They had been seeing things for days; patches of water, clouds, and strange beasts had all presented themselves, but all only at a distance. None could be reached, and so they had given up trying to catch the illusive demons.

Staring at the cloud, it erupted into small puffs of darkness, as if a fungus growing in the bark of a tree at an accelerated rate. Expanding, moving, rolling with flashes of light. Blinking at it, he knew at any moment it would be gone. Focused on it, his scattered mind recalled the storm that had come to them on the raft, rolling in from a great distance. "A squall," he muttered hoarsely.

Tearing his eyes away, he stared at the unconscious creature in his arms. She still breathed, but only just. She had not opened her eyes since they lay in the tent the day before. Not daring to look up, he focused on her miniature form; the perfection of her tiny hands and delicate face as he caressed them with his dry cracked hands. He knew if he peeked, the clouds would be gone and all hope would be lost.

From outside, the glow of the quilt evidenced the sun beating down upon it. A strip of the material had been ripped loose and flapped wildly in the wind, slapping against the taut material that they had stretched over the poles to keep the heated rays at bay. Snapping and popping as it fluttered, the scrap flipped back and forth a few times, then dropped and lay still against the side of their shelter.

His gaze drawn to it, next to his right arm, he blinked repeatedly, as if to force it back into its chaotic whim. But the sliver of cloth refused. Raising his left hand, he leaned far enough to punch it through the tarp, flicking it and urging it to continue its struggle against the wind. His mouth dropping open, he glared at the impudent rag, then gritted his teeth as he growled.

Sitting back against the pole, his chin lifted and he stared out through the doorway at the approaching tempest. His jaw relaxed, his dentures parted in gaping awe as the dark storm rolled towards them, quickly covering the scorched earth. "Holy shit," he breathed.

Kicking his feet wildly, he screamed, "Dragon!"

Instantly awake, the Mate's head swum with delirium. "Dragon," he mumbled, rolling over and fumbling in the sand for his sword.

Animir and Bally joined him, and Amicia rolled onto her belly, barely alive and oblivious to her surroundings. The wind returned with an angry gust, tearing their covering away as a wall of water cascaded from the heavens.

Instantly refreshed, the Mate looked around him wildly, taking in the condition of the others. Looking up into the sky, he could hear or see no sign of the beast. Seizing one of the quilts, he shouted, "Help me! Spread it into the hole that it may collect the rain for us!"

Huge drops pelted their arms and faces, stinging them into red welt covered splotches of skin. Pulling the blanket across, they shifted what remained of their gear to the edges to keep it in place as the water pooled in the center of it, holding it against the wet sand below.

Surprised his storm had been real, Rey stared into the writhing clouds above him, then felt the stir of the creature in his arms. Wiping her hair from her face, she stretched, pushing her arms and legs out, as if drinking the precious fluid as it coated her.

Overcome with emotion, he rocked her back and forth, his shoulders shaking with his ragged breaths as he cried. Her mind clearing, Amicia joined him, clinging to his shoulder as she admired the beauty of the siren in her semi-delirious state.

Bending over their collection, Piers scooped goblets and bowls, first handing them to his comrades, who drank greedily from the vessels, then sitting them in the sand to be filled with the nectar of life. "I can't believe this is happening!" he shouted, expecting to awaken from his dream at any moment.

Her eyes open, Oldrilin stared at him, then shifted her gaze to the girl, who cried openly with joy. Burrowing against Rey's chest, she appeared calm, as if she had expected the storm all along.

"It's real!" Animir shouted, helping their leader locate every receptacle that they carried to be set out around their camp.

"Do you see the dragon?" Rey called, squinting against the spray that pummeled them.

"No dragon!" the Mate replied. "Just rain!"

Nodding, Reynard laid the siren upon the sand so he could aid in their search. Pushing at the granules, he formed a second hole and pulled a soggy blanket into it. Watching the water run in and collect, he shoved his face into the basin and drank until he thought he might vomit. Lifting himself out with his arms, the water slid down his face and dripped from his chin.

Above them, the clouds parted, and the deluge ended as abruptly as it had begun. To the west, the harsh rays of the sun punched their way through the clouds, fighting to regain control of its domain.

"Get the poles up!" Piers commanded. "Get the sides on it and cover the water."

"You think the sun can steal it away that fast?" Bally asked, fighting with the water-weight of the blankets.

"We can't take that chance," the older man replied, helping to lift the rain-soaked cover back into place. "We'll gather as much as we can. Maybe even stay here tonight and tomorrow, just to rest. Leave out tomorrow night with full bellies."

Working quickly, the group secured their camp. Syphoning the water out of Rey's smaller hole, they filled the waterskins, then used the remaining bit to rinse the mud from their clothing before spreading the articles across the sand to dry in what remained of the day.

"It's going to get cold," the Mate informed them. "We need to dry out everything we can before the sun sets."

Thinking of the drizzle after the rain on the raft, Amicia agreed with a nod. Looking down at her fingers, wrinkles cut deeply into her flesh, and she shivered at the thought of the miserable night to come. "I hate the desert," she mumbled as she pulled her clothing off, stripping down to her undergarments and spreading her sweater, shirt, and pants upon the sand.

All down to the bare essentials, the ground surrounding their camp held the majority of their belongings, all laid out to be dried by the relentless sun. As the last cloud disappeared overhead, Amicia announced, "We might as well have a bite to eat and catch a nap if we can."

"You have reservations about spending another day here?" Piers inquired, hoisting her pack to parcel out the rations.

"I do," she agreed. "We've been given a second chance, and I think it would be squandered lying about and waiting." Looking down into Lin's clear blue eyes, the round face did not smile. "Our reprieve is small, and I fear hardly enough to preserve us for long."

"Aye," Rey agreed. "We should pack at sunset, as usual, and push on." Looking around at the others for approval, he waited for Baldwin and Animir to weigh in.

"This is not up for discussion," Piers growled, realizing immediately that holding a heavy hand over the others would be impossible. Cutting his eyes over at the girl, he said more softly, "Are you sure?"

Toying with her merdoe through the thin material of her silky undergarments, she hesitated. Staring, as if off into some distant place, she sighed, "I'm sure. Let us eat and rest, and we can pack when the sun is low. There will be almost no moon tonight, so we will want to be ready to leave before the last light is gone."

"We have your light," Bally pointed out with a laugh, holding his hand up and imitating the way she had held the goblins of the foreboding forest at bay.

"Oh," she giggled, recalling the event as well. "Yes, we will have my light from the hamar gem if we need it."

"Then we walk tonight," the Mate agreed, handing her a portion of the dried meat and cheese. "Our food was wet by the deluge, so tonight will likely be our last meal of it; perhaps moving on is best after all."

Each locating a section of moist sand beneath the shade, they ate their food and then curled up for a nap. When they awoke, the sun had completed its journey and hung only half visible, the lower half hidden by the horizon.

Gathering their clothes, they dressed in optimistic silence, and the litters had both been rebuilt before the last of the light had disappeared. The last blanket soaked, their water hole still held a few inches, so they each scooped out a goblet and formed a ring around it to devour the last of their food.

"Who has the story?" Piers asked with warmth in his voice as he clung to their hope.

"Please, not a story," Rey begged. "Can't we just enjoy a single evening in one another's company?"

Chuckling, the Mate stroked his beard, giving the younger man a twisted grin. "I suppose for a single evening, we can let it go."

Allowing the silence, the group ate for several minutes before the ground around them began to boil as thousands of insects pushed their way to the surface and took flight. Pillars of tiny bodies formed clouds against the starry sky, and a moment later, they began to light up and blink wildly in a thick cloud around them.

Slapping at the swarm, Bally cried out, rolling on the ground. "Get them off!" he screamed.

"No, stop!" Amicia shouted, leaping to her feet. "You're hurting them!"

Frozen in mid roll, he glared at her, "Hurting them?"

The rest of the group sat still, staring at the girl as she opened her hand flat, palm to the sky. A dancing ball of light landed upon it, a tiny body no more than half an inch tall, fluttering glowing wings.

"What the hell is that?" Rey gasped.

"It's a desert fairy," Ami breathed, smiling as she spoke to the miniscule creature. Blinking rapidly, she laughed. "They live here, beneath the sand, and enjoy the night after a rain," she imparted to her friends. "Oh, yes," she agreed, speaking to the fairy on her hand.

Nodding, the conversation seemed to take hours, but in fact only a minute or two passed before she had learned all that she needed, and the pair of wings fluttered to carry her informant away. Sinking back into her place in the sand, she watched around them as the flow diminished until it was gone. The dancing lights blinked all around, but their number grew thinner as the fairies disbursed to enjoy their single evening.

"Well?" Piers prodded.

"They will spend the night mating, tonight and maybe tomorrow if the moisture lasts. Then they will burrow beneath the sand to await the next rain," she sighed.

"But that could be days or weeks from now," Bally observed.

"Months or even years," Amicia corrected, swiping at a tear. "What a beautiful life, living for a few moments in time."

Shaking his head, the Mate chuckled, "I suppose you find it romantic."

Snapping out of her trance, the girl stared at him, "What?"

"Forget it," he smirked. "Did they share anything useful. You know, about the desert or the oasis that's supposedly around here somewhere?"

"Oh, yes!" she exclaimed. "Whitefair. The city is to the north, and we should reach it tonight if we get moving; but there's a problem," she revealed, glancing between her comrades anxiously.

"So what's the problem," Rey scowled, aware that there always seemed to be one on their little holiday, as no event had ever gone completely according to plan.

"The oasis is filled with unsavory sorts of creatures. The desert fairy has warned of a collection of bones, where the bodies of those outcast by its inhabitants have been dumped over the years, and they are not given a proper burial. The people of Whitefair are savages, and apparently, they do not take kindly to strangers. The town is more like a trap than a haven," she warned, her features drawn into an unhappy frown.

"Unsavory or not, we'll cross that bridge when we get there," the Mate informed them, rising to have a look around. "We need to be sure we have everything and get moving as soon as we can."

Amicia had removed her braid after the deluge, and wild frizz stuck out around her head. "We should tie your hair up before we go," Rey observed, patting it playfully.

"I thought you liked it down," she giggled, pulling her mirror and brush out of her pack.

"I do, but this isn't the time," he informed her sternly. "We need to be comfortable to walk the last few miles, and having your hair flying around and distracting you won't do."

Sitting still, she allowed him to tame the curls and pull them into a tight bun at the base of her skull. Using her father's mirror, she inspected his handy work. "Thank you, Rey," she offered, pleased with the result.

"Don't mention it," he replied, getting to his feet with the others as they hoisted their litters and formed their line, headed north through the desert of Peaswan and towards the oasis of Whitefair.

THIRTEEN

Oasis of Whitefair

THE NIGHT DARK, the thin sliver of moon that eventually emerged did little to light their way. Off in the distance, to the north, a group of rocks jutted out from the surface and grew larger as they marched towards it.

"I think I see it," the Mate announced when he felt certain his eyes did not deceive him.

"We should be careful," Ami called, reminding him of the desert fairy's warning.

"Aye," he agreed in a quieter tone. The load heavy upon his shoulders, he kept the pace until the jagged stones were large enough to discern more clearly, then he stopped, calling everyone to form up.

"We need a plan," he informed them as they gathered around, dropping their loads onto the soft earth. "To the east, this small gathering of hills tapers off. I think we should hide our supplies there before we enter the city. With nothing visible to steal, we will make less of a target."

"Aye," Rey agreed, helping himself to a swig of their water, then passing the waterskin to the others.

Accepting the drink, Amicia's brow furrowed. "I have an ill feeling of this place. Perhaps a few of you should enter the town and scout ahead of us, maybe find a hiding place that we may slip into unseen," she suggested, placing her hand on Zae's shoulder to include her in the group needing protection from the unknown.

97

Exchanging glances, the men nodded, then the Mate replied, "Agreed. Let's move to the trailing edge of the stones and get you hidden. Rey and I will venture in and prepare a place for us." His eyes flicking over the horizon, he puckered his lips. "We'll need gold or something of value to barter with."

Producing her pouch of coins, Amicia recalled the day she had collected it in her parents' cottage. Handing it to him, she sighed, "This was to buy my passage to the west."

Bouncing the sack a few times, the pieces jingled. "Perhaps it will buy you sanctuary instead," he mused, placing them in his pocket and indicating the litters. "We need to get moving before the sun rises and we are seen."

Resuming their single line, the group ambled across the sand, arriving at the line of boulders as the first streaks of pink decorated the sky. Choosing a pair that would provide a bit of shade, they studied the view of the city from that vantage point, discovering that there was none.

The tall rocks that lay between them and Whitefair obstructed their view, but the sound of the city coming to life was unmistakable as voices and other noises carried across the sand. "Build a small canopy to hold off the sun while I have a closer look," Piers instructed, leaving the group while he slunk between the over-sized stones.

Dropping her pack, Amicia unpacked one of the litters to retrieve the poles. Balancing them against one of the rocks, she draped the quilt over and climbed inside, her companions joining her.

Sitting at the entrance, Rey waited for their leader's return. When he came around from the opposite side from that which he left, the younger man leapt up to meet him. "Is something wrong?"

"No," the Mate chuckled. "Just being sure I wasn't followed. The two guys I saw are covered head to toe in some kind of wrap; maybe to protect them from the heat and sun. I think we can replicate it if we strip down one or two of these blankets and use a bit of the rope as a belt to hold it closed."

Using Ami's dagger, he cut the edge of one of the padded quilts, gently removing each of the small knots that kept it from bunching up with laundry and use. The front made of a colorful pattern and the back a plain dingy white, they wrapped themselves and placed a flap of the swath over their heads to act as a hood.

"How do I look?" Rey asked with a chuckle, feeling ridiculous.

"Like you might pass for a local," the Mate informed him with a slap on the shoulder. "All right, we're set. I'm taking what I can for trade, so wish us luck and stay out of sight. Animir, you and Bally are the girls' only defense if you are discovered, so keep your swords handy and be ready should anyone get too close."

"Aye," Baldwin agreed, giving him a salute.

"I can fight, too," Zaendra mumbled, clutching her staff as their leader turned to go.

Smiling down at her as he caressed her dark cheek, Piers confirmed, "Of course you can, but I wouldn't want you to be hurt. If anyone comes, let the boys handle it, ok?"

Cutting her eyes up at him, she frowned while she nodded.

"Good lass," he praised, patting her shoulder firmly.

Satisfied they would be hidden and as comfortable as they could be, Rey and Piers left the group and began the trek around. The rocks sticking up from the ground gave way to a massive barrier constructed from bricks formed with desert sand.

"This place has been here a while," the Mate observed, dragging his fingers over the rough surface of the wall. "I wonder how we get in?"

"There must be a gate," Rey surmised, indicating they should keep moving. "Unfortunately, that negates the probability of entering unseen. Someone is going to know we are here."

"Aye," the older man agreed, shading his eyes against the sun as he studied the barrier ahead of them. In the distance, he could make out the opening, as well as the men who appeared to be guarding the entrance. Adjusting the strap to his bag, he thought about the items he carried inside, things he hoped to trade for their safety.

"Hello," he called as they got closer, waving at the pair of men who ambled back and forth across the entrance.

Placing his claymore against his shoulder, one of the men faced the seaman and scowled, "What right of passage have you here?"

"We are travelers," the first mate replied calmly. "We've been told of this oasis and wish to replenish our stores before we travel north."

"North," the man grunted. "We don't take in many strangers," he informed them bluntly."

"We will trade for our supplies," Piers insisted, opening his pack and producing one of the fine elven goblets. Holding it up and turning the cup made of gold, the jewels encrusted in the sides and base caught the morning light, creating a brilliant display.

The second man pushed his way in, reaching for the offering, but the Mate pulled it away; "For our passage."

"Sure, come in," the first man agreed, "but be warned. We deal harshly with rule breakers and thieves."

"We're not thieves," Rey informed him tartly, adjusting his pack as he followed his superior through the gate and down the dusty path.

Inside, they cleared the gate and moved through the crowd. "Keep your head down," the Mate instructed. "Don't speak to anyone unless I say."

Ahead, the path broke into different directions, lined with buildings formed from the same sandstones as the wall that surrounded the place. People moved all around them, about half of them covered head-to-toe in the same fashion as the two men who held the gate. Grinning to himself, the first mate felt certain they would blend in well enough with their disguises.

There were few windows in the structures that were topped with wood slat roofs, which hung over the sides one to two feet. Just below them, the walls did not meet them, leaving large gaps to aid in the circulation of the air inside.

Pushing forward, they entered the center of the city, and a natural spring bubbled from a stone pillar in the center of a courtyard, reminding Rey of the elves and their fancy fountain. "That must be it," he observed. Looking up, large wooden beams crossed the wide expanse, providing a degree of shade that lowered the temperature, while at the same time allowed in enough light to keep it well-lit in the bright sun.

"Aye," the Mate agreed, pausing his step to also have a look around.

The buildings surrounding the spring all had wide windows that overlooked the area, one on each of the six sides. Each window had a covering made of dried reeds, held open by a long stick. Children laughed and played in the shadows, and large clay pots lined the walls, with women carrying in new ones and exchanging them at random intervals.

The fountain itself was guarded by a second pair of men, who stood watch as more women filled the clay vessels and lined them up to await their exchange. "It's all very organized," he observed, indicating for the other man to follow as he fell into step behind one of the women, this one dressed in a simple dress, rather than the head-to-toe robe.

Her long dark hair bleached by the sun, lighter sections caught the rays and glowed with a red hue. Her skirt a bright orange contrasting against her green top, it swished as she walked, her bare feet silent as they made contact with the soft earth. The jug balanced on her shoulder, she probably had made the same journey every day of her life by the look of her.

Admiring the sway of her hips, Piers grinned at the seductive attitude in her strut before a man tumbled in front of her. Catching her as she lost her balance, his hands landed on her waist, keeping her on her feet as Rey helped her secure the unbalanced load.

"Easy, girl," the Mate soothed, the two who had brought the disruption rolling around in the sand and exchanging punches before a third stepped in and separated them.

"There'll be no fighting here!" the one in charge bellowed, grasping one of the lawbreakers by the scruff of his neck and dragging him to his feet. Giving him a shove back down the path they had entered by, the other brawler stumbled along after, holding back the flow of blood from his brow with the palm of his hand.

"Rough place," Rey observed.

"Aye," the Mate agreed, turning his attention to the woman, who gazed up at him with large brown eyes accented with flecks of green. Caught in the moment with her, he bowed, offering his name, "Piers Massheby, ma'am."

"So I see," she breathed, her chest rising and falling as she panted heavily. "New to Whitefair?"

"Passing through," he offered, giving her his best smile. "Only just arrived and looking for a place to stay for a day while we prepare to head north."

"North," she echoed, her features scrunched and hinting at her years with fine lines around her eyes.

"Aye," he laughed. "Would you know of a bed and breakfast we might rent for the night?"

Breaking their connection, her hair floated as she turned away, searching for her canister that Rey had relieved her from. Seeing him holding it patiently as she had done, she stared up into his clear hazel orbs. "You are men," she breathed.

"That's the general idea," the Mate chortled quietly, surprised by her reaction.

"No, men," she repeated, then clarified, "mortals of the rim."

"Ah, yes, we are that as well," he confirmed, his hand grasping a few strands of her hair and pulling at the curl of them.

Staring at him, Rey could not believe how easily the other man appeared to be toying with her, almost certain he would have her into a bed before the sun had set. "I can carry the water if you'd like to lead the way," he offered, feeling as if the couple had forgotten he even existed as they shared their connection.

"Yes, of course," she snapped out of her trance. Standing straighter, she grinned, "I'm Meena. Meena Gavaan," she supplied, offering her hand.

Giving it a firm shake, the Mate smiled with all his charm, holding the appendage for a moment before raising it to his lips to plant a gentle kiss upon it.

Clearing his throat, Rey adjusted his load, again interrupting their connection.

"Please," Meena said with a smile, "this way." Pushing past the two men, she continued her stride down the narrow road until she arrived at a set of stone steps carved into rock that formed the wall of one of the houses.

Following her up to the landing above, they arrived at a patio covered by another section of bound reeds that held out the sun. Beneath it, a table with four chairs stood in the center. Around the outside, a short wall held a long bench on the far side, with small potted plants hanging over the edges and lining the other.

The plants heavy with strange fruits and vegetables, they had enjoyed the morning sun as it rose. Currently midday, a pleasant shade covered the area, keeping the air significantly cooler than the rest of what they had seen.

To the left lay an entrance into her two-room apartment. Holding back the brightly colored blanket that covered the door, she permitted them to enter. Inside, their eyes adjusted to the darkness as only a pair of small lamps burned, located on opposite sides of the room from each other. Rey placed her jug on the table that sat squarely in the center of her kitchen as he looked around.

The wall on the left formed the corner of the door, so that the entrance opened up straight back and to the right. On the far wall, a long table served as her workspace for preparing meals and caring for her plants. On the wall to the right of the door, a long, cushioned bench served as a place to sit or lie down. In the right wall, they could see another door that led into the bedroom, but they could not discern what it held through the narrow gap as a thin swath of material hung over to give it privacy.

"Your place is nice," Piers offered, smiling at her with a squint to his eyes.

Looking him up and down, the woman did not return the grin. Instead, she demanded in earnest, "Why have you come to Whitefair?"

"We told you. We're just passing through," he assured, holding up his hands in a form of surrender.

"And our tongue happens to roll off your lips," she accused, crossing her arms as she glared at him evenly.

Rocking his jaw slowly, the Mate studied her, then asked, "Have we done something to offend you? I thought we were being neighborly, carrying your jug for you and all."

"Neighborly," she smirked. "No one is neighborly in Whitefair, and no services rendered without a price," she wheezed, taken with a cough. Serving herself a cup of water from her new supply, she cut her eyes over at the younger man, then drank the liquid in a few quick gulps. "How long have you been in Eriden?"

Clearing his throat, Piers growled, "All right, that's enough. Sorry we bothered you, *ma'am*." Grabbing the younger man by the arm, he pushed him towards the door ahead of him.

"No, wait!" she hissed, holding up her hands as he had done only a few moments before. "Please, I do not mean to be ungrateful. It was kind of you to provide your aid," she added with a hint of a smile. "Would you like some of my water?" she offered, hoping to appease the newcomers.

Accepting the cup, the pair each had a drink, their eyes roving as they studied her small home further.

"You live here alone?" Piers asked in a relaxed tone, removing his bag from his shoulder and dropping it on the bench, next to the door.

"Yes," she agreed with a nod. "I have been here many years. It belonged to my husband, and we shared it before he died." Her lids heavy, his passing brought her obvious pain.

"I'm sorry," he said more quietly, lifting his chin towards the exit, indicating for the other man to go out.

Doing as he had been silently directed, Reynard dropped the curtain over the outer door into place and took a seat on one of the chairs. Propping his feet up in a second, he hunched over and prepared for a nap, as he felt certain the Mate would soon make his first conquest of Whitefair, so he was going to be there a while.

FOURTEEN

Hiding Places

"WOULD YOU LIKE SOMETHING TO EAT?" Meena offered, keeping the table between them as she moved around her small kitchen.

"No," the Mate replied. Removing the protective layers of mangled quilt he had added to his clothing, the cooler air of her home felt nice. "We really need to find a place to settle for a day or two," he confessed.

"As I said, there aren't many such places to be had here," she informed him. As he came around the table towards her, she took a few steps counter clockwise, keeping the distance between them. "I could show you a bit of hospitality," she offered, then added, "for a price," more softly.

"Hospitality," he repeated, frozen in his pursuit. He had been working his way around, hoping to get close enough to put a few moves on her that would make her more receptive to giving them aid, but her mention of payment had him on edge. "You mean, *hospitality*," he slurred the word, raising his eyebrows at her a few times.

"Of course; for a fair sum," she replied, clasping the leather bag that hung at her waist, the few coins inside tinkling against one another.

His eyes wide with horror, he made the connection at the same moment she realized her mistake. "Oh, shit," he muttered. "You're a –" he caught himself before he said the word.

Pressing her lips together, she raised her chin defiantly. "I'm a what?" she

105

spat. "A woman working hard to make ends meet in this god forsaken hell hole?"

Her words sharp, he could see the pain in her eyes. Pressing his hand flat against his chest, he stammered, "Look, I'm sorry; I didn't mean... " His voice trailed away as he searched for the right words. Exhaling loudly, he straightened himself and tried again. "I need to find a place for us. A place for a few days that we can rest and prepare for the next leg of our journey. I'm not really interested in... anything else," he faltered.

Her cheeks flushed with indignation, she tightened her jaw, then spat, "I'll rent you the patio for the night if that's all you're after."

"That's very generous," he agreed, smiling with relief that she was at least still speaking to him after their misunderstanding. "But we have other friends," he explained, chopping the air with a stiff hand as he clarified, then swinging it wide as if indicating the others through the city walls. "We really need a little more protection."

"What kind of friends?" she eyed him warily, dropping the pouch and moving slowly towards her collection of knives, not sure what to make of the stranger and his odd behavior.

His demeanor less than his typically collected self, Piers fidgeted with his clothing for a moment, then laid it on the line, "I have a few friends hiding outside of town. The kind I wouldn't want to see injured. How much to have your bedroom for a few days to hide them in? No hospitality required."

She had reached the back table, and he could see her fingers sliding towards one of the blades.

"You're not going to need that," he clipped with a sigh. "If you say no, we'll go and look elsewhere. We don't want any trouble; we just want a few days to rest up before we head back out." Leaving her to think about his offer, he darted out the door, dropping the curtain back into place and plunking down into one of the unoccupied chairs.

"Wow, that was quick," Rey observed, removing his feet from the other seat.

"Hardly," Piers spat, holding his face in his hands, his elbows digging into his knees. "She comes with a rate," he informed him quietly. "I told her we just want to rent her room for a few days, and I'm giving her a minute to decide. If she says no, we'll go back to the spring and try someone else."

"You'll get yourselves killed, more like," she informed him from the doorway. Glaring at him with her deep brown orbs, there was something intriguing

106

about his behavior. Nothing fit with the two men; not their clothing, their demeanor, and certainly not their ability to speak her language.

Joining them, she took the seat next to Rey and rested her arms on the table before her. "How many friends?"

"Five," Piers spat. "And we need a way to get them into the city unseen."

"Unseen," she laughed. "You do like a challenge. That will cost you. But I know someone who can arrange it."

"Fair enough." Opening his pack, he produced the second of their elven goblets. Placing it on the table before her, he could see her eyes grow wide, but she didn't ask where he got it. Relieved, he exhaled loudly, then asked, "Can it be done tonight?"

"Do you have another one?" she cut her eyes up at him for a moment, then returned them to the treasure he had presented.

Growling under his breath, he opened the pack and placed a second by its side. "That's it," he grunted.

"It will do. At dark, my associate will take you to retrieve your friends, and they can hide in my bedroom. You get two nights, and then you must leave. After that, there's too much risk of detection. I have regulars who will notice..." she informed him quietly.

"Aye," he nodded, gazing at her dolefully. "I understand."

His face taking on a hot flush, Rey also understood. "Well, now that that's settled, do you have a place around here to have a pint? Or is beer out of the question?"

Laughing again, Meena studied the younger man. "Whitefair is filled with pubs," she informed him curtly. "It's about the only thing we do here. Go back down to the path and hang a right, then follow the noise. But watch yourself and keep covered as much as you can. We have few men of the rim in the oasis, so you'll stand out like a sore thumb."

"There are other mortals here?" Rey asked in surprise as the Mate recovered himself with his wrap and hood.

"Yes," she affirmed with a nod. "About a dozen, along with elves, dwarves, a few satyrs. And most would cut your heart out for what's in that bag of yours," she sneered, certain that wasn't the last of his trinkets.

"We'll be careful," the Mate agreed, standing beside his young friend as he hung his pack over his shoulder. "Make the arrangements, and we'll meet you back here at dusk."

Following his leader, Rey marched down the stairs, and they turned onto the path as she had directed. Arriving at a bar a few blocks down, they made their way inside, where they took a table in a dark corner and prepared to stay out of sight until they could make their next move.

"Are we all set?" Piers demanded, arriving on Meena's patio as the last golden rays disappeared.

"We are," she replied with a crooked grin. "This is Geoffrey Tabard and Humphray Heron, fellow mortals of the rim," she introduced, presenting each with an open palm. "They are going to help get your friends here to my quarters, safe and sound."

Nodding at each in turn, the first mate quickly assessed the pair. Geoffrey stood near his height, maybe an inch taller, with short spikes in his near black hair. His build slender, his beady blue eyes watched around him anxiously, and the Mate felt certain he was the brains of their duo.

Humphray on the other hand stood about five-foot-ten and nearly as much around the middle. His fingers stubby, he offered his hand, and Piers wiped the sweat from his fingers after he accepted it. His hair and eyes dark brown, his round face held a vacant expression, and the Mate flicked his gaze back and forth between the unlikely pair for a moment before he decided they would do. Satisfied, he announced, "Fine. Let's go before anything crazy happens."

Her eyes wide, the woman glared at him, "Is something wrong?"

"Nope," he clipped, shaking his head firmly as Rey came stumbling up the stairs behind him. "Rey, you stay here, out of sight," he instructed, pointing at one of the chairs under the canopy.

"Aye, aye, captain," the younger man replied with an exaggerated salute, then spitting as he broke into a loud laugh.

"Shh," Meena hissed, grabbing him by the chest and pulling him to the furthest point before shoving him into a chair. "You'll be heard!"

Nodding his agreement, Rey leaned against his fist, propping himself up against the back of the chair and closing his eyes.

"He's drunk!" Geoffrey observed.

"Aye," the Mate agreed with a disgruntled scowl. "Hours we've waited, so the sooner we get the others here and under cover the better."

"We'll get them here," Humphray promised, clamping him on the shoulder as he hoisted a large coil of rope. "Which direction are we headed?"

"East," Piers replied more calmly as they scurried down the stone steps. "There's some large boulders…"

"Yeah, yeah, we know the ones," Humphray agreed, turning to Meena as she brought up the rear. "We'll get them over the wall, but you must keep watch," he whispered so that only she could hear.

"Right," she replied, pulling her hood up to cover her head as they followed the first man through the narrow passages.

The sun gone, the only beings out would be those up to no good, so they did their best to avoid contact with anyone. Arriving at the east wall a short time later, Geoffrey scaled the rough surface with ease, then dropped the rope back for his cohort to join him.

A much larger man, Humphray huffed loudly as he pulled himself up, only making it about three feet off the ground before he lost his grip and crashed into the soft sand below. Shaking his head in disgust, Piers smacked him on the arm, "Forget it. We'll get them. You go find us some food and deliver it to Meena's; I'm sure my friends will be hungry when we get them there."

"Food? At this hour?" the fat man grunted.

"Aye," the Mate replied tartly. "You don't look like you miss many meals. Food for five and some broth if you can score it."

"Broth," the other man laughed, dropping the rope before he strutted away. "Fine, I'll bring the meal, but it's going to cost you," he called over his shoulder.

Shaking her head, Meena sighed, "Sorry, Piers. Everything costs, but don't worry; we'll see that they're fed."

Taking hold of the rope, he hoisted himself up, straddling the wall next to Geoffrey, who had been anchoring it for him. "Do we leave it here?"

"Naw, you go down, and I'll join you, then I'll bring it back up when we've gathered the rest," he stipulated.

Using the line to walk down the wall, Piers observed as the other man seemed to know where all the hand and foot holes were without looking as he followed. "You boys do this often?" he asked, concern growing in the back of his mind over what might happen if they were caught.

"Once or twice a month," the other man sneered. "We have a guy who makes regular deliveries for us, so sometimes we use this wall; sometimes we use the west."

"What sort of deliveries," the Mate insisted, squaring his shoulders and folding his arms across his chest as he waited for the reply.

"The secret kind," Geoffrey laughed. "Which way?"

Seeing that a real response was unlikely, Piers pointed, "Over there," leading him through the boulders. Without lights or torches, he feared that they would have a difficult time finding the group, but his companion seemed to know the maze of rocks well, and they found the rest of his friends sitting on the ground, watching around them anxiously when they arrived.

"Piers!" Ami squealed, leaping to her feet and throwing her arms around him.

Getting to his feet, Baldwin followed, observing, "We weren't sure you would make it. We realized after you left we really hadn't come up with a backup plan in case you didn't."

"No need," the Mate observed, giving the girl a squeeze before placing her feet back on the ground and handing out orders. "We don't want to take most of this stuff in with us; only what we'll need while we gather our supplies. Is there somewhere around here we can hide it until we're ready to leave?" he asked, addressing their guide, who was inspecting their gear.

"Sure," Geoffrey shrugged. "I know about a cave over on the north side of these boulders –" He stopped, noticing the mermaid. "What the hell is that?"

Staring up at him with wide eyes, Oldrilin sidled around behind Baldwin so that only a sliver of her small form could be seen.

"A friend; leave her be," the Mate growled, selecting the items they would carry over the wall. "We'll want to fill these waterskins and the wine bottles. Most of the rest we won't need, except a few empty packs for carrying food and such."

Nodding, the local man agreed, his eyes still trained on the siren. "Yeah, bring some empty packs, and we'll get you stocked up."

Fitting her pack over her shoulders, onto her back, Amicia placed Lin's carrier on her chest and offered to hoist her into it.

"I'll walk," she replied, pushing her hands away.

"That ain't right," Geoffrey chuckled, her words indecipherable. "I've learned most of the languages that come in here, but I never heard that one." He looked from one group member to the next, awaiting an explanation.

"Show us the place," the Mate insisted, carrying their poles and weapons with folded arms.

"This way," the other man grunted, waving his hand for them to follow. On the other side of the band of large rocks, he located one with a hollow space underneath so that a small cave was formed. "No one'll see them in here," he promised.

Immediately realizing that could be a lie, the Mate said in a low voice, "Leave nothing of value."

"Aye," Bally agreed, stacking their blankets on top of the poles. "I'll take my sword and ax."

"I'll bring Amicia's bow and quiver, along with mine," Animir volunteered.

Sorting their belongings quickly, the six friends quickly grouped for their departure and followed Geoffrey back to the wall, where he climbed once again and dropped the rope below for them to use.

"Let me take her," Piers instructed, pointing at Oldrilin's bag, which still hung in front of Ami.

"I shall climb," the siren insisted.

"Look, we let you walk, but if you fall, you could be hurt. This isn't something easy, like swimming, so let us help you," he replied, bending over so he could keep his voice down. Accepting the pack, he placed his arms into the rope supports and offered her his hand.

Wearing a full pout, she accepted his digits, and he hoisted her up and placed her firmly against his chest. Using the rope, he made quick work of the climb, and the rest of the group followed, Bally bringing up the rear.

On the other side, Meena still waited, pacing anxiously as they each landed on the ground with a heavy thud. When Amicia turned, standing before her, the older woman stared at her with wide eyes. Her hands trembling, she seized the edges of her hood and pushed it back, dropping it onto her back as she searched the girl's eyes for some hint of recognition.

When none came, she stammered, "I'm Meena Gavaan."

"Amicia Spicer," Ami replied with a grimace.

"No time for that," Piers snapped, lining everyone up after pulling his blanket-cloak around him to keep the siren hidden. "We follow Meena straight to her place. Don't stop, speak or make eye contact with anyone until we are safely inside. Everyone understand?" Garnering their agreement, the rest followed as he led them down the path to their haven.

FIFTEEN

Any Price

CUTTING through the streets of the city, they met few and none who seemed interested in conversing. Leading the way, Meena kept her back stiff, her hood in place as she kept them moving, only pausing when the need to let someone pass arose.

Behind her, Bally followed, with Animir close behind. His height more than the others, he stood out, and the point of his ears and slant of his eyes indicated his ancestry quite clearly, which put him on edge. However, they had passed or seen three others by the time they reached the stone steps to her home, which gave him some relief that he wouldn't be an unusual visitor to the area.

Behind him, Ami kept pace, pulling her sweater around her despite the air remaining quite warm at the moment. She could hear Piers's heavy steps behind her, and they brought a little comfort that he was there. He carried the siren, which would keep her safe as well. So far, they had met two people, and they both had reacted strongly, which had her on edge.

Bringing up the rear, Geoffrey followed the line of outsiders, his mind turning with every step. They had been in Whitefair more than a decade, and the pair had learned fairly quickly that money above all else made for a happy life in the middle of the desert. Without it, they would have nothing and nowhere else to go at that. Taking care of this lot would pay handsomely, and

113

if the midget woman turned out to be what he suspected, he just might turn a year's worth of profits in a single night.

Arriving at the last turn, each climbed the stairs while looking around over the streets and houses below. Only a few were built with a second floor, so they were able to see many of the roofs spread across the vast metropolis.

"How many people are here?" Baldwin asked, surprised at the size of the town.

"Near a hundred thousand last time they took a count," Meena supplied, surprised by the random question.

"Ignore him," Piers suggested. "He rambles about nonsense frequently." Stepping into the kitchen, he opened his robe and helped his charge to the floor, then indicated the bedroom. "Go in and rest, Lin. We'll call for you when it's safe to come out, and we can have a bit of dinner."

When she had done as he asked, he turned to join the others on the patio, only to find Geoffrey peeking through the curtain that served as her door. "Do you mind?" he demanded, pushing his way out and pulling the cloth closed.

Wearing a satisfied grin, the other man placed his hands on his hips and spat, "Not at all. When shall I return for the pickup?"

"Night after tomorrow," Meena replied, handing him a fistful of coins.

Opening his palm, he studied the lot for a moment, then closed his hand around them, giving them a shake so that they jingled as he turned and marched down the stairs.

On the table, a meal had been spread, complete with a bowl of broth. "I guess the fat man does know where to get the grub," the Mate chuckled. Turning back to the door, he called inside, "Oldrilin, dinner is served."

Scurrying out on her tiny feet, the siren joined them, where she was handed her bowl of broth as she sat upon the bench next to a few potted plants.

Staring down at her, Meena breathed, "Holy shit!"

"What?" Amicia asked, accepting her bowl of stew and a hunk of bread.

"I didn't see her when you came over the wall," the older woman gasped. No, she had been too awestruck by the girl to notice. "Did Geoff see her?"

"Aye," the Mate nodded, also taking a bowl and a chair. "He seemed quite interested now that you mention it."

"We have to get you out of here, tomorrow night at the latest," the older woman replied in a shaky voice before she darted down the stairs.

"Hey, that was not our agreement," Piers spat, getting out of his seat to follow her. At the bottom, she spun around, running into him. Catching her as they collided, he paused, staring down into her deep brown pools, the green flecks sparkling in the dim light.

"She's a siren, isn't she," the woman whispered, her hands pressed against his chest as she joined him on the bottom step.

"Aye," he agreed, squinting at her with concern. "What difference does that make?"

"They are rare," she breathed, looking over her shoulder before catching his hand and leading him up a few steps before pausing. "Elves, nymphs; those are common here. We even get a few trolls once in a while. Mermaids are a different story."

"And?"

"Geoffrey and Humphray are traders. They buy and sell; that's what they do. Something so rare wanders into the village, you can wager he already knows who would be interested in acquiring one," she hissed, keeping her voice low.

"Lin is not for sale!"

"Shh," she warned at his raised voice. "Of course not, but that doesn't mean they won't try to steal her. I'm sorry. If I had known she was among you…" Her voice trailed away.

"Ah, you could have set up your own buyer," he accused.

"No!" she spat, instantly angry. "I would never sell another living being, not for any price!"

"Pfft, you sell yourself. I find that hard to believe."

The slap landed with a loud crack, catching him off guard. "You listen to me, Piers Massheby. A harlot was not my first choice in this life. I've spent many days starving and many nights sleeping in an alley; too many not to realize how much I am worth or what my life costs me."

His hand sliding over the wounded cheek, his beard tingled. "Careful. I might like it rough," he growled.

Thrown off by the banter, she blinked at him. "Are you always an ass?"

"Aye," he chuckled, "just ask my friends."

Her lip twitching, she fought the smile. *Something else about him that doesn't quite fit*, she observed. "Well, your little friend is in danger," she reminded him curtly. "We have to get her out of town before they can come to take her."

"All right," he agreed with a small nod. "We'll discuss it after they've eaten. Maybe tomorrow. They could use a good night's rest as well," he stipulated, turning to complete the climb to his dinner.

Piers glanced around at the group, noting they had all near finished eating by that time; save Rey who stirred his portion aimlessly. "Still drunk?" he asked.

"Aye," the younger man replied. "That was the strongest beer I've ever had."

"Well, some of it was liquor," the Mate chuckled. "Those smaller glasses you were downing. Do you have any gold left at all?"

"Nope. I didn't have much to begin with."

"It's ok," the Mate let him off easy, considering his condition. "We'll have enough." Reclaiming his seat, he ate a few more bites, then pushed the bowl away. "Meena thinks we can't wait. We need to get our supplies together tomorrow so we can leave out tomorrow night."

Instantly sober, Rey sat up straight. "Why's that?"

Watching the siren as she finished off her broth, Piers laid his hand over his heart, feeling it beat heavily inside his chest. It was no secret he had never cared for the tiny creature, or her kind. However, realizing she could be in danger disturbed him just the same.

"I don't want to get into that," he said, avoiding the reason for the change in plans. "Suffice it to say there is nothing fair about Whitefair, and the sooner we get out of here the better."

"Where will we go?" Amicia spoke up, drawing her sweater tighter around her as she listened in on their conversation.

"We're still headed north," Piers informed her. "Although I'm not totally sure what we will find when we get there."

"Trolls and wolves," Meena dropped flatly, taking a seat next to him. Pouring herself a drink from a bottle of wine, she raised it in a toast. "Might as well bid you the best of luck now."

"Why is that?" Rey demanded, glaring at her.

"Trolls are a right nasty bunch; they don't make friends. Even the few who have ventured here keep to themselves. The wolves, well, they aren't much better. They take crossing their lands kind of personal," she sneered, having a hefty taste of her beverage.

Her eyes wide, Ami considered the possibilities. Clutching her merdoe through her shirt, she swallowed hard, then asked, "Is there any way around?"

"Depends on where you're going," the other woman smiled.

"We're not really sure," the Mate confessed, running his hands through his hair, pulling at the knot to free it and let it hang down loosely upon his shoulders. "We're looking for a ship, or a place we can build one, so we can return to the rim."

Spitting into her cup, Meena glared at him. "You're serious! Hasn't anyone told you? There is no leaving Eriden." She cut her eyes over at the blonde, blinking at her a few times. "Only the dragons have ever seen beyond the barrier that protects us."

"We've been told," Amicia agreed, meeting her stare. "Call us slow learners. That, or hard-headed fools who refuse to give up," she laughed, glancing at their leader. "Either way, that's where we're going."

Her hand trembling, Meena placed her cup on the table, then rubbed her palms across her skirt. "Let's say that it was even remotely possible. You would need help."

"And how much is that going to cost us?" Piers snapped.

Staring at him, Meena curled her tongue for a long moment, then tears formed in her eyes. "Perhaps you would consider a trade," she replied softly.

"Ah, and let me guess. You require a place within our company and passage to the rim," he chuckled, rolling his eyes.

Shocked, she glanced around at the others, "Is that not what each of you seek? A way out of Eriden. An escape to a better life?"

Her dark features crinkled, Zaendra observed with a raised chin, "Certainly not. I wish to explore more of my homeland, not that I ever wish to leave it."

Pursing her lips, Meena turned on Animir. "And what of you, elf? Do you desire to visit the realm of mortals?"

Cracking a wide smile, he laughed, "I'm sure I wouldn't make it far there," indicating the pointed tips to his pierced ears. Wafting his hand at her, he nodded, "But you on the other hand. You might walk among them unseen. But why would you care to leave? Is your life here among your people truly so hard?"

Rising, she left them, moving into her quarters, only to return a moment later with a small golden orb in her hand. Sitting in her chair, she held it up before her.

"An orb of truth!" Amicia gasped.

Cutting her eyes over at her, Meena stifled a laugh. "An orb of truth? So, you have seen one of these before."

"I have," Animir intervened. "What I don't understand is what a wan such as yourself would need of one."

"Wan? What's a wan?" Piers demanded, shifting his gaze among the trio curiously.

At that moment, Oldrilin fell off her perch and landed on the floor, jarred awake by the tumble.

"Lin!" Rey gasped, leaping to his feet and scooping her up.

"Sleepy, Rey Daye," she whined, rubbing at her eyes.

"Oh, I know," he agreed. "Where will we be sleeping? Or she... be sleeping?" he asked of their host.

"I'll make her a pallet on the floor in the bedroom. That way, a few of you can take the bed, and I'll sleep here on the patio or on the bench inside," the woman of the house offered, placing her orb on the table and showing him through the portal.

As soon as she had gone, Animir snatched the glittering ball and gazed into it. "A wan is a female wizard," he explained. "Wizards are the closest relatives to mortals of the rim here in Eriden. Males hold great magical power, while females hold no magical ability whatsoever."

"Most females," Meena corrected, rejoining them. Taking the device from him, she held it before her, where it took on a subtle glow.

"Is that why you want to come with us? You don't fit in here and you want to get away; escape to a new life somewhere better?" Piers teased. "Well, let's set the record straight. If and when we find a way out of here, we aren't taking any of you natives with us, so if that's why you've come along on this crazy adventure, you can exit any time." His voice grew loud, his blood boiling at the thought of the consequences taking them back to the rim could hold.

Shifting his gaze angrily between them, he continued, "Secondly, we don't want anything from you that you aren't willing to give. No tricks, no empty promises. We'll pay if we must, but be assured, we aren't thieves, and we mean no harm."

Lowering her prize, Meena studied him over the top of it, then sank down on the bench next to Amicia. Turning to face her, she smiled, "Tell me about this orb of truth. Where did you learn of it?"

"Lady Cilithrand," Ami whispered. "She had it and used it to show me a few things."

"And did you believe what she revealed?"

"No," Amicia grinned, having realized the elf's deceit. "Every bit of it was a lie. I think she was trying to manipulate me with it."

Giggling for a moment, the older woman nodded, then offered hers to the girl. "Take it."

With trembling digits, Amicia accepted the small globe. Staring into it, the golden glitter shifted to clouds that parted before a dragon flew across her view. Gasping anxiously, she covered her mouth with her free hand as the image faded and the orb returned to its normal opaque state.

Accepting the trinket back, Meena nodded, "You are unique, Amicia Spicer."

"And you are not the first to recognize this," Piers accused, his eyes narrowed as he leaned towards her. "Perhaps you should do some explaining before I have to amend my statement about not harming anyone."

SIXTEEN

Wizard's Bounty

NODDING, Meena offered a crooked smile. "It's been many years since I have spoken the truth about such things openly," she confessed. "Would you like a glass of wine?" she offered, helping herself to a fresh cup.

"I'll take some," Ami agreed, hoping it would calm her nerves. Glancing between the other men, then up at Rey as he rejoined them, she asked in a calmer voice, "Why did I see a dragon in your little magic ball?"

"The better question is, how do you, a mortal of the rim, see anything within it," the older woman replied, pouring glasses for the others. "Piers, be a dear and select another bottle for us. They are in the rack under the back table," she requested, giving him a warm smile.

His gut wrenched at her familiar behavior, but he stood to do as she had asked. Placing it on the table, he returned to his chair, an odd feeling tingling over him. "What sort of magical powers do you have?" he quarried.

"My, we are full of questions," she observed, looking at each of them in turn. "Let's start with me, shall we?" When no one protested the suggestion, she took a large sip and began.

"I was born near fifty years ago. And you are right, Animir, wans are understood to be non-wielders of magic. When my powers manifested themselves early on, my parents did everything they could to hide that fact. Whitefair was a safer place back then. Ziradon was the Supreme Dragon, and all of Eriden was at peace," she said with a smile, having a noisy sip.

121

"I married when I came of age to the wizard my parents had chosen for me." She cut her eyes over at Amicia as she explained. "We seldom marry for love, you see. But I grew to love him, quite deeply in fact. He wasn't troubled by my powers, helping me to keep them hidden, and together we flourished. The routes between the north and the south were well established, as well as those between the east and the west."

"People used to visit Whitefair regularly," Piers qualified.

"Oh, yes," she agreed with a nod. "We sit almost square in the center of the Peaswan Desert, and our springs are the only source of water within it. For centuries, the wizard community has enjoyed the bounty they have provided."

"So, what happened?" Bally asked, enthralled with her story.

"He died," she supplied with a shrug, not elaborating as to how or why. "It was near the same time much of Whitefair and the rest of Eriden suffered a great loss."

"Ziradon," Animir agreed with a nod. "When Gwirwen stole the throne."

"Shh," she warned, pressing a single digit to her lips. "Gwirwen has many supporters here, as it is his rule that has allowed such vile men to rise to power. But legend says that our great leader lives, imprisoned by his successor, where he might one day be freed to reclaim what is rightfully his."

"Oh boy," Piers laughed, pinching the bridge of his nose between his finger and thumb. "Ok, so we have the dragons, who are like the great guardians of all the land, but a not so great dragon is now in charge. As a result, your town has fallen into its currently deplorable state, and you have been forced into... whatever you want to call this now. Taking care of yourself the best you can," he offered, raising his glass towards her in a small toast.

"Yes," she agreed with a nod. "I have faced many hard choices. At first, I was resigned to my principles, but I quickly discovered that I could not eat them. I was evicted from my home, and all I had was taken from me."

"Aye, you said this was your husband's house," the Mate recalled.

"It was, and it was our home while we were married. There are a few wealthy men, wizards who run most if not all of our city. One of them had me removed," she explained, lowering her gaze to pick at the fringe on her skirt. "Once I agreed to his demands, I was allowed to return. I have stayed here ever since," she sighed. "I provide hospitality to those he requires and to others when I have the opportunity to make a little extra on the side."

She did not look up at him as she spoke, and Piers could feel the twist in his gut. He never paid for flesh, and this was why. "You have no shame here, Meena," he whispered. "You are among friends."

"Am I?" she clipped, raising her chin and shaking her dark locks. "You made it quite clear your group is full and you have no intention of taking us with you."

"That doesn't mean we won't help you leave Whitefair if you choose. We will see you to another place, another town, where you may begin again," he assured.

An angry tear spilling over, she shook her head once more as she studied the girl beside her. "Now that you have heard my tale, shall we hear yours?" she asked firmly.

"I don't really have one," Amicia denied, pulling her legs up and hugging her knees to her chest with her left arm, her right still holding her cup. Sipping at her wine, she hoped Meena would move on to someone else.

"No, I insist," the older woman spat with a nod. "You wanted to know of the dragon. Tell me how you are able to use the orb."

"I don't know how," Amicia sighed. "It started as soon as we got here. The sirens gave me a magic shell so I could talk to them." She patted her chest and the device underneath.

"You are able to use it, though," Meena pushed.

"Yes, and later I used some crystal from the elves and now your magical ball. I don't know why though. I swear it," the girl insisted with a sob.

"It's ok, love," Piers soothed, his gaze fixed firmly on the wan. "Why don't you tell us why. You obviously know something about it."

Her glass empty, Meena considered pouring another before placing the empty cup on the table. "As I said, I have had my powers since I was a young girl. I have done all that I could to hide them, as well. But, there are some who can see our gifts within us even when we do not wish them to see," she observed, staring into Ami's clear green eyes.

The air caught in her chest, Amicia struggled to breathe. This was it; this was the moment she would discover the truth. "Who am I?" she whispered, scarcely able to form the words.

"I do not know," Meena confessed, placing her hand over the girl's atop her knees. Giving her a pat, she smiled, "I only know what you are not; you are not a mortal of the rim."

"No shit," Rey gasped, standing slowly. "And how do you know this?" he demanded, squeezing his empty cup in anger.

"I am a wielder of magic," the woman replied. "Would you like another drink, Rey?" she offered, deciding she did need another glass. Pouring a generous amount, she could feel the tension in those around her. Releasing a deep sigh, she sat back into her seat next to the girl.

"The orb can be used for many things," she explained, holding it up and producing a scene across it; a meadow from the glen. "I can watch all the corners of Eriden. People, places, events. I can watch what is in the past, and I can see some of what lies ahead."

"Some?" Piers asked.

"The future is an ever-changing thing, like a glass of water being carried by a person who runs. Sloshed one moment, flat calm the next, with bits being splashed out from time to time," she chuckled. "To ever think we can know what it will be like would be folly, as every step we take changes what it will be."

"I see," he agreed, studying her. "You have watched Ami, then. You know who her parents are."

Catching the question in his observation, she cut her eyes over at the girl. "You do not know the line of your birth?"

"No," Amicia whispered. "The parents who raised me were not my own; my mother confessed it upon her deathbed. I have come to Eriden to discover the truth behind the blood within my veins."

Her heart aching, Meena sighed, "I wish that I could provide you with that which you seek. Alas, I have never lain eyes upon you before this night. Not even in my magical glass have you appeared."

"But when we met, you seemed to know me," Ami denied.

"I recognized the power within you. You are a very powerful being, Amicia Spicer, and I see you, one to another. I have hidden my talents, but they are well practiced. I would make a good addition to your group, and I assure you I would do all that I could to further your cause," she promised glancing around at the gathering. "Should I leave you a moment to decide?"

Realizing she was asking if they needed time to take a vote, Piers folded his hands, extending two of his fingers and tapping them against his lips. "Anyone opposed?" he asked gruffly. His eyes darting around the group, he waited. When none voiced a concern, he smiled. "Well then; I guess you are officially in. I'm beginning to think we need a name for our little troop of vagabonds," he laughed.

Rising, he placed his glass on the table and announced, "We need to get some sleep. We will gather supplies first thing and head out as soon as the sun sets tomorrow."

Rising in agreement, Meena led the two girls inside, where they were given her bed to share. Pulling out the remainder of her blankets, she brought them out for the men, who would stretch out on her patio to sleep.

"Where are you going?" Piers demanded when she started down the steps.

"To sit below and think," she replied with a smile. "I am accustomed to the late nights."

Nodding, he followed her, sitting beside her halfway down, the point at which she had slapped him earlier. When they were comfortable, he leaned towards her and asked, "So, is there anything else you'd like to share?"

"I'd like to hear a bit about you if it would be acceptable."

"Aye, it's acceptable," he grinned, looking up at the stars before he began.

After he had shared a bit about his youth, he told of a few adventures on the sea. Finally, he explained how he had come across the girl, hiding in their hold, followed by the dragon, the raft, and washing up on Eriden.

Meena smiled as he spoke, drawn in by his gravelly voice and the way he commentated on everything. "You have enjoyed your friends, now that you have found them," she observed.

Staring at her, taken off guard, he blinked for a moment before recovering with his best smile and pushing on. Completing their quest, up to that point, he finished with a shrug. "And that's about all there is to know about me."

"Ah, but you have left out the most important thing," she giggled, leaning away from him. "Piers Massheby is a liar."

His grin gone in an instant, he growled, "What's that supposed to mean?" Here he had thought he was being suave and in the least winning her trust, and this was her reply?

"You speak well of your friends, but you pretend that they annoy you. You take charge of them but act as if it is a burden. You care very deeply for them, but you never tell them so," she replied quietly. "Amicia is quite taken with you, but I am certain you have never mentioned that you share her feelings," she finished.

"Ok, that's enough," he spat, holding up his hands and preparing to leave her there.

"What's the matter? Can't bear to face the truth? Or just upset that I have seen what lies within you?"

Glaring at her, he could not believe she had been so bold. "Do you always talk this way to people? Cause it seems like this would be bad for business," he made the jab with a laugh.

Smiling, she waited patiently.

"Come on, you don't have something snappy to say?"

"You are a good man, Mr. Mate. An excellent guardian and provider. Why have you not married that girl?" she asked in earnest.

"Because I'm too old for her," he bit angrily. "You know, you reach a certain age, like we are, and you just know things, and that's something I know; I wasn't meant to have a wife and a family. Not like other people." Blinking rapidly, he looked away, his eyes focused on the street below them.

"Our age," she chuckled.

"Aye," he nodded, pointing back and forth between them. "We're the same age. I'll be fifty in another year. And don't you tell them that!" he spat, realizing the blunder. "They don't know I'm a day over forty!" Staring at her, he gave a small grin at the joke.

"You think people our age don't deserve it, or are you punishing yourself for something in your past?" she insisted.

"Maybe both," he agreed, losing the smile. "I really am too old for her. Someday, I think she and Rey will make a go of it though, at least I like to think so."

Her eyes wide, she demanded, "You think I don't know what you are up to? Either you plan on sailing that boat with only you and Bally or you know you are never leaving Eriden," she accused. "If she is not a mortal of the rim, you cannot take her away from here. This is her home."

"Aye, it's her home." He raked his hand through his hair, twisting his locks for a moment, then setting them free. "I'm working on it. I don't know what we're going to do." Cutting his eyes over at her, he swallowed. "You're really starting to scare me with this telepathic shit, by the way."

"I'm not telepathic," she laughed. "I just know people. And I am a smart woman; I see things, and I listen to what people say."

Shaking his head, he glanced up at the stars, observing, "It's getting late."

"Yes, tonight is spent. But we will speak again, Piers Massheby, of this I am certain."

Cutting his eyes over to glare at her, an odd feeling twisted in his gut. "I'm a womanizer. I chase women, young and old. I get them into bed, and I never look back. You should watch yourself."

"Oh, so now I am a conquest to be had?" she observed with a laugh. "You are certainly full of surprises, Mate."

"You called me a liar, and that isn't true. I may not always tell everything I know, but I don't make a habit of lying to people I care about."

"No, you only lie when you must. And to yourself," she sighed, getting to her feet. Stepping through the curtain without looking back, she stretched out on her bench in the kitchen and closed her eyes to sleep.

SEVENTEEN

Day Traders

THE GROUP AWOKE with the sun the following morning, each rising and taking care of their personal needs. Meena poured water for them to wash and provided bread and dried fruit for their breakfast.

Watching her as she moved, Piers felt as if a rock had settled in his gut. He had so many conquests to his name, young and old, and he preferred the young. There had been few who could resist his charm.

Speaking with the wan into the early hours of morn, he had shared far more of himself than he ever had before, given her parts of his past even the others in his company had never heard. Accepting his basin to scrub, he smiled down at her, a flutter of happiness sparked by the green flecks in her eyes.

"Where shall we go to gather what we need?" he asked, then washed his face and pulled his hair back into the scrunch, fastening it at the top of his neck.

"We have a market," she supplied, helping herself to a small plate of the food. "We can't all visit, though. Amicia definitely will need to remain here. As the siren. The rest of you may come, but we must be careful."

"Why can't I go?" Ami asked with a small pout.

"You would be recognized, my child," Meena soothed, having taken to the girl. "We do not know what you are, but others will recognize that you are unique."

"Aye," Piers agreed, taking a seat and tearing a large chunk of bread off of

129

the loaf. "Don't worry, love. We'll get everything we need and be back as soon as we can. You will stay here, along with Rey and Bally. Sit tight, and for the love of God, do not attract attention to yourselves," he commanded, giving the two young men a stern glare.

"Aye, sir," they replied in unison, genuinely afraid of what he would do if they disobeyed.

Donning the robe and hood they had fashioned for Rey, Animir joined Piers and Meena as they slunk down her stone steps and marched along the path. Making a few turns, they arrived in a large market, where a vast open area filled with small stalls spread before them, the roof made of large beams such as those that had protected the spring from the harsh sun.

Some of the cubicles had wooden or reed roofs, while others were open to the sun and sky above. The air stifling around them, most of the people wore the coverings, and Piers felt glad that they had sacrificed one of their blankets to make them. Arriving at their first stop, he pulled the fourth of their elven goblets from his bag and placed it on the table in the center of a short round merchant's stall.

"How much for my elf cup?" he asked, noting the man appeared to be sizing him up.

"Thirty pieces," the wizard replied.

"Come now, you know it is worth three times that," Meena intervened with a shake of her head.

His back to them, Animir kept his eye on the street, watching as others moved along, not seeming to notice the trio.

"Yes, but where is the profit in it if I give him so much?" the merchant groaned. "I must leave room to earn a few pieces for myself!"

"I only want a fair price," Piers replied with a frown. "Sixty pieces," he offered.

Pursing his lips, the shop keeper studied him, then nodded. "I'll give you fifty, but you must sell me two. That would be a hundred for the pair."

Holding the dark expression, the Mate considered the trade. If he gave him the second, that would be the last of the goblets, and they had little else of value to barter. Realizing it would be hard to make any further transactions without coins, he sighed, then produced the final cup. "Here; take it."

Accepting the gold pieces, he dropped them into his pouch, then growled, "We need the blacksmith and someone who can sell us a few more arrows."

"Follow me," Meena commanded, leading them through the maze of paths. "Will we also need water?" she asked as they moved.

"Aye, we have waterskins, but if it will take us so many days to clear the desert, we will need a few more," he agreed.

"That much water will be hard to carry," she observed.

"You have a better idea?" he demanded, stopping to face her.

"I can get us a water stone," she informed him, her face grim. "It holds many times what your water skins can carry, but the price will be steep. What else do you require besides the arrows and the weapon you seek from the blacksmith?"

"Food," he clipped. "We don't want to starve to death, either."

"I'll do what I can," she promised, pointing ahead of them. "The black-smith is in the corner, at the end of this row. Tell him of your need for arrows, and he can provide you with those as well. And I'll need fifty of your coins," she stated calmly, opening her hand.

Studying her for a moment, he hesitated, not sure of her intent. Deciding he didn't have much choice but to trust her, he worked the strings open on his pouch and poured a generous amount into the outstretched palm. "Is that enough?"

"Yes," she agreed, dropping them into a bag of her own. "Shall I meet you here or back at the house?"

Scanning the market, he sighed. They had seen no sign of danger since they had arrived there, only crowds of people eager to buy and sell their pitiful wares. "The house is fine," he agreed. Ready to finish his business there, he turned his back on her and pushed his way to the end of the row, the elf close behind.

Stepping into the smithy's stall, he inhaled the scent of the fire and sweat deeply, a smile curling his lips as he did so. "Hello," he greeted the shop keeper warmly.

"Hello," the man before him barked. Matching the first mate in size and stature, his bright red hair stood out among the locals. "A fellow mortal of the rim," he observed, offering his hand. "Shamus Smith."

"Aye," Piers agreed, giving him a firm shake. "I'm in need of a blade for a spear and a few dozen arrows if you can swing them."

"Of course," Shamus agreed. "One hundred quid and I'll get you fixed right up!"

"A hundred," the Mate faltered, aware he would fall far short after what he had given the woman. "Can we trade for something else?"

"I'm afraid I only deal in gold," the smithy laughed.

"Well, what can you get me then," Piers grumbled, dumping his resources into his hand and counting them. "I have sixty-six pieces left, and it's all that we have," he snorted.

Studying the lot, Shamus pursed his lips. "I have an older blade I could sell you for that. Been meaning to rework it, but it would get you by in a pinch."

"May I borrow your forge?"

"Borrow my forge!" the other man laughed. "What the devil for?"

"I'll rework it myself," Piers offered, pulling at his covering and shirt, revealing his broad muscled chest.

"Well, if you insist on a new blade," the shopkeeper laughed, accepting the coins. Placing an old strip of iron on his anvil, he grinned. "If you're going to work it from scratch, I'll take sixty; leave you enough for a pint at the pub when you're done."

Handing him the money, Piers lifted the hunk of metal and inspected it, then set to work. Wiping soot across his sweaty brow soon after, he hammered against the hot ore, forcing it into shape.

Watching anxiously, Animir noted the number of onlookers who had gathered around in the street. Casting his gaze over them cautiously, most seemed harmless enough, as quite a few were local women, obviously enjoying the show. He chuckled to himself, considering if they should have charged for the view.

"Where shall we acquire the arrows?" he asked, allowing his partner to continue his work.

"I'll fetch them for you. Twenty you said?"

"Two dozen I believe was the agreed sum, but twenty will suffice," the elf agreed.

Disappearing for a few minutes, Shamus returned with the group of shafts bound tightly with a section of twine. "Count them if you want," he suggested as he held them out.

Accepting the bundle, Animir gave them a quick survey, satisfied that they were very close to the right amount, if not exact. "Thanks," he replied, throwing them over his shoulder to hang on his back. Seeing that his friend was going to be there a while, he left the stall and wandered down the way.

Moving slowly, without any real purpose, he peeked into the different booths to discover the wide variety of goods and services that could be found there, not to mention the different species all gathered in the one place. He passed a few elves of reigning descent, none of which gave him a second glance, and many more who were serfs among the City of Jerranyth.

When he happened upon a shop run by a pair of dancers from the queen's royal court, he paused, a broad smile on his lips. "Now I have seen everything," he quipped, stepping onto their carpeted floor. "Why and how did the pair of you come to be here?"

Looking up at him in surprise, the couple moved closer together, fear on their faces. "You a bounty hunter?" the male asked in a shaky voice.

"No, no," Animir laughed. "I'm just a traveler. Happened into the city yesterday."

"No one happens into Whitefair," the woman sneered, pressing herself into her husband's grasp for protection.

"No, I swear it," the taller elf clarified, licking his lips. "I have left the queen's city behind me. I've made some new friends, and we're headed north," he explained.

"North?" The other male appeared doubtful, then remembered his shop. "Would you be interested in some material then? Make a nice winter coat for yourself," he offered, drawing his eye to the rows of material that lined the walls of his stall.

Stepping forward, the elf examined the variety of colorful cloths, each wound into thick rolls, which the locals used to make their robes for protection against the heat and sun. Walking aimlessly through them, he felt certain they had no need of any or means with which to purchase them. In a back corner, he discovered a stack of animal hides; leather tanned for cold weather clothing.

"How much?" he asked, doubtful they would be able to afford it.

"I can sell you three yards for twenty gold pieces," the shorter elf offered.

"How much for the lot of it?"

"You want it all?" the female gasped.

"Yes. How much for all?"

"What have you got?" the male sneered, sensing desperation might drive the price up, or down if he weren't careful.

Placing his hand flat against his chest, Animir could feel the necklace pressed against his skin; a small white stone at the end of a string. Tiny compared to the larger version that Lady Cilithrand had presented to Oldrilin; still it was more precious to him than anything else that he owned.

Reaching inside his shirt, he lifted the shimmering stone, pulling the string to break it. Holding it out, he opened his hand as he offered it to the couple, maybe the only two in the entire market who would appreciate its value. "This is all that I have."

Staring at it with wide eyes, the woman looked up at him suspiciously. "Where did you get it? Is it clean?"

"Yes, of course," he scowled, daring to look at it briefly before turning his gaze away. "It belonged to my father; it is the last of our treasures."

"And why do you trade it?" the man growled.

"I have no use for such trinkets," Animir replied quietly. "My house has been ended, as I am the last of my line. I was forbidden to use magic, and my power is weak; I daresay beyond repair." Cutting his eyes over at the couple, he gritted his teeth, "Do you wish to trade or don't you?"

"Yes, yes," the woman agreed, warming to the idea. Reaching for the stone, she curled her aged fingers around it. "We have been away from Jerranyth for many moons," she explained. "Galiodien still sat upon the throne when we left. We danced in his halls for many moons."

"He was a great leader," Animir agreed, blinking against his tears as she took his sacred crystal. "Treat it with care," he commanded.

"Will you carry this alone?" the male inquired, eyeing the size of his purchase.

"Can you deliver it for me? I am staying with a friend by the name of Meena Gavaan," he suggested.

"Meena," the older man breathed, his eyes wide. "Yes, we will see that it arrives by this afternoon."

"Good, and thank you," Animir replied with a smile, turning to leave and find out if his friend was ready to return to the others.

EIGHTEEN

Flight of Fancy

USING the water that had been left for them, Ami stripped down and washed herself head to toe. Thinking of the bath she had enjoyed in Jerranyth, she laughed for a moment at the simplicity of the porcelain bowl before her.

Using a small cloth, she dipped and then wrung it before she ran it over her sticky flesh. Dust polluted the water quickly, as they had spent days marching across the desert to even get where they were. *And we're only half way across*, she sighed, *judging from what Meena said about Whitefair's position.*

Thinking of the older woman, she wondered what it would be like, to grow up as a wielder of magic, especially one who must hide their gift from others. *In a way, that's the way that Animir must have felt as well*, she surmised. She knew the Mate was not pleased Meena wanted to join them, but she herself felt as if the wan belonged with them; *an outcast, a lost and forgotten soul.* "She's one of us," Ami whispered aloud; she could feel it in her gut.

Shaking out her clothes before she returned them to her cleansed body, Amicia took her brush and mirror out onto the patio, where the others sat fanning themselves gently beneath the shade. "Come now, surely this isn't so bad," she teased.

"No, but it ain't the best," Bally replied in a surly manner.

"What's eating you?" she demanded, pulling the braid from her hair and sitting on the long bench to brush it out.

"He's upset that Piers made him stay here instead of explore the city," Rey chuckled, watching as she completed her grooming.

Across from him, Lin grinned, "Amicia Rey's special friend."

Caught off guard, he sat up straighter in his chair, giving her a dark glare, "You are all my special friends, Lin," hoping she wouldn't say anything else.

"It's ok, Oldrilin. I know about his infatuation with my hair," the girl laughed, parting it so she could replace the braid. "You want to do this for me?" she offered, cutting her eyes over at him.

"Sure," he agreed with a chuckle, taking a seat next to her.

Smiling at Baldwin, Amicia soothed, "Don't be cross, Bally. From what Meena says, this isn't a great place for looking around."

"Pfft," he spat, "all of Eriden is filled with evil little creatures. I don't think there's a great place here to be found."

Zae's eyes wide, she threw her arms across her chest, clicking her tongue in disgust.

"I'm not talking about the glen," he corrected, rolling his eyes as he got to his feet. "I mean, they can't protect us from everything." Moving to the top of the stairs, he stared down at the street, watching as people came and went.

"I'm sure the mate knows that," Ami laughed. "Besides, you're not the only one who would have liked to have a look around, so you needn't feel special."

His features twisted in a heavy pout, the cabin boy held back his retort, as it would have only hurt her feelings; besides, she wasn't the one he was angry with. A few minutes later, his eyes grew wide as he continued to watch the crowd.

Turning slightly towards the table, he whispered, "Hey, Rey; come here," motioning with his hand for his friend to join him.

Finished with the braid, the taller man stomped up next to him. "What?"

"Shh," Bally commanded, indicating the path below. "Watch. In a minute or so, a guy in a dirty white robe is going to pass, going that way." He pointed to the left. "He's carrying a long parcel under his arm."

Almost upon his finishing speaking, the man walked by, not looking in either direction.

"How did you know that?" Rey hissed, his heart pounding.

"That's his fourth trip by that I've seen," his friend whispered back. "Maybe we should get Lin inside."

"No, if they are watching us, they already know she's here."

"What are you two whispering about?" Amicia demanded, standing to join them.

"I think we need to leave," Rey suggested quietly, turning to face her. "Go inside and see if Meena has any more of those wrap things that we can use to hide Oldrilin inside."

"We can't leave," Zaendra interrupted. "The Mate told us to stay here, and we are going to do as he says," she informed him, still angry about the jab at her homeland.

"HEY!" Bally shouted taking two steps down the stairs to block them.

Pivoting, Rey could see the men coming up. "Get her into the bedroom, now!" he instructed with gritted teeth.

Moving to help his friend block access to the upper deck, he waved. "Geoffrey, isn't it? I thought you wouldn't be back until tomorrow night, when we're ready to leave."

"Yeah, well, I decided to renegotiate our payment arrangement," the other man said with a scowl.

"Oh, that's too bad," Reynard frowned, shoving his hands in his pockets and shifting to help hide the door as Oldrilin slipped by behind him. "Meena isn't here right now, but we'll let her know that you came by."

"This doesn't concern Meena," a bald man at the bottom of the stairs called up to him. "I hear you've got a siren up there."

"A siren," Amicia gasped, joining her friends. "Now where would we have gotten one of them? They're water creatures, aren't they?"

"Only by preference," the bald man laughed. "They got legs when they want them, sure enough."

"Oh, you speak as if you've seen one," Rey replied, not about to move over and let them by.

"Why as a matter of fact, I have," he laughed. "Let's all have a seat there on the patio and talk about it."

Leaving them, Amicia stepped through the door and looked around. Her heart pounding, she pushed herself to think. *How can we defend ourselves against these thugs?* She could hear the debate escalating outside. In panic, she ran her hand across her chest, searching for her merdoe.

"Maybe I can reach him," she whispered, pulling the shell from between her breasts. Clenching it within her fist, she searched, crying into the darkness.

"*Piers!*"

Hearing no reply, she tried again, a tear running down her face. *"Mate, please, help us!"*

"Ami?"

Across the city, in the midst of the crowd, Piers pulled his robe on to cover himself, shoving the new spear he had forged at Animir to carry.

"Ami's at the house, is she not?" the elf asked in surprise.

"Yes, but I can hear her calling to me. I think she's using the telepathy," Piers replied, pushing his way through the throng. "I need to get somewhere quiet where I can hear and concentrate." Fighting between the bodies, he located a small alley and took a few steps in.

Closing his eyes, he drew a deep breath and focused on the girl. *"Amicia, are you there, love?"*

"Piers, oh thank God!"

"Ami, what's happened?"

"Men are here trying to take Oldrilin!" she replied. "Oh, shit!" she screamed aloud, a hand clamped on the back of her neck and pressing her face against the left-hand wall of the kitchen, just inside the door.

The trio had pushed past their young guardians, knocking them flat on the patio. "Give us the siren, and no one's gotta get hurt," Geoffrey growled.

"If you take her, someone's going to get hurt," Rey countered, getting to his feet.

Holding Amicia firmly, the bald man took charge, commanding, "Check the bedroom."

The third man hadn't said much and appeared to be the muscle of the trio as he stepped inside, calling, "Yeah, I got her." Giving Zae a backhanded slap, the nymph collapsed. Screaming shrilly, Lin's tiny voice became muffled when he covered her in a large bag, scooping her up as if she were a wild animal to be trapped and claimed.

"Please don't take her," Amicia begged. "Anything we have is yours."

"Anything?" the bald man laughed, pressing his face against hers.

"We don't have time for that," Geoffrey warned. "Her friends'll be back, so let's take what we came for and get the hell out of here."

"Maybe next time," the man teased, licking her ear before he let her go. Rushing down the stairs, the men turned right and disappeared.

"Oh my God," Ami breathed, wiping the slobber out of her cartilage. *"Piers, are you there?"*

"I'm here. I'm almost to the house," he replied.

"They took her! They have Lin. Geoffrey, some bald guy, and a third. They have her in a sack, as if she were –"

"Shh," he soothed. *"We'll find them. Get our stuff together and be ready to get the hell out of here. Do NOT leave that house, any of you. Do you hear me?"*

Looking around, she found Zaendra crying, lying across the bed. No one else was there. *"It's too late for that,"* she called into the darkness. *"Rey and Bally are gone. I'm sure they've gone after them."*

"Shit. Ok, stay there, and we will be there shortly. We're coming to you."

Sitting next to Zae on the bed, Amicia held her, each of them crying. "It'll be ok," the older girl soothed. "They will find Lin and get her back."

"I h-h-ope so," the nymph stammered. The two had become quite close during their months together in the glen, and it terrified her that she might lose her best friend in such a horrific manner.

Arriving at the top of her stone steps, Meena glared at the overturned table and a broken chair. "Shit," she muttered under her breath, then pulled the curtain back as she darted inside, her robe floating around at her swift movements.

"Girls!" she clipped loudly, seeing the pair sitting on her bed. "Oh, thank God," the older woman squealed, sitting in an attempt to hug both at the same time. "What the hell happened?"

Before she could reply, Piers and Animir cleared the top of the stairs. "Where is everyone?" the Mate called, peeking inside.

On her feet, Ami ran out, pushing him onto the patio as she flung her arms around his neck. Hugging her tightly, he stroked her back as he soothed, "It's going to be ok, love. We'll get her back, I swear it."

Leaving Meena sitting on her bed, Zaendra joined in the hug, her smaller body trembling with fright. "They took her, Mate! Lin is gone!"

"What's going on?" Meena asked again, glaring at the four of them in turn.

"Someone's taken Oldrilin," the Mate informed her. "That Geoff guy from last night. I didn't see them, but he had two other men with him."

"Oh yeah," she scowled, the anger boiling in her deep brown orbs. "I knew this would happen. That bastard has crossed me for the last time."

Stepping back inside, she returned a moment later with a long staff. "You stay here. I'll get her and bring her back."

"Not a chance," Piers replied angrily. "She's my responsibility."

"Oh," Amicia interjected, wiping at her eyes. "You don't even like her. When did she become your responsibility?"

Glaring at the girl, their leader clenched his jaw. "The night we took her from Riran in a hail of dragon's fire. Look, we don't have time to argue. I just need to know which way they went. I can do the rest," he assured, locating his sword, then turning to the elf. "Do you stay to watch them or go with me for the rescue?"

"I should stay behind," Animir agreed. "We'll need to pack and be ready to leave."

"Aye," the Mate replied, wiping his beard anxiously with his arm. "Get everything together. Did you get the water stone?" he asked of their host. "We haven't filled the waterskins, so it will be the difference in our survival."

"Yes, I have it," Meena informed him, her voice thick, "but you don't know where they will take her. I do. And I can help fight."

"With that?" he indicated her staff with a shrug. "Sorry, love; too risky."

"I'm not asking your permission," she replied, pushing past him and heading down the stairs, stick in hand.

NINETEEN

The Great Escape

CLOMPING DOWN BEHIND, Piers turned right to follow her, skipping a few steps to catch up. Beside her, he demanded, "Ok, where have they taken her?"

"There's a slave trade on the south end of town. Exotic creatures and the like. He more than likely will put her up for auction, since that will net him the most profit," she explained, her skirt catching as her legs slid past one another in the heat. Pulling her hood to cover her head, she never broke her angry stride.

"So, we just bust in there and demand he give her back?"

Stopping abruptly, she faced him squarely. "You have a better idea?"

"Yeah. We have a look around, come up with a plan, and try not to get ourselves killed!"

"Great plan. What about your other friends, Rey and Bally? If they followed them, we can meet up with them. Four is certainly better than two," she clipped.

"Aye," he agreed, looking around anxiously. "All right, take me to this meat market, but do not let us be seen. We'll watch for the boys and go from there."

It turned out locating the pair had not been difficult; uncovered and brandishing two swords and an axe, they had cleared a path and gathered a good deal of attention. Entering the courtyard where the sale would take place, Piers picked them out and pushed his way towards them.

"Get out of my face!" Rey screamed, raising his weapon as a threat to an old man before him.

"What's going on here?" Piers demanded when he had reached them.

"This guy says we're not allowed in here," the younger man shouted. "But they've taken my friend, and I'm not leaving here without her!"

"It's ok," the Mate soothed, looking around at the size of the gathering. "We'll get her back."

"No, you won't." The bald man stepped forward, tapping his lacky on the shoulder, waving him off. "Sirens are deemed lesser beings by the laws governing magical creatures. They're like fairies; you can trap and trade as many as you like in Whitefair."

"Well, this one doesn't belong to you," Reynard bellowed. "You broke into my friend's house, and you stole her!"

"Is that right? Well, since she didn't come through the gate, that makes her illegal cargo. We consider her confiscated," he informed the younger man, poking him in the chest. "Beat it before I have you arrested," he stated calmly, cutting his eyes over at Bally as he leveled the threat. "The whole lot of you."

Grabbing his arm, the Mate pulled him back. "Come on, Rey. There's too many of them to take on here."

Jerking himself free, Reynard turned his back on him, squaring his shoulders as he walked towards his friend. When he reached him, he leaned in close. "You ready to fight?"

"No, mate," Bally replied. "Piers says when we cross blades with these bastards."

"Bah!" Rey kicked at the sand as the older man joined them.

"Don't be too upset, son. The fight will come, I assure you." His eyes roving over the crowd, he searched. "Where the devil did that woman go?"

"What woman?" Rey clipped.

"Meena. She brought some long staff with her, plenty pissed I might add. Apparently, she and Geoffrey aren't the best of friends," he chuckled, noticing that several of the men carried similar wooden poles. "What do you suppose they're for?"

"I have no idea," Rey fumed, his arms flailing as he paced back and forth, making sharp turns every four to five feet.

Rolling his eyes at his surliness, the first mate turned away, searching for a place he could reach out to the girl. Spying a stack of crates, he sauntered over and leaned against the wall behind them, enjoying the shade as well as the solitude. *"Ami."*

"Piers?"

"Aye, it's me," he chuckled, amazed he had reached her so easily. *"Are we set to leave?"*

"Yes. Everything is packed. Animir got some hides for us, so we will need some help carrying them, but otherwise, we are set."

"Hides? What sort of hides?" he asked in surprise, then thought better of it. *"You know what, never mind. Just be ready. If this goes down the way I fear that it might, we may be running all the way to the gate."*

Breaking off the connection, he rejoined the other two men. "They have everything ready, but they are going to need some help carrying part of it. Something Animir secured for us; I'm not sure what."

"Ok, so what about Oldrilin?" Rey asked in a calmer tone.

"I'm working on that," Piers replied with a chuckle, spying Meena on the far side of the courtyard, near the stage. "What the hell?" When she made eye contact, he could tell she was up to something.

"Do you think you guys can make it back over the wall?" he asked in a hushed voice, while never taking his eyes off of her.

"Now? Won't someone see us?" Bally asked, perplexed that they would attempt such a thing.

"Ah, well," the Mate shrugged. "If she does what I think she's going to do, no one's really going to care."

"You know what she's got planned?" Rey gasped, fear twisting his gut.

"No, but remember what she said about being a wielder of magic and always having to hide it?"

"Yeah."

"Well, I think she's about to educate them."

"No shit."

"No shit," the Mate chuckled. "I think you two should get back to the others. Take everything you can carry and get over the wall. Wait for us at the cave, with the litters."

"Aye, Mate," Rey agreed, pushing his friend by the arm to get him moving.

Working his way through the crowd, Piers inched towards her, still watching for her next move. On the stage, a variety of small creatures were brought out and sold to the highest bidder. Rage roiled in his gut at the inhumane way they were treated.

"And now we have desert fairies," the auctioneer called, holding up a clear wine flask filled with tiny bodies flinging themselves against the walls.

"Oh man," he breathed. *Twenty more feet*, he reminded himself. *Keep moving; desert fairies are not what we came for.*

Listening to the bidding, he kept on. At fifteen feet, she turned and looked at him. Giving her a quick smile and a nod, he kept moving.

Her face stoic, she held her frown firmly. Shifting her gaze back to the stage, she gripped her staff with both hands, choking it between them. She had never used the device publicly. Truth be known, it had belonged to her husband, but now it was hers, and she knew how to use it.

Peeking again, she found Piers only a few feet away. Waiting, she made no move towards him. "Nice to see you made it," she said with a small laugh when he joined her.

"I had to take care of the boys," he informed her, putting his back to the wall beside her and sweeping the crowd. "What's the plan?"

"When I grab the siren, you get up there beside me. We'll only get one shot at this, and I've never done it with three. Actually, I've only ever done it alone, but there's a first time for everything," she laughed again.

"What are you going to do?" he asked anxiously.

"It's called a transposition," she replied, turning so that she faced him and could speak in a softer voice. "Basically, I'm going to –"

"Transport us somewhere," he finished for her, not liking the sound of that one bit. "What are our other options?"

"There are none," she sighed, shaking her head. "If they get her off that stage, we'll never see her again."

"Damn," he muttered, not daring to ask what would happen if she failed to pull off her little magic trick. "Then we'll hope you make it. The others are going back over the wall, to the place where we hid the rest of our gear. How far does that trick work?"

"Not far," she confessed, studying his masculine features. "I have an idea. I have my orb. If I can see the place they're going, maybe I can target it for the transposition."

"Where were we going?"

"My home. It's a place that I know, and it's within range. But if we go there, we still have to get away and out of the city," she lamented.

"Then let's try for the boulders. What do you need from me?"

Pulling the golden sphere from beneath her robe, she shook it slightly towards him. "Hold it with me and close your eyes. Picture the place you speak of," she instructed.

Closing his eyes as he laid his hand over hers, the tips of his fingers brushed the smooth surface. Envisioning his party there at the cave, waiting for them, he exhaled in a loud sigh.

"Is this it?" she asked anxiously.

Cracking his lids, he looked down at the image between their fingers, grinning. "Aye. Exactly as we left them."

"Ok, I will try for it," she decided firmly. "Now we wait for your friend."

Unfortunately, the wait was long, and several other creatures were presented and bargained for, each tearing at Piers's gut in their pitiful state. "I can't believe they are treated this way," he whispered, sliding his arm around her waist as he leaned closer to converse.

"I don't come down here; it's deplorable," she agreed.

"So, tell me this. Why is Whitefair even here? A collection of scum in the middle of the desert."

"Like I said, it once was a beautiful place. The center of the desert; caretakers of the springs that give life in the middle of nowhere. There are wizard communities to the east along the mountains and west on the fringes of the sand to the sea, and they would pass through here on their journeys from side to side," she explained, happy for the distraction from the cruelty before them.

"And you were raised here," he recalled.

"I was," she agreed. "My father was a merchant, who sold antiquities in the square."

"I'm sure you miss them," he observed. "You do not see them often, or have they passed?"

"They are gone. I have no family, as my brother took his wife and children to Mopea, which is a township to the east, when Gwirwen came to power and everything changed," she explained. "I have not seen them in near twenty years."

"Exactly how long has this fellow been the Supreme Dragon?" he asked, his brow furrowed. The change in the throne seemed to have brought disruption across the land, as several had mentioned it as of late.

"Seventeen years," she supplied. "It was sudden. No one expected it, but when it happened, word spread quickly. Many tested the limits, and Whitefair fell into chaos. Some say that he prefers it this way, as it restricts travel between the communities."

"That's too bad, isolating people," he observed, catching a glimpse of a small form being marched up to the stage. "Shit, that's her, poor thing!"

Her face drawn, she nodded. Oldrilin wore large cuffs around her wrists with a chain dangling between them. Her lip stuck out in a heavy pout, her eye and face bruised from being struck.

Tightening his grip on his sword, the rage boiled in Piers's eyes.

"Don't," Meena warned.

"I want to kill them," he hissed. "They're barbarians. They don't deserve to stand here, breathing our air."

"We haven't come for that," she warned. "If you attack them, our chances of getting away will be destroyed. Is that what you want? To leave your friends without you to help them make it home?"

She knew exactly how to reach him, as the thought of leaving the others to their own means snapped him out of his rage. "You're right," he agreed, blinking a few times. "How do we get her?"

"Follow me close," she commanded, pushing her way to the steps of the platform as the bidding commenced. Marching up them, her robe flowed around her. "Unhand her," she bellowed, brandishing her staff in warning.

A tall man held the end of the rope, which had been tied around Lin's neck. Yanking it, as if she were a dog, he pulled her back with him as he moved away. "This here is my siren to sell!" he declared loudly.

"Not anymore," the Mate growled, pulling his sword out as he marched past Meena and removing the man's head with a single swing. The lifeless eyes wide, it fell in slow motion, landing on the stage with a thud and rolling so that the empty orbs stared up at him. Coughing, Piers stood frozen for an instant before Oldrilin screamed, grabbing at his legs in joy twisted with fear.

Scooping her up with his free arm, he swung around as Geoffrey and a few of his friends came up the stairs, while others leapt up onto the short platform. Moving up behind Meena, he shouted, "Do it now!"

Instead, she stood tall, her hood falling from her head as she raised her arms, lifting her staff straight in front of her. Bringing it down with a pounding motion, as if to drive a hole into the stage, she screamed, "AayA!"

A bright flash of light followed, white streaks shooting from the tip that bolted out in all directions. A wave of energy, the men who were on the stage flew off, propelled back by the blast, with those in the courtyard knocked to the ground. The place flattened, as if a cannon had been leveled at them, their movements were slow as they recovered.

Rolling over to his belly, Geoffrey glared at Meena. "You wretched whore," he bellowed. "What right have you to use a staff against us?"

"I have every right," she screamed back. "Wan I was born, but I have been gifted with the power. Do not follow, or you will die."

Turning, she claimed the Mate in an embraced in the same motion transporting the three of them to the place where they had hidden their gear, leaving the crowd in the market bewildered at what had taken place.

Arriving in a puff of smoke, they found the others gathered against the rock, sitting out of sight and waiting for their arrival. Not expecting it to be so spectacular, the gathering screamed in surprise, then recognized the trio an instant later and breathed heavily as they recovered from the shock.

Dropping onto the sand next to them, Piers gasped for air. "That was amazing!" he panted.

"Yes, quite fun, actually," Meena chuckled softly, taking a knee beside him. "Do you think they will come after us?"

"Only if they wish to die," he laughed. "You told them you would kill them."

"Yes, I might have exaggerated that part," she confessed, her eyes darting around nervously as she caught her hair around her face from blowing in the wind and smoothed it.

"Are we leaving?" Rey asked, glaring at the chains on his small friend. "We need to get these off of her."

"We can remove them," Animir offered, holding Baldwin's axe. "Lay the chain here," he instructed, pointing at the rock.

"Don't!" Meena intervened. Kneeling before her small friend, she held her staff between them while whispering a few words. Popping open, the shackles fell from her wrists, and the chains clinked as they hit the ground.

"Amazing," Rey breathed, lifting Oldrilin to comfort her against his chest.

"Aye, she's a right talented wan," Piers agreed, then informed him, "and no we aren't leaving yet." Looking around at the others huddled there against the rocks, their gear had been stacked on the litters, ready to go. "They'll see us for sure. We'll hide here until nightfall and then make our way out, east for a few hours before we turn north. Too many of them have heard us say that we are headed that way not to cover our path at least some."

"They know where we hid our packs," Rey pointed out, indicating the stacks of supplies.

"If they come, they will die," the Mate insisted through gritted teeth. "Meena may not have been serious about killing them, but I won't hesitate."

"I saw," the older woman laughed, thinking of the beheaded man. "You are good with a blade."

"Aye," he agreed, grinning at her like a kid. "I –"

Cut off, Geoffrey leapt over the rock and landed between them, knocking them away from each other as he swung his sword wildly. On their feet, Bally and Rey joined the fight as the interloper had brought five friends to help him reclaim his prize.

Hiding under the edge of the rock, Amicia cradled Oldrilin under her arm. Covering her ear, she soothed, "Shh, shh, it's ok. They won't hurt you anymore." Thinking of her bow and quiver of arrows, she wondered if she shouldn't join the fight.

Not waiting to ponder the sanity of it, Zaendra grabbed the spear the Mate had formed for her that very day, running past him and impaling one of the men through the chest. Dropping the handle, she screamed, falling to her knees and joining the other two girls in their hiding place.

Outside, the metal clanged loudly when it collided. This wasn't a play match, and the adrenaline coursed through Baldwin's veins as a burly man traded blows with him. Holding his sword with both hands, he swung it precisely, blocking and dodging as he forced the scoundrel away from the rock that sheltered his friends. His confidence stronger, he grinned, pressing the fight.

Next to him, Rey used his own to swing and stab his aggressor, his teeth clenched tightly in a fierce growl. "You bastards," he seethed, landing a jab that sent blood dribbling across the sand.

Leaping onto one of the rocks, Animir drew his bow, releasing an arrow that caught one of the men trying to drag Meena away through the heart. Falling to his knees, the arrow broke off, shattering with a loud snap. Free of him, she swung her staff at Geoffrey, the second man, growling angrily as she did so. "I've so longed for this day."

"Save the arrows!" Piers commanded. "Grab the axe."

Dropping his bow, the elf obeyed, scooping it up by its long handle and bringing it down with a crack against Geoffrey's skull, splitting it so that thick blood splattered. Catching some of the goo on her face, Meena screamed in horrified surprise. "Oh, dear God!"

"Fight or get down!" Piers snapped.

On her knees, she slid under the large stone, her hands shaking as she wiped at her face.

"It's ok," Amicia soothed, holding her hand as the sounds outside grew disturbing. Outnumbered, the three men begged for their lives as they were hacked and chopped by the swords and axe until no sound remained.

TWENTY

Blood of the Wicked

"OH, DEAR GOD," Meena breathed, rocking back and forth as she knelt in the sand. Her face splattered and smeared, she stared at her blood-stained hands. "Piers," she breathed, hardly above a whisper.

"I'm here, love," he replied, kneeling beside her, his arm tenderly draped across her back.

"I need water," she croaked.

"Yes, I think we may have some," he agreed, turning to their packed gear.

"The waterskins are empty," Rey informed him in a shaky voice. "We have no water."

"I have the water stone," Meena recalled aloud. "It took all that I had to acquire it," she informed them, still glaring at her fingers. "I have blood on my hands."

"The blood of the wicked," the Mate growled. "Pay it no mind. Where's the stone, love? And how do we use it?"

"Inside my robe. Open it and you will find it in the pouch. Ami, can you fetch it, my child?" the older woman begged, cutting her brown orbs up at her, her face still downturned.

In silent agreement, Amicia pulled at the rope that held her robe, freeing the material. The bag hanging at her waist, she used two fingers, working them inside the mouth and widening the gap. Digging for it, she pulled out the golden sphere, which sparkled in the bright light. "That's not it," she

151

mumbled, dropping it on the ground. Pulling out a smaller, smooth blue stone, a smile flickered across her lips. "How do we use it?" she repeated the question.

"We need a receptacle. Something to hold the water," Meena explained, her voice stronger. Her hands clenched into fists, she tried to ignore their soiled state.

"Use the cookpot," Animir suggested, loosening the ropes on one of the litters to retrieve it.

Placing the stone in the bottom, Ami stared down at it. "Now?"

Leaning over it, Meena whispered inaudibly, and water began to bubble out of the rock, putting about six inches into the bottom. "Remove the stone," she commanded.

Reaching in, Amicia pulled it out, holding it in her dripping hand. "It feels cool," she observed, amazed at what she had seen.

"Yes," Meena replied, dipping her hands to wash them, then moving to her face. "When we are settled, I will teach you how to use it," she promised.

Kneeling beside her once more, the Mate pulled her hood back, examining her face and hair. "You're all right, love," he soothed, his lips close enough to kiss her if he had wanted.

Glaring at the display, fire burned within Ami's chest.

"How tenderly he holds her," a deep, growling voice said within her head.

Looking around, her heart smoldering, she replied, *"He is free to hold whomever he wishes. He has taken no vow with me."*

"Lie to yourself, but you cannot lie to me," the gravelly tones replied.

Standing abruptly, the girl announced, "I need to be alone." Stomping away from the group, she picked her way through the large boulders.

"Don't go too far!" Rey shouted after her, distraught to see her go.

"Let her be," Piers instructed. "We've all just had our understanding of life adjusted. Let her have a moment to let it sink in."

Scowling after her, Rey did as he was told but wasn't happy about it.

Across the way and out of sight of the others, Amicia leaned against one of the large rocks. *"Who are you?"* she demanded, searching her mind for the one who had spoken to her. *"Uscan? Is that you?"*

"Uscan," the voice laughed. *"No, I am much closer to your heart than that fur-covered traitor."*

"Traitor," she breathed, turning her back to the stone and sliding down to

sit. *"Who are you then? Have we met before?"* she demanded, pulling her merdoe from her cleavage and grasping it tightly.

"Silly child, have you not learned you do not need the siren's toy? You are stronger and more powerful than all of them combined," the stranger declared.

Blinking rapidly, the girl fought to process his words. *Who the hell is this? "Please, give me your name,"* she begged.

"I am called Lamwen. Captain, if you will."

"Captain," she panted. *"You command a ship?"* a moment of excitement gave her heart a flutter.

"Hardly," he laughed. *"I need no vessel to wander where I will. No bonds can hold me, as I am as free as the open air."*

"Oh," she breathed aloud, the realization coming to her. *"No, please go,"* she begged, then screamed, "Please go!"

"Ami!" Rey's voice echoed through the rocks, drawn to her by the loud cry.

"Rey," she whimpered, finding her feet and running to him.

Catching her, he squeezed her against him. "I heard you crying."

"I –" she stammered, unsure what to say about the voice between her ears. Could it have been real?

Of course it was real. She knew it in her gut. "I just needed a moment," she sobbed. "Please, don't tell the others."

"It's ok, love; they understand," he soothed. Turning her towards their friends, he held her against the side of his chest. When they reached them, he pulled her down to sit next to them, where he continued to maintain his grip on her.

Not pulling away, she cried against his white shirt, thinking of the day she had wet Rupert's best suit. *The day we buried my mother.* Her would-be mother. *Shit.* Her life was wrong. Nothing in it fit. Not when strangers stole her friends, men tried to kill them, and dragons whispered within her head.

Lying upon the sand, her temple resting on her arm, Amicia watched as the others stirred around her. The sun hung low in the sky, only a small sliver of it left.

"I killed him," Zaendra lamented, standing a few feet from the man she had impaled.

"Aye," the Mate agreed, "but be assured he would have done the same to you, given the chance." Holding out the spear, which he had cleaned, he offered it to her. "You did well for your first time to use such a weapon."

"It was fear," she replied, cutting her eyes up at him but still wearing the pout. "I will never be the same."

"No," he shook his head, resting his free hand upon her shoulder. "None of us will. But life is dangerous, both here and in the rim of mortals. You have no cause to mourn what you have done," he offered with a small smile. Holding the shaft before her, he waited for her to decide.

Slowly, she raised her hands, folding them around the hard wood. She had been pleased when she first saw it, on Meena's porch. Now, standing over a corpse with the sun glinting upon the blade, her stomach ached. "Thank you, Mate," she offered, gazing up at him once more. "Things might have been different if all I had was a limb from a tree."

"Aye," he nodded, smiling more fully. "Which is why I have given you this. I always want you to be able to stand up for yourself; it's a big world out there."

"Aye," she smiled back, forcing her sadness away.

Sitting up, Amicia glared at her. She had hidden under a rock while the girl fought to protect them. Her stomach turned at the stench the bodies had left hanging in the air. "When can we move?" she gagged.

"As soon as everyone is ready. We'll work our way across, to the end of the boulders. There, we can have a bite to eat; Meena secured us a few rations, and the boys have brought everything edible from her stores," the Mate supplied.

Flushing, the older woman knelt beside her. "They have even packed me a bag, as if I were away on a holiday," she laughed, then sighed.

Taking pity on her, Ami frowned, placing her hand upon her knee. "I'm sorry. We did not mean to remove you from your home. From the only life you have ever known."

"Tis quite all right," Meena replied, patting her gently. "It wasn't much of a life. I can't believe they thought to bring my hairbrush," she laughed, putting a smile on the girl's face.

"They are accustomed to caring for a woman," she grinned. "They will have you spoiled by their devotion in no time," she added, flicking her gaze over at the Mate, who watched them covertly.

Standing, Meena offered her hand and helped Ami to her feet. Rummaging around, they secured all that needed to be added to the litters and then put their packs upon their backs. Carrying their weapons, in case anyone else cared to stop their departure, they followed the mate as he led them through the maze.

"I scouted while the lot of you rested, so I've marked the path for us," he explained, pulling his hood up to protect his head. "These robes are nice. Hard to believe being all covered up would make you cooler."

"You don't spend centuries in the desert and not learn a few tricks," Meena laughed.

Arriving at the spot he had picked out for their break, the group formed a circle, and Meena provided them with a pot of water to share. "I will miss my plants," she observed as they passed out the fresh fruits and vegetables she had had on hand.

"Did you grow much of your own food?" Bally asked.

"A fair amount," she agreed. "All of the pots on the patio provided something that could be eaten. It would have been a waste of the water if they had not."

"What about your magic rock? You have all the water you could ever want," Rey observed, indicating the kettle full of the precious liquid.

"I'm afraid not," she laughed. "It is enchanted, but there is a limit to the amount it can produce. Eventually, it will run dry."

"Oh," he grunted, pursing his lips. "Will it last until we clear the sand?"

"I believe that it will. I only ask for what we need each time, and that will stretch the supply a bit," she reassured.

"Just the same, let's pour the leftovers into one of the waterskins," the Mate suggested.

"Oh, it won't keep," Meena countered. "It will go sour in a few hours."

Scowling, he clipped, "What kind of magic is that?"

"I don't make the rules," she sighed with a shrug. "But it feels good to use my powers in front of others. I've lived a very secret life; kept few friends for fear someone would discover it."

"What could they do about it? I mean, if you were born that way," Bally informed her angrily.

"Oh, it was forbidden just the same. Girls who showed signs were removed, probably killed. For centuries, it has been so. My parents hid me, hid my talents. It's the only way I survived," she informed him sadly.

The sun gone and the meal eaten, the Mate advised, "We should get moving. We'll follow our usual routine and make camp as the sun rises. If it takes us six days to get to the northern edge, we will spend seven because of the walk to the east."

"Do you really think that's necessary?" Rey asked, gathering his things before lifting his end of their litter.

"We can't risk someone catching us; it's the best way to hide our direction. We'll walk until midnight to the east, then turn for the north."

Forcing down his grumble before he let it escape, Bally hoisted his end as Animir got the other. Falling into line, Piers and Rey took the front, their four girls walked in the center, with Amicia carrying the siren on her chest, while the two younger men brought up the rear.

Her head covered, Meena walked behind Ami. Watching the back of her head as they moved, her mind turned over what she had learned of the girl. Things had moved so fast since she met this unlikely group of travelers, and already they had left death and chaos in their wake.

She would like to think that things were going to get better, as she feared that they wouldn't. They were headed into the realm of the trolls; a right nasty group of creatures. So bad, in fact, they would make what happened in Whitefair seem like that holiday they were talking about.

TWENTY-ONE

Dragon's Breath

THREE DAYS into crossing the desert, the group came across what had once been a great tree growing in the middle of the sand. "What an odd place for a sapling to take root," Reynard observed, as it had fallen over and rotted from the root.

"We should salvage some of the wood. We can carry it for a fire tomorrow night if we want a small one," Piers suggested.

"Or hold on to it in case we get drenched again," Amicia suggested, resting her hand on the massive old trunk.

Using the axe, the men took turns, each of them removing one of the dead branches and paring it down into suitable logs, then finding a place for them on their litters, wrapping each one in a section of the leather in case it did rain on them.

"How did you come by all these hides?" Piers asked of the elf. "You said you had no coins when we were taking up the collection," he observed, cutting Animir a doubtful glare.

"I didn't trade it for gold," he replied, not meeting his gaze. "I had a family heirloom. The couple in the shop were dancers," he explained.

"From Jerranyth?" Amicia gasped. "Did you know them?"

"No. They left before Lady Cilithrand came to power, so they have been gone from our homeland for centuries."

"What type of heirloom," the Mate frowned.

157

"The sacred kind," the elf snapped, glancing at the girl. "Hamar gems come in many sizes. My family held one, a very small one, that I kept upon a necklace. They were eager to have it, and I the hides."

"What are we going to do with them?" Amicia asked, her features doubtful about the value of the trade.

"When we reach the north, it will be colder," the elf supplied, standing tall as he finished securing the load. "We will need protection, and we can use them to constructs coats for everyone, and even have a few pieces to spare."

Smiling, Meena grasped his arm. "How kind of you to care for the group so, providing us with this thoughtful gift." Her words to the point, no one could argue with his logic.

"Well then," the Mate interceded. "Since we are at a pause, we should discuss our direction." Stepping over to a smooth area they had not disturbed with their tracks, he used a thinner limb to draw upon the sand. "This is White-fair, and we are here. These are the edges of the desert, and I presume out here somewhere is the coast and the ocean," he explained, referring to the east and west sides of the map.

"We can't reach the eastern coast," Animir observed. "The mountain range on which the elves have settled runs far into the north, with dwarves on the other end. We would have to go completely around, and that trip would take months."

"What about the west," Meena observed, taking the stick to add a few details. "The wizard villages line this side of our continent, and there are many, but none extend into the forest of the north," she explained, adding a jagged line for the boundary.

"Afraid of a few trees, are they," Rey snickered.

"The trolls own the forest of Yilaric. Only those who wish to die invade their lands," she explained in a subdued tone.

"We'll stay on the coast, then," Piers pointed. "We'll cross the rest of the desert, then turn west and visit the northern most city to stock our supplies. We can march over to the coast and make our way north, stopping as soon as we find a suitable location for building our vessel and getting the hell out of here."

He neglected to point out that not all of them would be leaving, nor did he suggest what would happen to those left behind. Instead, he commanded, "Let's finish packing and get a move on. We still have a few hours left this night, and we shouldn't waste them."

"Are you certain we will be able to leave once our ship is built?" Bally asked as they enjoyed their dinner the first evening off the sand. They had spent the day lying about the creek to rest and would sleep through the night to get back on a normal schedule.

"I'm not certain of anything," Piers laughed, devouring a fresh bowl of stew. "I'm glad to see your hunting skills are still sharp. This rabbit is delicious."

"I've never eaten rabbit," Meena informed him, taking a small bite. "It does taste appealing," she agreed with a smile. The connection between them had grown at every stop, and they sat side by side, toying with one another as they dined.

Across from them, Amicia's gaze smoldered. Plunking down on her log next to her, Rey bumped her shoulder gently.

"Leave them be," he whispered. "He's happy, and her age suits him. Let them have this, love."

"Is it that obvious?" she growled, digging at her meal, pulverizing the chunks of tuber and meat.

"Always," he laughed, "but you will heal." He didn't say the rest, afraid doing so would spoil his hopes and dreams.

Across the way, Zae and Animir played along the edge of a brook, while Oldrilin squatted down, examining the rocks that lined its shore.

"I can't believe we found this place," Piers breathed. "In a few days, we'll have reached the sand of a suitable beach."

"Are we building shelter or setting straight to constructing the boat?" Reynard asked, hoping to cover Amicia's foul mood.

"A shelter will be in order. It will delay our departure, but should the weather turn cold before the craft is ready, we will need protection from the elements. That and I'm certain we don't want to all sleep under the tent from now on," he laughed.

"I bet," Ami spat, drawing a few glances from the others. Dropping her bowl, she stood and marched down the bank, to a wide stretch where the water pooled. The edge there protruded above the water, hanging over the top with the ripples a few feet below. Sitting, she dangled her legs, her boots only inches above the gentle waves.

Pulling at her braid, Amicia let her hair down, enjoying the cool air as she ran her fingers through it. Leaning back, her arms stiff behind her, she gazed up into the growing darkness. Searching the sky, she saw nothing; no sign of the beast she felt certain followed them.

Lamwen had not spoken to her since they departed Whitefair, and she had not said anything about it to the others, not that any of them would care. Piers was too wrapped up in Meena to deal with such concerns. Kicking her feet, her boots made contact with the earth beneath her, knocking small bits of dirt and rock into the water below.

"You should not let their affair trouble you so," the familiar voice echoed within her mind.

"Lamwen," she replied. *"I'd been wondering when you would return."*

"I never left," he laughed. *"Come further down the shore; let us rendezvous as lovers,"* he hissed.

"Certainly not," she spat, outraged at the idea of it.

"Come then, child. Let us share a few moments face to face."

"Why? Is there something you can't share with me here?" she asked, her face twisted into a crooked grin as she toyed with him.

"I wish to lay my eyes upon you," he growled. *"What would it take to bring you to my side?"*

"I doubt that you could convince me," she dug at him deeper, considering if she could hurt him with her words and enjoying twisting the dagger she used to impale him.

"Shall I threaten the lives of your friends? Their wellbeing is so fragile, you know," he groaned.

That got her attention. *"You wouldn't,"* she declared, sitting up straight, her feet still.

"Do not tempt me, princess. Mortals of the rim and vagabonds of the realm are hardly worth a second thought."

Looking around, her heart pounding, the sun had all but disappeared, and she knew the others would be looking for her. *"I can't stay long,"* she offered, getting to her feet. *"I don't want them to know that you're here."*

"Ah, a secret between us. Splendid. Come to the bend, then walk into the trees."

Doing as he asked, she crept gingerly along the shore. Stones of all sizes littering the path and her footing often unsure, she was careful not to fall over any of them in the near darkness. Leaning over a particularly large one, her hands splayed across the cool surface, giving her a chill as the smooth and roughness pressed against her palms. Working her way around, she straightened, catching her hair and holding it out of her face as she peered the way she had come, measuring the distance she had placed between her friends and herself with an inkling of fear.

"That's it; turn and come to me."

Her hands trembling, she shook them, unsure if it were caused by the cold stone or sheer fright. A hundred feet into the trees, she entered a small clearing. Even in the darkness, she could see the outline of his massive form as his hot breath poured over her. Thinking of the gem of hamar, which she still carried in her pocket, she knew she could use it to illuminate him if she chose.

"What do you want?" she said aloud, unsure if he could speak to her with a normal tongue.

"Kaliwyn," he hissed.

The word tickled her flesh, sending a flurry of prickles across it, as if ants had discovered her and poured over her skin. "I do not know that word," she breathed.

"It is your name, princess."

"My name is Amicia," she lied, knowing full well that was the moniker given to her by the humans who had raised her.

"I told you before, you cannot lie to me," he growled, swinging his head so that his massive eye stared her in the face. "Do you fear me?"

"Should I?" she stammered, then raised her hand, placing it upon his chin. The feel of it excited her, and she ran her fingers along his jaw. Pulling the stone from her pocket, she lit it, examining the soft green of his scales, pale and alluring.

Noting a scar as she worked her way down his neck, towards his body, she sighed, "I can't believe they bound you."

"You speak of the satyrs."

"Of course. They had no right to attack you. I saw you come down to converse to Preivia. I have often wondered what was said," she supplied, her fingers trailing along as she studied him with her left hand, her magical stone in the right.

He could detect every touch, even through his thick hide. The feel of her mortal skin teased his senses, and the scent of her stung his nostrils. "Your dragon heart is strong, Kaliwyn."

"I told you, that isn't my name. If you must address me, you shall call me Amicia or Ami. That is what I prefer," she scolded, turning to face him.

His large glossy eye blinking at her, he laughed with a low rumble that filled the air.

"Shh," she commanded, stepping towards his head. "The others will hear!"

Bumping her chest with his muzzle, he groaned, "Fine. I will remain your secret."

Her heart beat wildly at the offer. "I do not wish to see you again," she informed him tartly. "Say what you must and be done with it."

He had intended to kill her; that had always been his plan. To have her stand before him, with that bravado of hers. To inform her of her name before he stole her last breath. "What you wish matters not, princess."

Narrowing her gaze, she squinted angrily, certain he had been listening to them all the while, as Bally and Rey often insulted her snidely using the same term; *princess*. "You infuriating beast. Why must you torture me?"

Rising to tower above her, he glared down at her small form, considering how easily he could end her. Recalling what had transpired the night he had stood before the council, he growled, "Take care, Amicia, mortal of the rim. I have watched over you, but in the forest, I will not always come to your aid."

"Watched over me?" she spat, but he leapt into the air, knocking her down as he took flight, headed south out over the desert.

Watching as he disappeared, Amicia sighed. Picking herself up and dusting away the dried pine needles and dirt, she used the stone to light her way back to the brook. There, she darkened it and returned it to her pocket as she followed the stream to their camp.

"There you are!" Rey scolded, catching her at the place she had sat only a while before. "Where the hell did you go?"

"I went for a walk. Do you mind?" she bit angrily. "I don't need you hanging over my shoulder every second of the day."

Her hair catching the moonlight, floating around her like a shimmering golden halo, he couldn't help himself. Looping his arms around her waist, he pulled her firmly against him. "You scared the shit out of me, disappearing like that," he growled, the swear punctuating the depth of his emotion.

"And?" she pushed against his chest, fighting to free herself.

He didn't reply. Instead, he nuzzled her cheek with his beard before he kissed her. She ended her struggle and yielded to it, a slow searching connection between them. The feel of him scorched her, after standing in the warm air spewed by the dragon, her breath shallow with emotion.

"Ami, if you don't know how much I love you by now, you never will," he breathed. "You can stop waiting for Piers. You can stop pretending I'm just some man caught up in this crazy adventure with you."

Staring into her clear green eyes, he waited. His hazel orbs holding her there, as if in a trance, she scowled. "Do you think I could be won so easily?"

"No," he confessed, releasing her to stand on her own but maintaining his grip upon her back. "But I wish the chance to court you. Please. Allow me to prove myself to you."

Dropping to his knee before her, he caught her hand, pressing it to his lips. "I've been so patient, Ami. I've waited for you since the day I met you. Walking you to the head, my heart screamed you were the one."

"That's romantic," she clipped. "I'm sure that line works with all the girls."

Standing slowly, he pursed his lips. "Laugh at me then. Go on, have your fun. It doesn't change the way I feel about you."

"Rey, you don't even know me," she whispered, thinking of her meeting with the dragon and the secrets she kept from him. "I don't even know myself," she confessed, shaking her waves. "I promised Piers I would leave him alone because I need time to discover who I really am." The hurt in his eyes clear, her heart softened. "Please don't look at me that way."

"What way?" he sniffed, fighting not to cry.

"As if I've torn out your heart and stomped it on the ground," she sighed, sliding her hand into his. "I've always known of your caring. Even when I have tried to discourage it, I knew it was there."

"But you long for Piers."

"Yes. I have always wanted to be his," she acknowledged, her chin dimpling. "But I won't ever be his."

"No, you won't," he concurred, catching her hair and pushing it away from her face. "Tell me yes. Agree that I may court you."

Raising her hand to catch the side of his face, her fingers ran along his jaw. Thinking of the dragon and the familiarity of the touch, she laughed in spite of herself. "You're a silly man, Reynard Daye. To push so hard…. To wait so long."

"I'll wait longer if you require it," he said softly. "But I know letting him go would be easier if you had a love of your own."

"I'll consider it," she said with a gentle nod. "Would that be enough?"

More than he had, he agreed with a broad grin, "You know it will." Taking her hand, he kissed the inside of it gently, then led her back to the others. They

163

had stretched out with their heads next to the fire, their feet pointed out and away, like tips to a star.

"Our group has grown too large," she teased. "We don't fit next to the flames these days."

"We'll manage," the Mate replied, laying his arm across the rocks.

Removing her hand from her blanket, Meena reached for him and gave him a squeeze. She hadn't loved a man since her husband passed, but the one next to her made it difficult not to give in. Made it hard not to want to try again, even at her age.

TWENTY-TWO

Love's Treasure

ARRIVING on the outskirts of Heewan a few days later, the group hid among the woods to the east and formulated their plans. "Are you sure this is the northernmost city?" Piers asked, looking over the dwellings and people anxiously.

"I'm positive," Meena grinned at his cautiousness, always protective of his crew. "Have no fear, Mate. The rest of the wizard community will be much less hostile than those you encountered in Whitefair."

"They're wearing the same robes," Rey observed. "We brought what we found in Meena's closet. Maybe we should wear them and try to blend in, just in case."

"Aye," Piers agreed. "Hostile or not, it would serve us well to pass as locals, or in the least as if we belong."

Unpacking one of the litters, they located the hooded articles and held them up for inspection. "They are all pretty much the same," Amicia observed, glancing at the taller woman. "Such pretty colors," she added with a smile.

"Most of them are mine," Meena pointed out as the Mate pulled on a more masculine shade. Helping him secure the rope tie around his waist, she said more quietly, "This one belonged to Jaco, my husband."

When her eyes flicked up to meet his, Piers caught her hands and held them still. "Meena, I've warned you about me."

"Silly man, you think a woman of my age doesn't know how to take care of herself?" she laughed.

"I don't want you to be hurt," he said softly, giving her palms a firm squeeze.

"Let me worry about my heart, and you worry about yours," she replied, leaning forward and lifting her chin to graze his lips with a gentle kiss.

Noticing the silence around them, the Mate stepped back, dropping her and clearing his throat before he announced, "Very well, then. When we get inside, everyone stays close, but we can spread out a little. Perhaps pairs would be good for keeping up with everyone."

Reaching for Ami, Rey seized her arm and quipped, "Got my partner," with a loud laugh.

Glaring at him, she didn't argue. Glancing down at Oldrilin, she asked, "Is it safe to take her in? And what about you," she cut her gaze over at their newest friend. "What if they've heard about your abilities and want to arrest you?"

"I doubt that they have," Meena said with a shake of her dark curls before she donned her hood. "But, you are right about the siren. It would be best if she remained outside."

"I'll stay with her," Bally offered, taking a seat next to her on the ground.

"I thought you wanted to explore," Amicia pointed out in surprise.

"Well, the last lot tried to kill us," he chuckled anxiously. "I think I'd rather have a look at the forest here. Zae and Animir can form a team, and we'll poke around finding bugs and sticks to mess with," he added with a wink at Lin, knowing their smallest member well.

"Bally play with Lin," the siren grinned, wringing her small hands.

Amicia smiled at her response. The siren had slowly been regaining her personality after her rough treatment at the hands of her captors in Whitefair. Her black eye and bruised skin had healed in a matter of days, but it had taken much longer for her to trust again. She feared the mermaid's child-like innocence would never return, as she now looked at the world with changed eyes.

"Aye," Bally agreed. "As soon as the other's leave, we'll search out some things to explore."

"Just don't wander too far from camp," Piers instructed with a firm nod. "The rest of us will go in, get what we need, and get out."

"What are we looking for, exactly?" Animir asked.

"We need some sturdy line for making the winter coats from the leather. A punch for forming the holes for it, as well. Any dried food you can come by at a fair price, in case we run into an issue with game and scavenging," he listed.

"I want some cloth," Meena spoke up. "We could all do with a change of clothes, as these won't last forever," she observed.

"Then we'll need needles and thread for that, too, although I don't see that as a priority," he confessed.

Her brow furrowed, she countered, "I'll take care of that."

Rolling his eyes, Piers puckered his lips at her stubbornness but said no more against it. Head-strong and fiercely independent, he had learned quickly that she would form her own opinions about almost everything. "Fine, just remember we have to carry whatever you come up with."

"I won't," Meena nodded, pleased to get her way.

"How are we going to pay for all of this?" Amicia demanded. "We spent all that we had getting out of Whitefair."

Glancing at each other, Rey and Piers each looked away, neither of them caring to explain.

Seeing their displeasure, Bally leapt at the chance to share. "They took it off the dead guys that attacked us," he beamed.

"You stole money from the bodies of men?" Ami gasped. "What a horrid thing to do!"

"Hey!" Piers snapped, putting a pointed finger in her face. "First off, they attacked us, so the fact that they died was mostly their fault. Second off, they didn't need it anymore, and we did."

"You searched their corpses and stole their last coins," she pushed in disbelief.

"Exactly," he agreed, removing the digit from in front of her and placing the hand on his hip. "And now we're going to spend them to get what we need to make it to the north."

Amicia held her breath, not wishing to argue further over things that could not be changed. "Fine," she grunted, holding out an open palm. "Let's have it." She glared at him angrily as he opened his bag and passed out the supply, handing each of the women a third. Her eyes wide, she gaped at the amount. "They had all of this on them?"

"Yes, almost a thousand coins between the six of them," the Mate informed her with a somber expression. "It's all we have, so spend them wisely," he commanded, glancing at Baldwin and Oldrilin before he called, "That's it. Let's get in there and get back out."

Placing her newfound riches in her coin bag, Ami turned to Rey and sighed, "That's us." Placing her hand in his, he led the way, the others only a few yards ahead of them.

No gates guarded this sprawling town, as the houses were constructed differently, even if the people appeared much the same. Entering via one of the streets, where carts were pulled by beasts of burden, they followed one such wagon down to the center of town where the market stood in a wide-open courtyard surrounded by other structures and shops.

Once there, they paused, taking in the vastness and variety of the stalls. "It will take all day to explore this," Rey breathed.

"Aye," the Mate agreed, "I think we should regroup. Meena and Ami can go in search of the material and sewing supplies. You and I can visit the black-smith, and you other two see if you can scrounge up any food. We all need to be back here before the sun disappears behind the buildings."

"Ok," Ami agreed, glancing at her female comrade doubtfully before handing her bag of coins to Piers. "You'll need these, I'm sure."

"Aye," he nodded, accepting the pouch and leading Rey into the throng of the crowded market.

"I believe we should start on one end and work our way across," Meena suggested.

"Good idea," Amicia agreed, following her to the southern wall of the arena. Her plan sound, they found a large shop in one of the adjacent buildings to the plaza of stalls that had been filled with offerings to suit many needs. "Beautiful colors," Amicia observed, her fingers stroking a few of them as they entered.

"Hello," a young man with red hair and pale blue eyes welcomed them right away.

"Greetings," Meena nodded, taking charge. "We will need a large assort-ment this day. Can we be accommodated?"

"Of course," he grinned. Clasping his hands together eagerly, his eyes fell on her companion. "I shall keep a tally for you on the cost."

"Splendid," Meena praised, beginning her search.

Following, the clerk busied himself straightening the stacks of material but remained close at hand, presumably in case he was needed. When their gaze met, Amicia could feel a connection between them if only for a moment. Her heart beat faster, and her breaths grew shallow as he held her stare. *He looks familiar,* she mused, her mind drawn for a moment to the day of her mother's funeral and the boy who had presented her with a single rose. *Older, perhaps?* Surely not.

Spying the bolts of white in assorted weights and weaves, Meena offered one, "I think Piers would prefer this."

Drawn back to the present, Amicia giggled, "It's so drab." Running her hand over a silkier version, she suggested, "This would make nice under garments." Watching as Meena considered the cloth, she whispered to herself, "How many days does it take to fall in love?"

Hearing her, the other woman chuckled, curious at the observation; "Apparently not many."

Her eyes wide, Ami glared at her. "So, you are in love then," she accused. Flicking a quick glance to see the shop owner had given them some room, she pushed, "Does he feel the same? You know he will never marry you," she jabbed, striking out in pain. "He's too old for a wife and family, or so he says."

"Ah, but what does it matter?" Meena continued to smile, the glow about her unshaken. "If we never wed, we will have loved each other while we could. I'm old enough myself. I cherish what we have and will take whatever he is willing to give."

Blinking a few times, the girl hissed, "It does not bother you, sharing his bed as so many have before you?"

"No, I'm not a child. I will hold him for as many days and nights as I am able. It has been many years since a man touched me with the caress of a lover or looked at me with eyes filled with tender care. Those things are precious, Amicia, and should never be taken for granted or be wasted in demand of a vow," she finished in a huff.

"I'm sorry. I didn't mean to offend you," Ami sighed, averting her gaze, again noting they were not completely alone. "I'm a bit jealous, I guess."

"You wanted him to marry you, but he refused," Meena nodded. "I've heard. But it does not mean that he doesn't love you."

"I know," Ami agreed, deeper sadness leaking into her voice, "but it still hurts."

"You will have a suitor when the time is right."

"I had one," the girl informed her, raising her chin as if to brag. "I can't believe it's been so long ago. Back in Nalen, he courted me, proposing nearly every day."

"And you refused him?"

"Of course! He's at least forty and a family friend at that!"

Pausing her searching of the material, Meena faced her. "You refused because of his age, but with the Mate it doesn't bother you?"

Staring at her with wide eyes, Ami flushed. "That's different. I knew Ru all my life, like being courted by kin. Piers was far more exciting, hearing of his adventures and learning of his life, fresh and new as love should be."

"Well, I'll take what I can get. If he never makes me his bride, I can live with that," Meena blushed as well, resuming her weighing of choices.

Noticing the pink hue, Ami giggled, "Are you embarrassed? You look warm."

"I am not embarrassed," Meena replied evenly. "I'm thinking of the way he makes me feel. I have not been so happy in many years." Again dropping the material she had been inspecting, she turned to the girl. "I wish this for you, Amicia Spicer. Someday, I hope you will feel the joy of your life."

"I do feel it. At least, I think that I do," Ami sighed, looking away and fixating on the shop keeper still lurking nearby. He watched her covertly and smiled at her when their eyes met. She extended a slight nod in his direction, noting his firm jaw covered with red stubble; the face of a man, yes, but similar to the boy in Nalen, she was sure of it.

Pulling herself away from their rapport, she returned to the matter at hand. Considering the amount of time it would take to sew the new clothing, she changed the subject. "This is going to take us months to sew," she pointed out, glaring at her hands as she complained. "Perhaps we should be less ambitious in our purchase."

"No, we'll get a machine," the older woman suggested, indicating a contraption that hung on the wall.

"How does it work? I've never seen one before."

"They are quite simple and very useful," the clerk proposed, reminding them of his presence.

"Yes, it will look different once it's assembled," Meena agreed with him. "You use your feet to run it, like a potter's wheel."

Her features melting into a frown, Ami leaned in and whispered, "Can't we just use some magic and poof them together."

Laughing, Meena quietly replied, "Magic is useful for many things, and making suitable fitting garments isn't one of them." More loudly, she announced, "I'm getting this for the Mate, and a new robe for Animir. We'll get a second bolt for you and the boys."

"You care for all of us," Ami pointed out more meekly, feeling as if she had misbehaved. "Meena, you are so kind. I'm sorry if I hurt your feelings. I want you and Piers to be happy together. I really do," she said with a full smile. Noticing a bolt of sheer material, fine and soft to the touch, she sighed, "We should get this for you."

"I know what it's for," Meena shook her head. "I'd rather not."

"Why? Because you think he will never ask? So what. We can make the dress and you can keep it in case he ever does."

Glaring at her, Meena clenched her jaw. "You still think I should waste my time with false hopes, dreaming of something I may never have while missing out on all that I do."

"Hope is never false," the girl clipped, meeting her gaze. "Dreams are what keep us alive. Knowing that there is always more, whether we are meant to have it or not. This is why I came to Eriden, with the hope of finding my past and dreaming about my future. With Piers or without him, I still have things to look forward to, and so do you."

Nodding, Meena smiled. "I feel the same. But if we take this, Piers must never know. I do not want him to feel that it is expected of him. I am truly happy with what we have."

"Then we'll only take enough for the dress, and we'll hide it in with the rest."

"What about your gown? One day, I expect you will give a man your hand. The chance for you is even greater than mine," Meena informed her.

"All right, enough for two gowns," Ami agreed.

Wafting to the vendor, Meena listed their choices, "We'll take each of these, please. Do you have any heavier weaves?"

"They are over here," he directed, pointing out the next selection and remaining close to them once more in the new area of his store.

"For more pants," Ami observed, glancing down at her own. "You're not getting anything for yourself?"

"A few changes were packed for me when we left Whitefair. I shan't need any for a while."

"And how are we going to carry all this?" Amicia asked in dismay when the bolts for the trousers were added to their pile. "Piers will not be pleased."

"We'll manage. Perhaps a third litter that the two of us can carry," the older woman suggested.

Her features drawn further at the possibility, Amicia pouted.

"Don't look so glum. Are you in the mood for a skirt, or do you want to stay with the britches?" Meena asked in a protective, motherly fashion.

"A dress would suit you," the shop keeper observed, plying her with another grin.

Her cheeks flushed, Amicia looked down at her legs, then sighed. "I was given these when I was found on board the Sea Serpent. They actually belong to Bally," she recalled. "I had never worn pants before, but I do enjoy them. I guess we can make me a skirt if you like, but I wouldn't mind another pair of these," she insisted, refusing to abandon her wardrobe entirely.

"Very well then, I think we are settled," Meena confirmed. "I believe this will be all," she informed the shop keeper.

"Yes, ma'am," he agreed, moving to gather their selections and collect the sum. The young proprietor appeared to be only a few years older than the girl. He continued to steal glances at her as he worked, and his interest in her hinted he might care for more than merely selling her wares. He smiled fully when addressing her, which added a sparkle to his pale blue eyes. Touching the fine material of the special bolt when he came to it, he inquired, "You are betrothed?"

Meeting his gaze, Amicia spat, "Certainly not." Flicking her eyes between them, she could see the smirk on Meena's lips as the young man stared directly at her in awe. "I mean," she stammered, "wishful thinking, perhaps." Finding her manners, she managed more politely, "A girl can dream, yes?"

"Of course," the shopkeeper grinned. "You live near here?"

"We are new to the area," Ami replied, shaking her golden locks at him.

"I see. Then perhaps we will see each other again when you are in town," he suggested, his eyes fixed firmly upon her flushed features.

Noting the connection between them, Meena added, "We will need a large basket for each of us to tie on our backs for carrying it all, as we have some distance of walking ahead of us."

"Yes, I can provide those as well," he agreed, still sharing covert glances with Ami.

When he turned his back to pack their goods, Meena giggled, "And here I was thinking Rey would be your intended, but I see you might fancy another."

"What?" Amicia whispered, her thoughts distracted as she watched their haul loaded into the carts; she could not shake the feeling she had met this man before.

"Nothing," the older woman sighed. Despite the girl's claims, it was indeed fortunate Piers had never agreed to take her hand; Amicia was obviously not ready to commit herself to any one man if a cloth maker could so easily turn her head in such a short time.

Handing over the coins, the girls hoisted their loads and left the shop a short time later. Arriving at their meeting point, each of the men were equally weighted, but Zaendra and Animir had not been so fortunate. Only able to acquire a small amount of dried fish and fruit, they were able to help carry the bundles out of the city and back to their camp in the woods.

Dropping everything on the ground, the group gathered around and gazed at their additions. "I can't believe you bought so much cloth," Rey observed, pointing at it with an open palm.

"It'll be all right," the Mate defended. Rubbing his chin before taking a seat on a large stone, he observed, "It was bound to happen at some point; we've acquired more than we can carry."

"Nonsense," Meena laughed. Spreading one of the blankets, she stacked a few of the bolts of material upon it. Tapping the staff against the ground, she chanted a small spell, and the items shrank before their eyes.

"What the devil," the Mate spat, on his feet.

Catching one of the rolls of cloth, Ami held it up, in shock that it was now about the size of her forearm. "Incredible," she breathed.

"I told you magic does have its uses," Meena laughed, gathering another lot for adjusting.

"You mean you've been able to shrink this stuff down the whole time, and you let us carry it?" Reynard demanded, glaring at her.

"Well, I couldn't deprive you of your share of the work, now could I? Besides, this is my contribution to the group. That and making the clothes once we are settled," she informed him, finishing with the second collection of gear.

"You already contributed when you got Oldrilin back," Piers informed her, helping her repack the smaller goods. "We should only condense the things we won't need until we reach our destination."

"Very well," Meena agreed with a smile. "Whatever makes you happy, Mate."

TWENTY-THREE

Ruins of Abolia

WHILE THE OTHERS repacked their gear, Bally and Animir hunted down a rabbit for the stew pot, and Zaendra helped Ami locate the vegetables and herbs to flavor it. Setting it over the fire a short time later, they spread out their blankets and then sat around it to eat as the last rays of the sun disappeared.

Staring at the woman across from her through the dancing flame, Amicia thought about what she had said at the weaver's stall. Noticing the way that Piers seemed to fawn over her, she wondered if he would still act that way after he got what he wanted. Watching them kiss a moment later, she grew bright red as she realized he may already have.

"Are you ok, love?" Rey asked, scooting closer beside her, "You look a little flushed."

"I'm fine," she shrugged, fighting the urge to stare. Using him to draw her focus, she leaned over to examine his clear hazel orbs. "Don't you ever tire of chasing me?"

"Nope," he chuckled, catching her chin and using his thumb to trace the scar on her bottom lip.

Leaning against his chest and snuggling beneath his arm, she closed her eyes and listened to the beat of his heart. *He's right; letting go of Piers is easier with someone else to hold*, she mused.

Eating their meal, they spoke in low tones to avoid drawing attention in case anyone might be out wandering in those particular woods. Falling asleep soon after, they arose with the sun to pack away what remained and head out on an unmarked trail.

The going varied with the terrain as they reached for the western shore. Once they found the ocean, they would follow the coast north, only going as far as they must to find a place to build their ship, which turned out to be easier said than done.

Small groups of houses dotted the coast anywhere that a beach had formed, and the rest of the shore formed cliffs or reefs, both unsuitable for their needs. For two weeks, they kept up a steady pace, covering twenty to thirty miles a day but finding the place for which they hunted nowhere in sight.

"Is it me, or has the air changed?" Rey observed as they broke camp the morning of the eighteenth day since Heewan.

"I feel it too," Ami agreed. "The trees are thicker and it smells..." she inhaled deeply, "fresh."

"I believe we have crossed the northern boundary," Meena supplied, wrapping herself in her robe. "From here on, this is considered troll country, so we should keep our eyes open and take great care."

"I still don't think they will bother us," Piers disagreed. "We are going to stay on the water line, so I'm fairly certain they will never even know we are here."

Packed and ready, they had only walked a few miles when they noticed a set of rocks stacked in an odd fashion, with a second matching pile that had been toppled a few feet away. Lowering their packs and litters, the group took the opportunity for a break while they examined the stones. Running up on the second for a better view, Bally looked around, grinning widely.

"I know you're not going to believe this," he panted, staring down at the stones upon which he stood, "but I think this might have been a community."

"Why wouldn't we believe it?" Rey laughed. "Towns rise and fall. Why should those in Eriden be any different?" His hands on his hips, he breathed deeply, observing the tall grass that swayed in the northern breeze.

Observing the pillar that still stood, Meena remarked, "I believe you are right. The name Abolia is carved here."

"Abolia," the Mate repeated, joining her to inspect it for himself. "Does that name mean anything to you?"

"No," she replied with a shake of her head. "I've never known of a settlement this far north."

A sick feeling in her gut, Amicia slid her hand in her pocket and toyed with her hamar gem. She had taken a preference to it over the merdoe ever since a dragon had become a permanent fixture in her life. Focusing, she called to him. *"Lamwen, are you there?"*

"Always, my princess."

His reply brought a smile to her lips. Something about the way he used the word sounded like a term of endearment, a sharp contrast from a creature known for being the most brutal in the land.

"We've reached a settlement, or the remains of one…"

"Abolia."

"You know of it?"

"It fell before the great war," he provided.

"Are we safe here?"

"I like your hair when it blows in the wind."

Swinging around, she searched the horizon, then dared to look up for a moment, still not seeing him.

"Is something wrong?" Rey asked, standing beside her.

"No. Should there be?" she replied, a quiver in her voice.

"I don't know," he laughed. "You seem jittery all of a sudden."

"I'm fine," she lied, her heart ready to beat its way out of her chest. *"Are we safe? That's all I need to know,"* she added to the voice inside her mind.

"I'll warn you if I see anything," the dragon replied.

"You have your moments," the man before her was saying, "where I'm not even sure you're here. Like your mind has wandered off somewhere else."

"I'm here. I'm just worried about who might be around," she explained, forcing a weak smile.

"Aye," he nodded, offering his hand.

Taking the appendage, she wondered what Lamwen would think of her doing so as they followed the others to have a look around. Leaving their litters for the time being where they had laid them, she hoped the dragon would in fact warn them if they fell into danger or anyone else approached.

A few hundred yards to the east, they came into what could be none other than Abolia. Walls still stood in places, but most had toppled with time, and a few bore the signs of a fire.

"Could the dragons have done this?" Bally inquired, examining the marks.

Her heart in her throat, Amicia considered calling out to ask but decided it wouldn't be wise, as it could sound like an accusation. Instead, she followed Rey to a wide square of open grass, surrounded by a short fence. Rows of stones lay inside, and although the names on the rocks had all been hidden by time, the cemetery itself still remained.

"They were here a long time," she observed by the number of rows. Doing a bit of quick math, she frowned. "There are thousands of graves here."

"Aye," Piers agreed, turning slowly to take in the view. "I doubt we will find anything useful here. Perhaps we should get the gear and move on; we still have daylight left that we shouldn't waste."

"Hey guys, over here," Bally yelled, waving from outside the fenced yard.

Leaving by the way they came in, they gathered at his location, where bleached bones lay within the grass. The Mate knelt beside them, poking a skull and noting there were more hidden within the blades.

"These are not the people who lived here," he observed. "They are far too recent."

"How recent?" Ami asked, sidling closer to Rey. They had fought off the men to get out of Whitefair, and she still had nightmares about it.

"Hard to say," he shrugged. "One of these is crushed, which takes a lot of force. There's no smell or anything else left, which means enough time for the rest to decay. A few years," he guessed with a shrug.

"I think we should go," Meena advised. "These bodies aren't buried, so they were left out for a reason. A warning, perhaps."

Cutting his eyes over at her, Piers hated her honesty at that moment, as that kind of talk would only serve to scare the others. "We'll go then," he acquiesced, gathering their weapons and what remained of a helmet and chest guard.

"Why are you taking those? They don't look very useful," Rey observed.

"They can be reformed," the Mate advised. "You never know when a scrap of metal will come in handy."

Marching along the path, dark clouds hung low in the sky, threatening rain. Quickening their pace, the Mate urged them along. "We may have to find shelter and call it a night."

"Please not here," Amicia begged in a soft whisper. *"Are you bringing in a storm on us?"* she asked of her giant friend.

Laughter echoed between her ears.

"That's not funny, Lamwen. We don't wish to be wet."

"Well, it isn't me. Can't it just be time to rain?" he reasoned.

"We need some protection," Rey agreed. "Let's push across to those cliffs hanging off the mountains on the far side of this settlement."

"That's a few miles from here," Piers challenged, appraising the distance, keenly aware that would mean walking straight through the remains of a forgotten city. Looking at Meena, he laughed, attempting to lighten the mood. "Know any rain charms?"

Her eyes lighting up, she grinned, "Actually I might. Let's find a tree."

Moving quickly, they gathered their gear and continued on from there as they had been. A few hundred yards ahead, a small grove of trees stood, with a much larger one in the center.

"Will this do?" Piers asked as large drops began to splat against them.

"Yes, if I can do it," she agreed, dropping the basket she had been carrying and holding her staff with both hands. Chanting quietly to herself as she stood beneath it, she tapped the ground repeatedly.

"Well this feels odd," Rey observed, turning in a slow circle next to their litter, which they had set down.

"Oh my God," Amicia breathed, pivoting as well, noting that the rain had begun in earnest, falling all around them; but not through the tree. Dropping her head back, she began to laugh, "It's shielded. Like a glass dome placed over the top."

"Yes, precisely," Meena agreed, pushing her hood back to look up as well. Stifling her grin, her pleasure at her success refused to be hidden.

"Well done," Piers praised, clamping her on the arm. "The only problem is, it's getting damned cold." Casting his eyes about, he swore under his breath. "This wood isn't going to burn, either. It's too fresh," he advised, giving a lower branch a shake."

"We have the desert wood that Meena shrank down," Bally interjected.

"Ah, yes, let me just bring it to normal size," she agreed, searching for it among their things.

"Can you make it bigger?" Animir asked. "I mean, if you could, we would only need one piece."

Pulling one of the logs free, which she held easily with one hand, she laughed, "Let's give it a try, shall we? Where do you want it?"

Clearing the ground and gathering rocks to form the circle, Piers pointed, "Right here, love."

Placing the wood in the center, Meena gave the log three taps with the tip of her rod, and it grew tenfold in size. "Is that big enough for you?"

"It sure is!" the elf agreed.

Happy for the small number of rations they had picked up in Heewan, the group spread their blankets and had their meal, ready to call it a night. Lying around, enjoying their fire in their magical dome, they talked quietly about their adventures.

Getting to his feet, Bally stepped over to the edge, where a drip line had formed. Poking his hand out and then pulling it back in, his sleeve had been wet up the elbow. "This is really amazing," he spluttered. "Is there anything you wizards can't do?"

"Oh, yes," Meena assured.

Sitting cross-legged, staring into the flames, Piers muttered, "Transfiguration, perhaps." Glancing at the others, he explained, "You know, turning themselves into something else. Or death." The moment the word tumbled out, he regretted it.

Pivoting his gaze, the look on her face said it all. "I'm so sorry, Meena," he breathed.

"It's ok. Don't trouble yourself," she whispered, her eyes distant, as if reliving the horror of Jaco's demise. After a long moment she added, "Yes, there are certainly things no amount of magic can change."

"Did you try to save him?" Bally asked, still shaking his wet hand as he reclaimed his seat.

The entire party turning to look at him, Piers scowled, "Can you really be that thick."

"No," the younger man denied, glancing one to another, "I mean, you're the one that brought it up."

"I wasn't there," Meena provided. "Otherwise, I might have tried, even if it would have exposed me. It's a hell of a thing, to have someone knock upon your door to tell you your mate is never coming home."

Amicia's heart ached for the other woman as she recalled their conversation over purchasing cloth. "It's a hell of a price, loving someone," she agreed, shifting her eyes to Piers. *Eventually, it costs you everything when they're gone.*

TWENTY-FOUR

New Abolia

"HERE, let me help you with that, love," Piers offered early one morning a few weeks later. Meena was having difficulty tying the ropes for her baskets, and he felt more than happy to give her a hand.

"It's the damn chill in the air," she observed, rubbing her palms against each other briskly. "My fingers aren't as young as they used to be."

"I hope summer hurries up and gets here," Bally chortled.

"This is summer," Meena informed him, cutting her eyes over to catch his look of disbelief before she added. "Eriden is a vast continent. Did you think it was a little island, after all?"

"No, I…" he stammered, "I just didn't realize we were that far north."

"We've been walking forty-six days since we left Whitefair," Piers informed him. "I'm out of paper, and down to making simple tally marks on the side."

"Oh, wow," Amicia said in surprise, swallowing hard. "So, we really are in troll country."

"Aye," the Mate nodded, the pack adjusted. "Time is against us, and bitter cold looms in our near future."

"I'm beginning to think the western shore has no beaches that aren't claimed by someone else," Rey interjected, tending to their litter.

Amicia caught the glance that passed between their oldest members. "What's that for?" she demanded. "What is it that you know?"

181

"Nothing," Piers said quietly, looking at her over his shoulder. "We've been discussing what we will do if we don't find something soon. We may have to build a shelter and winter here."

"You've already been looking," the blonde accused. "That's why we assembled the coats and gloves from the leather. You think it's too cold already."

"Aye," he nodded, noting the others either had not heard or did not understand the implications.

"Shit," Amicia breathed. "How long before we must stop?"

"Three days," Piers clipped.

Angry, she turned to Rey and grunted, "Here let me help you with the load."

"Why?" he replied, tightening the ropes. "I can handle this, I assure you."

Pulling on the line on the opposite end, she examined his handywork, her breaths frosting in the cool air. Seeing her ignore his denial of the need of aid, he scooted around and took a knee next to her. "What's the matter?" he asked more quietly.

"Forty-six days," she whispered, cutting her tear-filled eyes up at him. "We're never going to find it."

"Then we'll build a shelter and put in for the winter; try again next year," he soothed, freeing the ropes from her grasp. "This wasn't a now or never deal, love. We'll get another chance."

Her heart ached at the thought of spending the winter watching Meena and Piers. As they had pushed forward, the relationship between the couple had become openly exposed. "He loves her," she choked, wiping at her damp face. "I don't know if I can share a cabin with them," she confessed.

"I'll be there as well," Rey pointed out, laying his arm across her shoulders and giving her a squeeze through the thick hide. "And we have four more days, the Mate said. Maybe we'll get lucky."

"Three days," the girl corrected, emitting a tiny, spastic laugh. Seeing the care in his eyes, she sighed. "Thank you. I know we'll get through this, and having to wait isn't the end of the world," she lied, almost certain that it would be.

On their feet, the group prepared to move out. Falling into line, Amicia's mind began its typical wandering, and she thought about how the changes within their group had been slow. She couldn't say exactly when she realized

Meena had been right about her life with the Mate. In the beginning, he had appeared self-conscious about their deepening romance, keeping it hidden.

However, he had eventually relaxed into his place by her side. He protected her as anyone in his company, maybe even more so. *A sure sign he is in love with her,* Ami observed. *And he goes to great pains to keep their rendezvous private,* she added, pursing his lips. He had never done so much for his previous conquests. But Meena Gavaan was far more than a notch in his belt even if he had difficulty admitting it.

Of course, as the relationship between Meena and Piers had grown, Ami had agreed to some of her Rey's demands. She allowed him to court her openly, and their relationship had deepened, although it had not been consummated physically. She still hoped to keep to that tradition, saving it for the night that they wed. *If we make it that far.*

Smiling as Reynard marched ahead of her, it lightened her mood to consider the depth of his caring. *He is faithful to a fault, and I should count myself lucky to have him.* She should have, but it had been far more difficult to convince her heart of as much.

Could she settle for such a thing? To simply give up hoping for something better. The thought rolled in her gut. She had become aware that she agreed with Meena, that there was nothing better than a man who held a woman with love in his heart and respect in his eyes. She had belittled the belief in Nalen, but through time and hardship, she had come to realize how much she had left behind.

At the head of the line, Piers halted without warning, having cleared the top of a small crest. Staring at the steep drop on the other side, he knew they would have to take the descent slowly, but that was not what had him in awe.

Before him, a wide beach expanded, lapping gently at the sloped shore. His eyes scanning the horizon, the water in the bay appeared clear with no reef to be seen. "Dear God," he breathed. "We've found it."

Holding his position, the others joined him, forming a line on the ridge above the alcove. "Oh my God!" Amicia squealed, covering her mouth with delight. Smelling the leather of her new gloves, she inhaled it, connecting it with the sanctuary before them.

Turning, she threw her arms around Rey's neck. She had been troubled all morning about her treatment of him, as if she were leading him on and eventually would break his heart. Standing there, looking down at what she hoped would be the place they could build their vessel, she was overcome with a mixture of joy and sadness.

If they weren't able to build the boat, he would remain with her forever, and she would make things right between them. And if they were able to construct it, he would leave her, and she would face the rest of her days in Eriden alone. At the moment she could not say which she hoped would be their end, but the stretch of sand implied their final path lay near at hand.

Recovering from his shock, the Mate announced, "Ok, we are heading down. Everyone stay focused. Don't let your joy at this discovery distract you from the trail."

Making the treacherous descent, the group soon arrived on the flat spread of the lagoon, its size and shape eerily similar to that of Riran. Dropping everything at the line of trees, they all hurried towards the water's edge.

"Will you be able to swim here?" Rey asked of his tiny mermaid, helping her from her pack on Zae's back and placing her on the ground.

Oldrilin gave no reply, her eyes bright as she inspected the flatness of the waters. The shape may have been similar, but the beach itself was quite different from the small grains of sand at Riran. Instead, it appeared more like small rough stones, with sharp jagged edges. Feeling the water kiss her toes, she paused, waiting for the others to join her.

Falling onto the rough sand, each pulled off their shoes and boots, ready to test their find; but the frigid temperature quickly drove them out of the surf.

"And I thought the lagoon was bad," Rey lamented, staring at his wet feet.

Sitting on the sand and wearing a small pout, Oldrilin studied the waves, aware this was not her home.

"At least give it a try," Ami encouraged. "If only to discover if you can transform."

Shaking her head, Lin curled her knees to her chest and rested her chin upon them. "I might get stuck in such cold water," she observed with a tremor in her voice. "Stuck in the ocean alone," she sighed.

"I'm sure you would be able to come back, but you can wait a few days if you would like," Amicia soothed, understanding her fear. "We will be here for many months while we construct the ship. You will have plenty of time to try."

Leaving the water's edge for the time being, the group explored the edge of the woods, which began a mere one hundred yards from the water. The distance perfect, all they needed was a clearing where they could construct their cabin and prepare their temporary home for the winter they would surely face before they could set sail.

Coming upon a suitable location, Bally laughed, "I knew we would find it! It's perfect," he screamed, slapping Animir on the arm as they ran to gather their gear.

"We'll help them," Rey volunteered. "You guys decide what we need to do next," he suggested, giving Ami a tug to come along and leave the couple to discuss their needs.

The air amongst them had shifted, and a great burden had been lifted. Hauling their things to the future site of their cabin, the group laughed and teased in a manner they had not shared in some time. Eager to hear their assignments, they knew they had a few hours of daylight left, and the sooner they completed their construction, the better off they would be.

Beneath the afternoon sun, they used thin limbs cut from young pines to lay out the foundation for their cabin. Then Bally showed the others how to fell and prepare the trees, training each of them for the job that would be theirs as the cabin was raised over the next few days.

Circling at a distance, Lamwen observed the group with his keen eye. He would not land and make his nest until the cover of darkness, but he knew the forest surrounding their new domain would provide him with all the cover he would need to continue his surveillance.

Seeing their progress in their first afternoon of construction, he reached out to Amicia. *"So, you have settled at last."*

Smiling to herself, Amicia continued to rake the bark off a long pine, removing it as she had been shown. *"It would appear so,"* she silently replied. *"Are we safe here?"*

"You fear so much, princess. But winter is upon the land, and the trolls have buried themselves to the north."

"And that's a good thing," Ami concluded. *"They will leave us alone then."*

"Until the thaw next spring," he assured.

"You will remain close?"

"Ah, you will miss me," he teased. *"I must travel to Adiarwen to stand before the council. My return is not a given, but I am certain it will be allowed."*

"They tell you what to do?" she asked in surprise, not realizing he had

been ordered to spy on them. The idea of it darkened her mood, as she had come to think of him as her friend.

"Ah, sweet Amicia; do not fret my presence, or the lack there of. Our connection has grown strong, and you will find me in your thoughts, though the miles between us may number many," he assured.

Smiling in spite of herself, she sighed, *"Be safe then, Lamwen."*

Be safe? Her sentiment stung him, like a thorn beneath a scale, digging into his flesh. Leaving the group to their construction, he turned to the east, the sinking sun to his back. *Surely, she has not formed an attachment*, he mused.

He had come to realize Amicia held great bravery within her, strength to stand whenever the occasion called for it. She had asked if they would be harmed, there in their new stretch of trees and sand, but he knew it was not for her own safety that she feared; it was that of her friends. *Be safe then, Lamwen.* Her words echoed in his mind, tearing at him from within.

His massive wings undulating gently, his thoughts churned. As captain of the king's guard, he had been assigned this task, by trust or exile he could not be certain. He had spent near on a year acting as her shadow, and in that time his heart had become fully divided.

He had briefly considered killing her, but the notion had been removed by the warmth of her touch. On the night they had left the desert, his decision had solidified when she stood before him, again without fear. Up to that point, he had oscillated between the two sides, weighing each but doing nothing to align himself with either.

As the cool wind flowed over him, he skimmed the tops of the trees, distracted as he prepared to face the strongest of their kind. *I must have control of my faculties*, he chided, as he knew this night would be far more dangerous than the last time he had faced the flames of their leaders.

Last time, he had neglected to reveal some of what he knew. Tonight, he would outright lie. He knew his thoughts were protected. He was strong, and no other could enter his mind without his invitation. Still, the idea he might be discovered in his treachery caused his heart to pound.

Foolish girl, he fumed, the smell of the sea greeting him as he arrived at the stone cliffs of his home. If he were not successful this eve, he knew that it would be Ami and her friends who would suffer.

The day not quite spent when he landed upon the rock of their meeting place, he glared at the pit that would soon burn brightly with the ceremonial fire of the elders. To the north, he could see the great prison, the scent of Ziradon reaching his sensitive nostrils in faint patches.

Growling to himself, he thought of Kaliwyn's father and longed for a moment to speak with him, to assure him that his child lived. Taken with a fit of folly, he imagined he would ask for her, as well, as the idea of her becoming his mate had become a recurring fantasy of his.

A fire had sparked within him the night she had touched him, examining him by the light of the hamar gem. It burned for her, yearning to see her returned to her true form, where he might pursue her as one of his own. Suppressing his laughter there on the sacred cliff, he knew it would never be; even if all were set right, it would not be permitted.

There were over a hundred male dragons but less than a dozen females within their realm. New dragon hatchlings were rare, and the privilege to mate was kept for only the most highly decorated members of the kingdom.

As captain of the king's guard, Lamwen held rank but not enough to be given a female. The knowledge of this drove him mad, as he toyed with the idea that he should kill her rather than see her given to another. Alas, it was a continuous debate, one that he felt he would lose, no matter which course he chose.

"You have returned," Ziewen growled, announcing her presence.

"I have," the male agreed, raising his chin.

Lighting the pyre with a hiss from her lips, she walked in a slow circle around him. "I have summoned our king," she informed him.

"And the others?" His heart fluttered with an instant of panic that his allegiance was in question.

"They will be along," she assured, noting the scent of his fear. "Tell me, before they arrive, what is it that brings you reservation?"

"My queen?" he replied, forcing down his trepidation.

"I smell the angst upon you. Do not lie," she accused, her eyes narrowing to thin slits.

"You would be a fool to challenge me before the arrival of the others if you believed me to be unworthy."

"I believe you serve your king but only when it suits you," she accused.

"As do all," he agreed evenly. "Tell me then, before we are interrupted. What would you have of me?"

"The girl. You have seen her, watched her, for many months. Have you observed any oddities that we should be aware of?"

"Oddities you would not want revealed to the council," he surmised, his lips parting as flames danced between his teeth. His loins ached as he thought of the princess. "She is a mortal female. I have seen nothing that would damn her or her companions." There, the lie had been told. The second time he spoke the words, they would come with greater ease, as nothing makes an untruth more solid than to repeat it.

The flutter of wings pulled their attention as Gwirwen scattered small stones upon his landing. "Begun without us?"

"Only the pleasantries," his mate replied.

Observing her, Lamwen's tail twitched. What game she played, he did not know, but she had her own secrets to keep, and that gave him power if he were cunning enough to use it. "My lord," he said aloud, bowing his head before the sovereign.

"What news have you?" his king snarled.

"You do not wish to wait for the council?" *My, my*, he observed, *is no one to be trusted these days?*

"They have duty elsewhere this eve," Gwirwen informed him with an air of discontent. "Inform us of your report."

"I have little to share," Lamwen grinned. "The humans are in the north and have begun construction for a cabin in the forest of Yilaric. It is my understanding they will build a vessel in the spring on which to sail from our shores."

Glancing at one another, the royal couple gasped in surprise.

"They cannot be serious," the king mused, followed by a loud boisterous laugh. "Do they think they can rebuild Abolia? New Abolia?" he gurgled.

"Fools," her ladyship agreed, her cackle echoing in the night. "They waste their time, as our shores are quite safe from any wishing to escape and carry word of us back to the mortals of the rim."

"Yes, quite safe," Gwirwen continued to chuckle. "What of the trolls? Will they be eliminating this problem for us then?"

"I'm afraid Yaodus and his people have already taken to their caves for the winter, as the snow came early to their mountain this year. It has not yet reached the beach where our quandary lies, but it will not be long before it finds them."

"And you will slumber over them once more through the long dark months," the king stated calmly, his humor under control.

"If that is your wish, I will construct a nest within the trees and spend my winter hidden beneath the snow," Lamwen agreed, painting his features with his best regretful expression. "Although I am certain we could leave them be. They have nowhere to go..." he observed, his voice trailing away to further enunciate his reluctance at the assignment.

"Vaudien has done quite well leading our guard," Ziewen informed him. "You needn't worry about your troops."

"Vaudien," Lamwen snapped, anger coloring his eyes. He had wondered how they had fared in his absence. "So, he has risen to replace me."

"Only temporarily. This matter of the girl is delicate. We could not trust this to just any dragon, but you have proven yourself loyal to my cause," the king soothed.

"More loyal than Vaudien?"

Studying the younger dragon, Gwirwen held his placid expression in place. "Return to the beach and ensure that the mortals have no surprises for us."

"Yes, your highness." Lamwen bowed, leaping into the air and leaving the fire upon the cliff behind.

TWENTY-FIVE

Watcher in the Woods

LYING in his preferred nest a few days later, Lamwen observed the progress on their cabin from above. *"You shouldn't tease him,"* he mocked the girl below, stripping bark from a tree. Focusing, he could see the smile on her face at his rebuke. *"Amicia."*

"I hear you," she replied, returning to her scraping as Rey walked away. *"You know I can't talk to you and him at the same time."*

"Exactly," he replied with a low laugh, toying with her. *"He might notice, and then where would our surreptitious romance be?"*

The banter they shared had grown lighter since arriving in Yilaric, and her cheeks flushed as her heart raced. She knew she should tell the others about him, but having a secret friend gave her a rush of excitement nothing else could match. Besides, she had kept his presence from them this long. What would it matter if she continued to do so?

"When you finish with that, we have another that is ready to begin," Bally informed her as he marched past.

"Exactly how did you get to be in charge of all this?" she gasped in reply. "Last I recall, you were the cabin boy."

"Aye, and I know everything about building cabins," he laughed, admiring the pun. Wafting his hand over her work, he observed, "It's about time I got to be useful to the group," a satisfied grin covering his features.

Glancing up to see the pride in his eyes, she stopped herself from making a

191

sharp reply. Instead, she showed him her right palm. "Well, have you any suggestions for preventing blisters?"

Grasping her hand, he inspected the wounds. "Bugger, Ami, you should have said. You need to let these heal. If we pop them, we risk infection," he lamented, running his finger over the pair, one along the top next to her fingers and a second smaller down next to her wrist.

"Maybe Zae knows of an ointment that we can make," she replied, pulling the injury away and picking at a bubble of skin.

"Don't!" he commanded, slapping her fingers to stop them. "If she can get the swelling down, you might try wearing your gloves. The ones we made from the leather."

"I get too hot," she whined. "This is hard work, not that I'm not used to work… but the sweat against the leather is unbearable."

"We'll have the cabin erected in a few days," the Mate informed her, joining the couple to have a look for himself. Shaking his head, he agreed with the boy, "Your attitude is commendable, not wanting to let us down, but you really should have mentioned this."

"Is it bad?" she asked more quietly.

"I'm sure we can deal with it, but you'll have to be given another job. Go and see Zaendra about the treatment, and I'll get to work on this stripping. We can't cut any more boards until this part is done."

"But you were chopping," she frowned.

"Don't argue. It all has to be done, regardless of who does what," he replied, smiling at her devotion.

Leaving the two men, she wandered in the direction of Zae and Lin, who were selecting branches to use when making their beds. Presenting the puss-filled pockets, she asked, "Have any remedies for this?"

Gazing at it for a moment, Zae looked up at her, shaking her head. "I'll wrap your hand, and you can help Lin with the beds. We need to gather more of the grass for the mattresses, and these are for the bases," she informed her, indicating their pile of limbs. "I'll see what I can find this far north that we can use to prevent the infection when they are drained."

Cutting a strip of cloth from their bolt of material, she bound the wounded flesh loosely, adding, "Be careful not to pop them until we're ready with the treatment."

"Ok," Ami agreed, setting to work on the grass. When she had finished the task, she wandered over to see that Meena was directing the laying of their wooden floor. Looking around at the final outline, over half the sections had been assembled. "This is going to be one heck of a cabin," she observed.

"Yes, it has to house a lot of people," Meena agreed.

"I grew up in a two-room house," Amicia added. "Gus and Arely had a bedroom, and I slept in the front room, which also served as the kitchen and sitting area, around the fire."

"They are the couple who raised you?"

"Yes, and they taught me how to run the farm. I know how to make preserves, spices and the like. When we need those things, I'll be the expert," she grinned, watching as Baldwin bounced around and directed the others. Her eyes following the outline of the walls, she could see that there would be a central room, which opened to face the beach.

On either side of the cabin, a long narrow room would hold three beds each, while a smaller room off the back of the structure would be for Meena and Piers. Swallowing as she glared at their quarters, her fingers picked at the dressing Zae had placed over her blisters.

"Is there something you would like to discuss?" Meena asked, seeing the girl's distant expression.

"No," she shook her head, sniffing as tears formed in her eyes. "I'm going to take a short walk and clear my head," she announced more loudly, stepping over the planks and marching up the hill. *"Where are you?"* she asked into the abyss.

"I'm above you, among the trees. Aren't you afraid your friends will see if you pay me a visit in broad daylight?"

"They won't see," she sighed. *"They're all busy working on our shelter."* Passing the place that Piers had dug a pit for an outhouse, she grinned at his attention to detail. They had planned it well, as there would be two stalls for them, one for the girls and one for the boys, so that they did not have to share.

Continuing on, she reached a thinner section of trees. Turning to peer over her shoulder, she shrugged. *"See, they haven't even noticed that I've gone."*

"Come to me then; make a left where you are, and I'll let you know when you're ready to adjust your direction again."

Smiling, feeling a little better, she speculated, *"I bet it's nice, being a dragon. No cabins to build, I would ponder."*

"No, we live in the side of a cliff," he informed her. *"The mouths of our caves open over the sea."*

"Ah, I bet it's splendid," she breathed, selecting her steps carefully as the

ground changed the further up she went. *"We lived on a cliff next to the ocean in Nalen,"* she explained. Noticing the coolness of the air, she shivered. *"I should have brought my coat."*

"You'll be warm enough," he soothed. *"Turn more to the east and continue up the slope."*

Making the adjustment, she caught a glimpse of his green scales through the trees a few minutes later. Bold in her approach, she did not hesitate to join him in the clearing, making it to his neck where she pressed her full body against his warmth. "There you are," she said aloud.

"It pleases you to join me," he observed, puffing heated air over her.

"I'm going to smell of smoke," she laughed.

"You have a fire, or will have when your meal is made," he pointed out.

"You are so practical," she chided, her hand resting over the scar on his neck. "I can't imagine hanging in the shadows, watching us all day when you could be soaring through the sky."

Catching himself, he held the thought, enjoying the moment with her and not wishing to spoil it. "Would you fly if you could?" he asked tentatively.

"But of course," she giggled. "If I were born with wings, I would know no different."

His heart pounding within his massive chest, he sputtered, "What if you could be given wings? Would you accept them?"

A tear dripping onto her cheek, she sighed, "Oh, Lamwen. What good does it do to dream of such things. I am a mortal of the rim while you are a magnificent beast of the air. I do not know why you have come to me, but I am grateful for your friendship. When the ship is built, and the others have gone, I hope that we shall still be friends."

"You do not intend to go with them?"

"No, I do not," she sniffed, stepping back to look into his massive green eyes. "I knew when I awoke on the sands of Riran that I had found the place that I belong. I suspect that this is why the Mate takes such care with the cabin he is constructing, as he knows this is where I will live out the rest of my days."

"I doubt Yilaric will be your final home," he observed in a gravelly tone.

"Regardless, I will remain behind, and although the other natives of Eriden may go forth from this place, I find a peace here I cannot deny. I will enjoy this cottage upon this shore and pray you will visit with me often and lay with me upon the sand." Placing her left hand on the tip of his nose, a nostril on either side, she wiped away her tears with her right, her cloth-covered blisters feeling odd when they touched her cheeks.

"I will be your friend and companion for as long as you shall need one, Amicia Spicer," he promised, lifting his chin to push against her flesh. He could not bring himself to tell her, as she had not responded well to the hearing of her name. Perhaps by the time her friends had built their ship, he could divulge more of what he knew.

For now, he would let them have their dreams, as unrealistic as they were. When the thaw came, the trolls would stand against them, and even if they did not, their ship would never sail. The waters around Eriden and had been enchanted some three millennia ago, at the time that Abolia had been destroyed in a rain of fire.

Blinking at her frail form, he thought about the stories he had heard of the ancient civilization, when mortals had shared their great land before their exile to the rim. It had been a trying time in the Kingdom of Eriden, one that had ensured that the divide between the magical land and the mortals would remain for eternity in its place.

"Ha ha, that's funny," Bally laughed, smacking his friend on the back.

"Well, you know being an elf isn't always easy," Animir replied, ready to delve into another story.

"Stop!" Rey commanded, bringing the pair up short.

Before them, the forest opened into a wide clearing, which they had discovered was not unusual. However, this one had an odd look about it, as all the grass within it had been flattened.

"What's wrong?" Bally clipped, not seeing the issue. "We need to get started on collecting our game so we can get it dried."

"Aye, you two go on, but skirt this clearing. Head east and you can cut around on the far side," he instructed, "and be sure to go around when you come back."

Shaking his head, the younger man didn't understand why but didn't bother to argue. "Fine. We'll go around," he sighed, giving Animir a shove before tearing into a run, with the elf in close pursuit.

Glad to be alone so he could think, Reynard knelt on the edge of the abused turf, touching a few of the blades tentatively. It could have been a family of bear or some other large animal making a bed for a few days. *Or it could be the dragon,* he realized with a stab of horror.

Eyeballing the width of the space, he figured the dimensions would be just about right. Pivoting, still low to the ground, he peered out over the expanse, only he didn't enjoy the view. From that location, whoever or whatever had been there had seen everything taking place at the cabin below.

Deciding this bit of news couldn't wait, he stood and stomped along the way that they had come, looking back periodically to get a landmark so he could recognize the blind from below. When he arrived at the cabin, Piers was busy setting up to cut a few logs.

"Are we starting on the ship?" he asked, glaring at the work in progress.

"Nah, not yet," Piers grinned. "Meena has requested a patio be added to the front here. I guess she misses the one she had in Whitefair."

"A patio," the younger man spat. "I thought we weren't doing anything else to the cabin. It's fine, and we're only going to be here until the ship is finished anyways."

"Aye," the Mate agreed, laying down his tools and facing the other man squarely. "Well, obviously you aren't here to help. Have you already rounded up a deer that we can dress to be dried?"

"No. Baldwin and Animir are still out. I found something, and I didn't think it could wait," Rey explained, dropping his gear next to the door.

"Oh?" Piers asked, his mind still on his project as he pinched his lower lip and glared at his selection of wood.

"I think the dragon has followed us."

His attention instantly redirected, Piers scowled, "Why would you think that? We haven't seen him a single time since we left the glen."

"We haven't seen him, but that doesn't mean he hasn't seen us. I'm not going to point in case he's watching us right now, and I don't want you to appear to be looking too hard either, but up above us, on the north ridge, there's a large rocky section where it forms a bit of a cliff."

Cutting his eyes up, but not obvious about it, the Mate agreed, "I see it, what of it?"

"Behind those trees is a clearing, and a very large creature has been laying around there. From the front edge, I had the perfect view of our whole setup here," the boy explained, pulling his arms across his chest.

"Shit," Piers replied. "So, you went traipsing across it, spreading your scent for him to find?"

"No, I sent the others around. He might detect we were there, but I doubt it."

Cutting his eyes up again, the Mate growled, "He's crafty, as no one has mentioned seeing him; but then again, we may have just not noticed in our comfort here. I think we should keep this between us. No sense scaring the girls."

"That's fine, but we need to forget this porch business and get to work on the ship," Rey suggested "We won't have to worry about the dragon when we leave here." Seeing the older man stiffen at the suggestion, he scowled, "The dried meat isn't for our voyage, is it. You plan on spending the winter here."

Piers turned his back on him. "I haven't announced it yet, but we don't have time to finish the ship this year; it will have to wait, and we'll begin construction in the spring."

"The spring!" Rey fumed. "Anything else you'd like to let me in on?"

"I didn't want to mention it until I had to," the Mate soothed, his mind turning.

"Aye, or maybe you've decided we're not ever getting off this rock," the younger man accused.

Turning on his heel, the older man glared at him. "I want to go home as badly as the rest of you. But we spent too much time getting here. I can't help that," he shrugged. Indicating their shelter with a stiff hand, his voice grew loud. "We needed the cabin, Rey, and not just for comfort's sake. Winter will be upon us any day now, with snow and ice. We can't afford to lose anyone when it comes."

His lips moving, the boy's face flushed. "Ok, what about the dragon," he hissed. "Fuck scaring the girls. They need to know he's here and that we could be in danger."

Shaking his head, the Mate disagreed, "I doubt we are in danger, generally speaking. If he meant us harm, it would have rained down upon us already."

Shifting his eyes over at their cottage, Rey stared at the door Piers had added to their fireplace, so he could access it from the outside. Thinking of how the beasts had toyed with his friends and family on Domania, he growled, "You know damn well they used to burn us out just to watch us rebuild. What if he's simply waiting so he can torch the place once the snow arrives?"

Blinking at him, Piers admitted in a calm voice, "I don't have a reply for that. I don't know what a dragon might be thinking. Honestly, I don't like this news any more than you do. If he's here, it could spell real trouble for us, but then again it could be nothing. I think we should keep an eye on Ami, and at this point that's about all we can do."

"I always look out for Amicia," Rey snapped, clenching his fists.

"I mean a very close eye. If he's here after one of us, I'm fairly certain it would be her."

His brow furrowed, Reynard clipped, "Why her? Why not your precious Meena?"

Laughing anxiously, Piers coughed into his fist as he collected himself. "Meena is a wizard. She belongs here. Amicia does not. You have seen how the people of Eriden react to her. I'm pretty sure the dragon, if there is indeed a dragon watching us, is here for her."

His eyes wide, the other man considered his logic. It was true, those they had encountered had been particularly interested in his intended. Could he be right, and she was the reason they were followed?

"I'll watch her," he quietly agreed, a sick feeling in the pit of his gut. "If he's here and she knows about it, she may be helping him hide."

His eyebrows lifting, the Mate growled, "Why would she do that?"

"You saw the way she protected him that night in the glen. She didn't want us to harm him," he recalled. "If he's here, she may still feel the same way."

His lips puckered, the Mate emitted a low whistle. "Well, that puts a wrinkle in things." He had trusted the girl implicitly to that point, but if she were thinking of changing sides, the last thing he could do was allow her to endanger the rest of their group.

"Watch her then, and share anything you notice, whether it seems important or not." Watching the other man turn, he called after him, "And don't worry about the ship, Rey. We'll get it built and be out of here before you know it."

TWENTY-SIX

Frost in the Air

"I SWEAR my balls are going to freeze off," Bally announced, slamming the door shut after he entered the cabin, returning from a visit to the loo.

"That's colorful," Rey observed, stoking the fire.

In the center of their common room, Meena sat at her sewing machine, her feet turning the wheel. Sliding the cloth across the flat surface, she leaned over to have a better look at her stitches. "Damn, my eyes aren't what they used to be," she complained.

Standing, the Mate gave her shoulder a squeeze. "Why don't you have a break, love. I estimate we have three more months before the thaw, and that gives you plenty of time to finish our changes of clothing."

Sitting in the boxed window seat, which the Mate had installed from glazed panes of glass, Amicia sighed loudly. Using an extended digit, she drew a square upon the frost. Longing to hike up the mountain to visit her friend, she didn't dare with the depth of the snow.

"Ami play with Lin," the mermaid offered, presenting her box of shells that she had gathered before the weather had crashed seemingly overnight, plummeting them into the worst winter any of them had ever seen, including the elf.

"Not now," the girl sighed.

"I'll play," Zae offered, accepting the small wooden carton. "Let's go in the bedroom," she suggested, indicating the room to the right, which the three girls shared.

"I could make us some tea," Baldwin offered, his voice cheerful.

Laughing, Animir croaked, "So bored you've taken to cooking?"

"Tea isn't cooking," Bally countered with a punch to the other man's chest. "It's called being helpful."

"And bored," Meena interjected, not looking up from her stitching. "Thank you. I'd love some." Their kettle had come from her home in the desert, another item it had surprised her they had thought to bring for her.

Opening another wooden container that held the dried leaves, Baldwin selected a few and placed them on their table. Then he filled their kettle and hung it over the fire. Finally, he selected their cups while he hummed.

"You're in a chipper mood," the Mate observed, taking a seat at the flat surface and observing the others.

"I'm used to winters," he replied. "We worked hard growing up and even in the cold we had to keep busy."

Hearing only half the conversation, Amicia turned her head. "Are you finally ready to tell us where you're from?" she asked tartly. He had told many stories when it had been his turn upon their flat, and she believed every single one had been a lie.

Glancing around, he swallowed, "What makes you think I haven't?"

"Oh, come on," she spat, getting to her feet to face him.

"Hey, hey!" Piers also stood, holding a hand up at each of them. "Some don't do so well at being locked up for long periods, so let's all calm down. If Bally has something to share, we can listen respectfully."

Glaring at him, the girl took a second chair at their table. "Fine. Tell," she spat, folding her hands in front of her.

Tending to his water, the boy kept his back to her for a few minutes, his mood greatly reduced. "I grew up on the northern continent," he sighed. "Wilderness, mostly. Like this here, filled with large trees, which grew up the sides of equally steep mountains. We felled them year-round and sent them down the river to the mill."

"A wood mill?" Amicia asked, not familiar.

"Aye," he agreed with a somber nod. Their water boiling, he opened the lid and applied the leaves, placing it upon the table to steep.

"I didn't come from a big family, like old Rey," he continued, giving his friend a slanted grin. "It was just me, my brother, and our pop."

"Was," Amicia breathed, a sick feeling in the pit of her gut. She regretted her previous comments, but it was too late to take them back.

"My mum, she passed when we were both little. Having babies, that's not guaranteed, and her third was her last," he said quietly, wiping at his eyes. "I didn't really know her; I have no idea why talking about her makes me cry."

"Oh, Bally," Ami sighed. "Let me take over the tea," she offered.

"I've got it," he replied, giving her a small grin. Pouring portions into cups, he presented them each with a steaming glass. "Like I said, we felled the trees. When the forest ran low, a few farmers moved to the mountain, and my pop helped them build their cabins and barns," he shared, his eyes roaming over the walls of their new home. "That's where I learned about building and how to make them sturdy against the cold winds and driven snow."

Watching him, the room had gone eerily silent, as if no one dared to even breathe as he spoke.

"We even got one for ourselves, there in the little community that was built," he stalled, taking a loud sip.

"So, what happened to it," Rey pushed, the tension wearing on him. "It can't be worse than being attacked by dragons."

"Oh, I dunno," Bally shrugged. "At least the beasts left you with something; some scrap of your life you could use to rebuild. We had only finished the house the year before, so it was a bit of a surprise that second winter when a great flood of snow cascaded down the slope."

"Oh, dear God," Ami breathed. "Your pop and your brother."

"Aye," Bally agreed. "We were asleep until right before it hit. Strange sound, snow crashing down the side of a mountain. It wiped out everything," he explained, swiping his hands in a wide flat arch to demonstrate the destruction. "Gone. The whole town disappeared in a single night. No more than twenty of us survived."

"Were you hurt?" Amicia dared to ask.

"Me? Not a scratch. Pop and Thomas, both dead when they were found, bloody messes. Frozen stiff from being lost in the snow."

Shaking his head, the Mate grunted, "That's a horrible way to go."

"I don't suppose there is a good way," Meena observed, sipping her tea as she worked.

Her words to the point, Bally wore a shocked expression. His smile slow, he tried to suppress the laugh before it broke out and the group laughed with him. Holding the smile when the fit had passed, he sipped his tea and then observed, "You got me there. I do miss them at times, though. I joined the cargo ship as soon as I was able. Told myself if I ever had to live on the side of a mountain again, it would be too soon."

Her eyes wide, Amicia glared at him, seeing his wide smile behind his cup. "You did it again, didn't you!" she accused.

"Did what?" he laughed.

"I swear, you are a practiced liar, Baldwin Carter. You talk incessantly about rubbish, and lies drip from your lips –"

"Like snow upon the mountain," he finished for her.

"It wasn't a lie, was it," Rey suggested, his arms firmly crossing his chest. "Was it?"

"Well, it was a good story," the Mate interjected with a toast. "It's a fine thing we are all apt at telling them, I give you that, with as many times as we've been trapped with only each other for company."

Returning to her perch beside the window, Amicia felt cross, almost certain she had been drawn in by another of Bally's tales. *At least this time it didn't feature a dragon*, she mused. Leaning her head against the glass, she called to Lamwen. *"Are you buried in snow?"*

"I'm higher up the slope, in a small cave," her friend replied. *"Do not trouble yourself for me,"* he commanded. *"I'm an old dragon. I know how to stay warm when the frost comes."*

Smiling to herself, she replied, *"I wish I could visit. I will miss not seeing you until the spring."*

"I'll try to arrange a visit for you if I can, my princess," he promised, lightening her mood as the evening fell upon them and darkness covered the land beyond their walls.

TWENTY-SEVEN

Dragon's Lair

AMICIA LAY IN HER BED, staring at the ceiling above her. Listening to the silence, she felt certain the rest of their company slumbered. Resting her hand on the blanket that covered her, her mind traced the nights she had slept beneath it, from the first in Jerranyth among the elves, through their flight to the glen. Her pulse quickened as they crossed the desert, then marched north through the forest of Yilaric, until she arrived at this one; *damn.*

Her bed the most comfortable she had rested in while in Eriden, save the spire in the elf city, she thought about how they had gathered the materials for them, laying a foundation of branches that had formed the mattresses from brush and grasses. After their walls were raised, Meena had sown a cover for each of them from the thicker cloth they had picked up in Heewan; the same one she had used to fashion each of them a new pair of pants.

Realizing her mind was too full to sleep, she slipped from beneath her cover and tiptoed from the room. In the kitchen, she prepared the pot for tea and stoked the fire. Waiting for the water to boil, she thought about gathering the leaves, along with a few other herbs and spices, before the snow began.

Who knew learning to be a spicer would come in so handy, she mused, her spirits briefly lifted at the quandary.

She had spent a few days working on canning a few preserves as well, all made from wild fruits and berries that they had come across. Everyone had

203

gotten into the picking, once she had identified the best candidates, and their pantry had been fully stocked on the delicious temptations.

The whistle of her pot rising behind her, she pulled it off the flame and added the leaves, allowing it to steep while she stood before the large window that faced the sea. The only one in the house, the Mate had taken the time to build a forge before they got too far into their construction on the cottage.

Once he had, all their efforts became more rewarding, as he was able to construct better tools from the scraps of metal they had gathered in the ruins of Abolia. Finally, he melted a mixture of sand to form the glass for the panes before her and the scraps from the metal to build the thin edges that held each in place.

Returning to her tea, she poured her cup, then sat with it, curling her legs beneath her as she observed the waves rippling beneath the moon. Sipping the warm beverage, her mind continued to turn, as the window before her took on a thin layer of frost. Touching it, she drew pictures in the mist.

Hearing a noise from across the room, she turned to see the couple's door remained shut. The other rooms, the ones the rest of the house shared, were only covered with a curtain, which afforded a minimal amount of privacy for them. The Mate had installed an actual wooden cover for him and Meena, which thankfully muffled the sound of their making love on the other side.

Ami's heart pained by jealousy, a warm flush tinted her skin as she considered their activities. Compelled to escape, she placed her cup on the table and slipped into her bedroom, where she put on her clothes as silently as she could. Then, carrying her boots, she returned to the window box, where she put them on, along with her coat and gloves.

Exiting, she pulled the door closed behind her, shutting it so gently that no sound had been made at her departure. Marching around the side, she left under the pretense of visiting the loo, but after she passed it, her thoughts continued to turn. Only after she was half way up the slope did she recall her dragon friend no longer languished in the clearing where she had seen him last.

Reaching out to him through the darkness, she called, *"Lamwen."*

After a long pause, he replied, *"Yes?"* sleep in his voice.

"I've decided upon a visit," she sniffed. *"How can I find you?"*

"Now?" he asked, his voice steadier and somewhat disturbed.

"Yes, now," she laughed. *"They are asleep, so I don't have to worry about being caught."*

"Very well," he agreed. *"Come up to the peak, and I will await you at the mouth of my den."*

"Your den," she chuckled, the word sounding more cozy and personal than cave. Marching through the snow, she pretended not to notice the cold, her heart set upon the stolen moments she would share with him.

The trail rough and difficult under the blanket of frost, she fought her way to the top, not stopping until she noticed a burst of flame to her left, the bright orange illuminating the sky above the slumbering trees. *"Is that the signal?"* she giggled.

"Yes, I see you have drawn near," he agreed.

Crossing warily, she arrived as he backed into the inner space. "Move to the back," he growled. "I'll warm the air, and you will be more comfortable."

His thoughtfulness cheered her, and she did as he instructed. Pulling her hamar gem from her pocket, she lit the small space with a bright glow. Puffing a few breaths of warmed air, he blocked most of the entrance with his large form so that it only escaped at a slow rate.

"Thank you," she said with a smile she did not feel.

"Something troubles you," he observed. "Am I the shoulder you wish to cry upon?"

"I guess that you are," she sighed, a quaver in her voice. Falling against his neck when he had settled down, she closed her eyes and listened to the beat of his heart. "I don't know if I will ever get over him," she confessed.

"Rubbish," the dragon replied. "The mortal is beneath you, princess. Think nothing of him. One day you will have a mate who matches your rank, of that you can be certain."

"You sound like an elf," she informed him with a quiet laugh, suddenly very tired. "Would you mind if I slept?"

"Slept? Here?" He could hardly believe she had climbed all that way to simply fall asleep. "I thought you wanted to whine over your human."

Shaking her head, she giggled. "I'm finished complaining; I want to sleep. I couldn't rest in my own bed, but now I feel completely ready," she explained, turning and sitting with her back against him.

"Very well, if you must," he agreed, curling a wing across her.

Comforted by his gesture, she toyed with the leathery skin that formed the appendage, thinking fondly of his ability to soar above the earth. The thoughts distractingly soothing, she relaxed as she closed her eyes, her fingers still wrapped around her elven stone.

Within a few minutes, her breathing fell into a steady pattern, and he knew that she must have been exhausted. Increasing the glow of her gem, he used it to illuminate her fragile form. "Kaliwyn," he breathed. Using an extended claw in the gentlest way he ever had, he caught her hair and removed it from her face so that he could observe her better.

Lamwen had never thought of mortals as attractive, but this one held a beauty stemming from deep within. Heating the air again, he watched her as she slept, his heart warmed that she trusted him enough to sleep within his presence. "Rest well, my queen," he growled gently.

Hours later, dim light trickled into the cave, indicating the coming of the sun. Stirring, the dragon woke the girl, warning, "Your friends will awaken soon if they have not already."

"Oh my God. I'm still in the cave!" she gasped, looking around wildly in dismay.

"Yes," Lamwen chuckled, "you cannot tell me this rock floor is as comfortable as your bed."

Frowning, she glared up at him. "It was comfortable enough wrapped within your wing," she confessed. Throwing her arms around his neck, she sighed, "Thank you. As much as I hate the thought of my friends leaving, I look forward to the day when you may always be close at hand."

Shaking his large head as she left him, he wondered if such a day would ever arrive. *"Be careful,"* he warned as she rushed down the incline through the trees.

Arriving back at their cabin, Amicia stomped her feet on the porch to remove the snow from her boots, then hurried inside. Pulling off her coat and gloves, she found that Meena had begun to prepare their breakfast. "Do you need any help?" the girl offered, hoping her long absence had not been noticed.

"Set out the bread and jam," the older woman instructed, ready to awaken the others and face the day.

Stumbling out of their room a short time later, Bally complained, "Why do you insist on waking us?"

"Aye," Rey agreed, taking his seat and eyeing their food. "We've nothing to do all day but stare out at the snow and walk up the hill for the occasional piss."

"We need the routine," Piers informed them, also falling into his seat.

"With the short days of winter, it's easy to lose ourselves and tumble into depressions or any other forms of mental infirmity."

"Mental infirmity," Bally parroted, sipping from his cup of warm morning tea.

"Don't fret," Amicia clipped, refreshed after her clandestine visit up the slope. "Just think; in a few weeks, the thaw will begin, and we can start working on our boat and preparing for the journey home."

Melancholy, Rey found it hard to agree with that sentiment. The cold of winter had surrounded them, removing the purpose from their days. What's worse, when spring came, he would likely be divided from her forever, causing him to feel as if all the happiness had been drained from the world by the ice and snow.

Watching the girl until she arrived at her home next to the beach, Lamwen spent the day lying in the mouth of his cave. Between watching and dozing, he thought about the stories he had heard about Ziradon and what became of his heir.

There weren't many, he had to admit, as Gwirwen had probably seen to it that any who knew the truth were either part of his legion or removed from their realm permanently. He did know of one, however, as there had been a young dragon who had told a tale a few times that earned him a reputation among the males of the dragon's lair.

Thinking of this informant, Lamwen wondered if he even still lived, as he had been made an outcast by the others; deemed a liar and unfit to serve in the king's guard. Watching as the boys came out of their cabin and ran up and down the beach for a few minutes before going back inside, he wondered if time would have altered the young dragon's tale.

Deciding he had to find out and hear his story first hand, Lamwen left his cave at dusk. Flying due east, he headed for the dragon cliffs of Adiarwen. When he arrived, he entered the bachelor's cave, the largest of those that pock the face of the cliff that hangs over the ocean. There, the majority of the unmated males spent their nights in the company of each other, while those who had been blessed with the duty of procreation were given private quarters in caves above, close to the rocky surface.

Ambling through the warren of passages, Lamwen sniffed at the slumbering dragons, searching for the outcast among them. He had to be careful, as the fewer who knew of his arrival, the better. The king and queen expected him to be at his post watching over New Abolia. Therefore, he certainly didn't want to incur their wrath, confident they would be angry to discover him there.

Almost at the point of giving up, the elder dragon finally located his target, finding Jarrowan as he slept alone in an alcove along one of the outside walls and away from the others. Waking the beast, he growled, "Jarrowan, I need a word."

"A word," the younger dragon laughed. "I'm sleeping, pops. Bother me some other time."

"Pops?" Lamwen felt certain the term had been meant as a slur. "Perhaps you are unaware of whom you are speaking to," he growled.

"I know who you are," Jarrowan snapped, adjusting himself to lie more comfortably. "Now go away."

"I am the captain of the king's guard, and I wish to speak with you," Lamwen stated more forcefully.

Glaring at him in the near darkness, Jarrowan replied tartly, "I'm not in the king's guard. I was banned, or don't you recall?"

"I recall," Lamwen agreed, walking a slow circle in the cramped space to ensure their conversation was unheard. "As I said, I need a word, but not here. Accompany me, and we will discuss that which has earned you disgrace."

Laughing, Jarrowan considered holding to his refusal. "Why should I? I've been an outcast for years. What is it that suddenly draws your attention to me?"

Pausing in his pacing, Lamwen studied him, then hissed, "If you saw what you claim, you will understand my need for secrecy. I leave you now and trust you will not disobey my command." Exiting, he dove off the front of the cliff, floating over the water a moment before flapping his large wings as he turned south and headed for the marshlands.

His curiosity piqued, Jarrowan followed the older dragon to the mouth of the cave. His eyes narrowed as he watched the captain disappear into the horizon, he leapt from his perch and pursued him to the swamp-covered grounds inhabited by the gnomes.

Seeing Lamwen below, Jarrowan circled twice, having a look around before deciding his confidence in the king's most trusted leader. "I'm here," he announced as he landed beside him, flapping his wings noisily. "What is it that you want?"

"Tell me about Ziradon, Kaliwyn, and Gwirwen," Lamwen replied.

Snarling a twisted laugh, Jarrowan spat, "I've shared all that I dare. I'm surprised my words haven't gotten me killed, or is that why you're here?"

"The king has allowed you to live, perhaps branded a liar better than murdered as a martyr. Tell me what you know," Lamwen insisted, pacing slowly around the smaller beast.

"I spied upon them the night he came to power," Jarrowan explained, looking around and swishing his tail. "They trapped him with a spell and then made him watch as they turned the dragoness into a human."

"A mortal of the rim?" Lamwen queried.

"Yes, a frail pink female with fair skin and wild blond waves." His voice confident, he had given up on anyone believing his words. Meeting the older dragon's glare, he waited for the laughter he had grown accustomed to hearing in response to his claims.

"And what did they do with this human girl?" Lamwen asked instead.

Uncertain, Jarrowan held the stare. "They removed her from Adiarwen," he said more quietly. "Ziewen flew her to the rim and dropped her there. Nalen, I believe, was the location Gwirwen specified."

His jaw tight, Lamwen breathed deeply for a full minute, considering his response. "What loyalty do you hold to our king?" he snarled.

Taken aback, Jarrowan broke the connection, turning in a slow loop and muttering to himself as he gathered his thoughts. Finally, ready to face his demise if it would come, he replied, "Which king? The real one they imprisoned in the stone cage or the one who masquerades as our leader while Eriden crumbles?"

Warmth in his tones, Lamwen agreed, "You have seen the truth in our circumstances. You will be rewarded for your patience. Tell no one of this and await my instruction. You may return to the dragon's lair."

"Wait!" Jarrowan shouted before he could leave. "Tell me what has happened. Why have you only now found faith in my words?"

Studying his new ally, Lamwen took a turn, looking around them again, then whispered, "Our princess has returned to Eriden. I alone know of her whereabouts. When the time comes, we shall rise against those who have wronged our kingdom."

His voice stolen, Jarrowan opened and closed his mouth a few times, then managed, "My captain, how can that be? Mortals of the rim... they do not come to Eriden easily."

"It has not been easy," Lamwen agreed, remembering what he knew of the girl's journey. "Return to the lair and wait. Fear not. I will have a place for you in my army when the time comes."

"Yes, my captain," Jarrowan agreed, leaping into the air to do as he had been instructed.

Leaving the marshes as well, Lamwen flew to the west, wanting to be back in his cave before the sun rose over New Abolia for another day. *I have made my first friend within our ranks*, he mused as he flew, certain that albeit the step had been small, it had been a worthwhile trip. *Jarrowan has confirmed what I have suspected, and one day, if we are successful, Kaliwyn will take her place as heir to the throne and the Supreme Dragoness of Eriden.*

TWENTY-EIGHT

Trolls in the Trees

"GOD, I'm so glad the snow is finally melting. We've been stuck in here for months!" Rey lamented, glaring at the beginnings of their vessel through the wall and looking forward to working on it.

"Can I get some more of that delicious bread and jam?" Bally asked, giving Amicia an encouraging smile.

"I suppose that you can," she replied, passing him the bowl of preserves. "We only have one other jar left, but there were plenty of them around last year, so I'm sure I'll be able to make more once they're ripe. I've never seen these berries before, but they are so sweet."

"I believe they are called freens," Meena informed her. "They grow all along the coast in wild patches, but there is a coastal village that has cultivated them to make large crops for wines."

"I think we should find a clearing or two and plant some of these and a few other things to grow while we build our ship," Rey suggested, helping himself to seconds as well. "We're going to need to stock up before we sail."

"They look like grapes," Piers added, "except for this odd pink color. I'm for the planting though. The more we have, the more we can take with us when we depart."

"Speaking of departing," Zaendra observed, "there will be some of us left behind. We'll need to plant enough so that both groups get to enjoy the freens."

211

Laughing merrily, the crew ate their breakfast before they faced the hard day ahead. The snow had been melting for a few weeks, and they would be felling more trees for ship building that very day. They had managed to construct the keel before the snow brought their efforts to the halt, and all seemed eager to continue their efforts.

Once they had eaten, they donned their leather coats and gloves, as the air was still quite cold beneath the trees. Outside, they broke up into work groups, with Rey and Piers taking on the chopping, Bally and Animir dragging them down, and Meena and Amicia stripping the bark so they could cut proper boards.

Humming while she worked, the older woman seemed quite content, but Ami had been troubled when the announcement came that the work would commence. Noticing her happy sounds, she sighed, "Doesn't this bother you?"

"What bother me?"

"You are helping to build the ship that will take your lover away. Shouldn't you be upset or something?"

"I suppose that I could be," Meena laughed. "But I love Piers. I know that he doesn't really belong here, and I want him to be happy. If he wishes to return to the rim, it is my duty to help him make that happen."

Scowling, the girl groaned, "I'm not sure I could be that unselfish."

Cutting her eyes over, Meena asked quietly, "Are you going to accompany Rey then, when they depart?" When the girl continued her scraping without a sound, she pushed, "Or has he decided to remain behind with you?"

"We have not spoken of it," Amicia confessed in a quiet voice, working furiously. "I can't go back there. I feel that my place is here, and he must make his own choices."

"And you have no desire in the matter?" Her hands still, Meena studied the girl, reading sorrow in the hunch of her shoulders.

"I cannot tell him what to do," she spat, stopping long enough to give her an angry glare. "I have taken no vow with him, nor given him any promise for the future. He is a free man, and he may leave if he desires."

At that moment, a shrill scream cut through the air from some distance away.

Her heart racing, Amicia sat up straight and looked around, then up the slope. "Oldrilin?"

Clearing the tree line, Lin and Zae ran towards them. On their feet, the two women met them about a hundred feet up the beach, north of their cabin. "For goodness sakes," Meena challenged, dropping to her knees before the smallest member. "What's all the screaming about?"

"Up there," Zaendra huffed, bending over to catch her breath. "We found something on the path."

Bally and Animir joined them, but the other two men were not to be seen and might not have heard the commotion. Glancing around, Baldwin considered if they should investigate or wait for the Mate. Making his choice, he demanded, "Show me."

Taking his hand, the nymph led him through the trees, the others close behind. They didn't have to go too far before they came upon a long stick, which had been stabbed into the ground. On the top end hung a dead animal, one that appeared to have been there several days but was decaying slowly due to the temperature of the air.

"Wow, that's attractive," the boy observed, reaching for the carcass.

"Don't touch it!" Piers shouted, joining them from the other direction. "We found another one up the trail on our way here."

"Well, it didn't get on that pole on its own," Ami observed, covering her face in disgust.

"No, someone has put them there. We're not alone in these woods," Rey snapped. All turning to look at him, it should have been obvious, and he clipped, "Trolls."

"Aye," the Mate agreed, lifting the animal slowly as he looked for booby traps. Finding nothing, he sighed, "We'll need to bury them."

"What a waste," Zae voiced, shaking her head.

"We can't eat them," Meena soothed. "We have no idea how long they've been dead. It would be a good way to poison ourselves."

Her eyes darting around, then up to the sky, Amicia searched for any sign of Lamwen. *Surely, he hasn't had any part in this*, she mused. Thinking it unwise to reach out to him and ask, she decided to keep this to herself. She had managed to visit him only once during the frozen winter months and still felt the need to hide his presence from her friends.

"I'll dig the hole. We can gather them and put them in, and we'll cover it up before we turn in tonight, assuming there will be more than the two we've already seen," Rey offered.

"That's good thinking," Piers agreed, offering him the find. "We'll take a short break for some water and get back at it when you're done."

"What are you going to do?" Meena asked, her voice lacking its typical confidence.

"I'm going to have a look around," he said with a nod. "See if I find any more and take them down."

Her lips pursed, Ami walked slowly back to her chore. Their morning had begun with happiness and hope, at least on the part of the others, but the discoveries had darkened her mood even further. Glancing around, she saw shadows behind every tree, as if unseen eyes watched them, waiting for their chance to attack.

"You've warned us about the trolls many times," Amicia observed as the two women reclaimed their tools. "Does it make you angry that Piers refuses to listen?"

Her arms pumping back and forth as she worked, Meena's features crinkled. "I do not wish to speak of this."

"Why not?" Ami clipped, her frustration obvious as she shrugged her shoulders. "You want to give me advice about Rey, let's hear about you and the Mate for a change. You share a bedroom with him. Obviously, you are husband and wife in practice even if he has given no –"

"That's enough," Meena hissed. Cutting her eyes over at the girl, she spat, "Piers is a good man. I told you before, I feel the caring in his touch and see it in his eyes even if he cannot speak the words. That is enough for me. As for this place, he believes the trolls can be reasoned with."

"But you don't."

"They are savages. They live in small groups of two or three, and they are not friends of any, not even each other," the older woman explained. Inhaling deeply, she calmed herself. "I fear that he thinks we will remain here after his vessel sails, but we will not stay in this cabin. Once he returns to the rim, those who are left behind will return south and settle closer to the wizard communities where it is safe."

"But you can't stay there," Ami pouted. "You are a wan. They would punish you for your talents."

"Then I will once again keep them hidden. I have done so for many years. It will not harm me to do so again."

Her lips pressed tightly together, Amicia thought of all the things the woman's magical abilities had provided and all the things they would not have had without her. "I'm sorry," she whispered.

"Tis not your fault," Meena replied more softly. "You are a dear friend, Amicia Spicer. I have enjoyed knowing you."

"And I you," the girl agreed with a small nod, blinking at tears. Bending over her work, she put her shoulders into it. She didn't know how they would get the ship away from the shore, but Meena obviously believed that they could; otherwise, why would she help to build it? *She must know a trick; some way to get around the magic barrier.*

While she worked, her mind wandered, and she realized that in the end, Piers might change his mind and take them all. *There are lots of islands within the rim*, she mused. *Perhaps he intends to find one for all of us, away from the evils and pitfalls both places present.*

Adjusting her grip, a darker thought tickled the back of her mind, one that brought a deep sadness to her heart. *What if the Mate is deceiving us and he never intends to leave here at all?* She didn't dare look at the cabin. She knew the detail and work he had put into its construction. *Don't*, she warned herself, but she knew things felt wrong. *You can only lie for so long before others see the cracks in your façade.*

Over the next two weeks, the group fell into a routine. While the girls prepared breakfast at sunrise, the men went out and combed the woods around the cabin. If they found more of the mutilated bodies, they did not divulge it to any of the four women.

The work of felling, stripping, and cutting wood planks continued the entire time, and each day felt only slightly warmer than the last. The snow, however, attested to the changes as it had all but disappeared from the places that the sun touched, and only lay in thin wisps in the protected areas beneath the trees.

Pulling on her coat and gloves to visit the outhouse, Amicia felt as if a rock had settled in her gut. Rey had asked her the night before if she had given any thought to her plans for the future, and it had ended in a spat when she insisted that she should not say or do anything that would sway his choice.

Marching up through the trees, she paused when she heard the sound of birds singing in the crisp morning air. Spying two large blue birds with red tips on their wings, she gasped, "How beautiful!"

Over her shoulder, she caught the hint of movement and swung to see that he had noticed her and come to join her. "I don't want to talk about it," she clipped, forgetting the chirping couple and edging closer to her target.

"I don't either," he sighed, ambling forward. "I just wanted to tell you that I've decided I'm not going with the others when they leave."

"What?" she gasped. "Rey, you don't belong here!"

"I belong with you," he defended, holding his hand up to stymie her protests. "Besides, there's only three of us. How the hell are three of us going to sail a ship?" he laughed, then sighed. "I don't think that vessel is ever going to sail, and if it does, I won't be on it."

Smiling as he looked up at her, he continued, "I just thought you should know. I mean, I know there aren't a large number of suitors around, but I'd still like to be considered if and when you're ready to be serious about it."

Turning his back, he walked away, leaving her to complete her business in the shed. Slamming the door when she entered, Amicia fumed. *He has no right to put this on me!* She hated the way it made her feel, as if she would one day be forced to accept him for lack of options.

When Ami finally returned to the cabin, the group had sat down to their meal and were halfway done with it. "Are you feeling all right?" Meena asked, standing to touch her forehead.

"I'm not ill," the girl sulked, cutting her green eyes over to glare at Rey. She did, however, feel anger roiling from deep within. Taking her seat, she clipped, "So, how many more dead animals have you found?"

The men did not reply, all frozen over their plates as they looked at one another. Folding his arms, with elbows on the table to lean on, Piers glowered at her. "None."

"You don't say," she grunted back. Narrowing her eyes at him, she knew it was more than that by the way the others were acting. "When do we start building more on the boat?"

"We will start back on the ship when we have a sufficient number of boards. A few more weeks and we should be ready," he replied calmly, sipping from his water.

Staring him down, she made her final attempt, "And how many men will it take to sail it?"

The silence that followed filled the room, as no one dared to breathe. Cutting her eyes around so that she could examine each face, she could see the truth etched in their features, as if she were the last one to discover it, or the first one to be bold enough to state it.

"I see," she whispered, pushing her chair back and leaving her empty plate where it sat. Lifting her coat off the rack, she opened and closed the door before anyone moved or spoke.

"What did you tell her?" Piers demanded as soon as she had gone.

"Nothing!" Rey shrugged, turning his palms to the ceiling. "I informed her I intended to stay here in Eriden with her."

"You didn't say anything about the bodies?" his elder grunted.

"Hell no! We agreed that we wouldn't."

"You found more?" Oldrilin sniveled, her bottom lip quivering.

"It's ok, Lin," her friend soothed. "Drink your broth. We've taken care of them."

"Unlikely," Meena inserted, laying down her utensil. "The trolls are displeased with our presence, and they won't be satisfied as long as we remain here." Glancing at the Mate, she sighed, "Perhaps we should go. The cabin is beautiful, and the forest is amazing, but they are no good to us if we're dead."

Her eyes wide, Zaendra squeaked, "Dead?"

"Now see what you've done?" Piers scowled, then changed his tone in an instant. "Do not worry yourself, love." He turned to the girl. "We'll take care of the trolls. Once they figure out we aren't going to hurt them and we get things worked out with them, things will be great here."

"Until you leave," Zae accused.

"Ugh," he grunted, rubbing his face with his hands. "You fix this," he commanded, eyeing Meena as he pointed at the nymph. "I'll go out and have a talk with Ami."

Shaking her head as he left, Meena frowned deeply. She knew things were getting out of hand. "I never should have allowed us to come this far," she sighed.

TWENTY-NINE

A Price to Pay

STANDING ON THEIR SHORE, Amicia stared at the frame which held the base of their boat. Behind her, Piers approached, cautiously creeping forwards. "I threw a fit when we left Riran," she observed, shaking her head. "Not this time."

"What about this time?" he replied calmly.

Nodding, she glared at the beginnings of a ship. "Who's the boat for, Piers?"

"It's for us," he replied flatly.

"No, it isn't," she turned to glare at him. Her eyes were drawn to the house they had taken such care with. "It will make a nice home next winter, as it did this one," she observed. "And the one after that, and after that..." Her voice faded into the future.

"A home for who," he clipped. "We'll be finished with the ship and be gone by then."

"No, we won't," she snarled. "Why do you keep saying things you know aren't true?"

Thinking of Meena's words the day he met her, he swallowed hard. "I can't leave her, and I can't take her," he shrugged. "What's a man to do?"

"Why are we building it then," she hissed. "Why did we even come here?"

"Because sometimes people need things," he informed her, blinking rapidly. "Things to remind them or things to believe in."

219

"And which is this?" she scowled.

Grinding his teeth, he studied her.

"You never intended to leave Eriden or to find a way home," she defended, standing taller and wrapping her coat tighter around her. "The night you told me you were leaving the glen, you said I could come, but you didn't mean it. You wanted to leave us there and be done with us, striking out on your own. Why did you then... let us come?"

"You wanted to," he whispered, swallowing visibly. "Have I ever been able to say no to you?"

"Oh, you know that you have. I've pushed you to court me since we met, or near enough," she sighed.

"That's different," he snapped turning away and staring across the water.

"Yes, it is. You like the fire, just not enough to let it burn you. You want the friends and the lovers. You just can't risk getting hurt," she assumed.

"Ami, I'm an old man. You promised we were finished having this conversation, and yet here I am, having to explain it to you once more."

"Only we're not talking about me, now are we," she countered.

"You mean Meena," he said with a quick laugh. "She is perfectly happy with the way things are."

"I know you love her, Piers. You should declare it and ask for her hand."

"I'd rather build the boat," he whispered.

"One that will never sail even if it could," she sighed.

"We need this, Ami. We need something to believe in, that one day we might see home again. Something to remind us this is not from where we came," he finished by wiping tears from his face.

Laughing, she turned her cheeks into the stiff breeze, feeling the chill upon them. "Anything to keep from admitting that *this* is home. We all belong here, Mate. Every one of us has a stake upon this land, only you can't admit it. Who hurt you so badly?" she asked, shaking her head.

"You've been talking to her, haven't you. She put you up to this," he accused, staring at the ground before him.

"No, I have not, and she never would. She understands you perfectly, all your flaws and weaknesses, but she also sees your strengths and the things that make you great. She loves you, Mate. More than I ever have or could. As much as I wanted to be called your wife, she deserves it far more than I ever did or will," she stated confidently.

The wind whipping around her, she marched into it, towards their home, leaving him to ponder the words that they had shared. Inside, she noted the others remained at the table as she removed her coat and gloves, hanging them over the back of her chair. Turning without a sound, she sat in her favorite seat, in the window that overlooked their beach, and curled her knees up before her.

"*Lamwen,*" she called into the abyss, her eyes staring out across the sea.

Getting no reply, she sighed. Slipping her hand into her pocket, she cupped the hamar and tried again. "*Lamwen, please speak with me.*"

"*I'm busy,*" he growled. "*Dragons have lives, you know. We don't lie about all day watching over flimsy mortals with untamed manes.*"

"*Something's happened,*" she replied, blinking back tears. "*Something terrible.*"

"*What's the matter?*" he coaxed, his tone softened.

"*We've found dead animals. They're gutted and impaled on long sticks. Out in the woods around the cabin.*"

"*Trolls,*" his voice echoed. "*Gather your food and stay inside,*" he instructed. "*Do not go out, and I will arrive as soon as I am able.*"

Smiling, she felt comforted that he would come when she called, only hoping it would not be too late.

"Where are you?" Rey demanded, giving her a shake by the shoulder and interrupting her thoughts.

"What?" she asked meekly, blinking up at him. Behind him, she could see the others had noticed her trance-like state, and Piers stood glaring at her. She hadn't even noticed he had come in from outside; she had been so deep in her thoughts.

"Who are you talking to? Is it Uscan, about the posts and corpses?" the older man inquired gruffly.

"Oh," her mouth dropping open, she moaned, "No, it isn't Uscan. I haven't spoken with him since we entered the foreboding forest and faced the goblins with the hamar gem."

"Then who is it?" Piers questioned more sternly.

"It doesn't matter," she replied, licking her lips. "He says that we need to gather our food and stay in. They are a message from the trolls, and we are in danger," she informed them, her voice fading as she confirmed the older woman's fears.

"It does matter," Meena intervened, gingerly approaching her to take the other half of the window seat. "Amicia, you have a rare gift. Some level of telepathy is common among magical beings, but few can use it so easily. Who is it that draws you away from us?"

"I…" she began, unable to form the words as she looked at their expectant faces in turn. A single tear spilling over to streak her cheek, she managed, "I should have told you. So many times, I've wanted to. We formed a connection that night in the glen."

"The dragon," Rey breathed. "You've been secreting away with him. I told you," he spat, spinning to face Piers. "I told you he had followed us, and he's gotten inside her head!"

"No," Amicia denied, dropping her feet to the floor, prepared to stand. "You've got it all wrong. Lamwen, he's looking out for us, and has been since we left our meadow. In the desert, he sent the rain that preserved us," she confessed. "He means us no harm."

"He went from wanting to kill us to our protector in a single night. How convenient," Piers observed, slinging his arms across his chest.

"It's not like that," she replied, shedding more tears. "He's away, but he will come and protect us from the trolls. We must stay inside until he arrives."

"We don't need a dragon as our protector," the Mate spat. "Rey and I will visit the trolls. We will offer peace and explain why we are here."

Shaking her head, Meena also began to cry. "I think that would be unwise."

"Unwise would be to wait here to be slaughtered," her lover growled, his eyes still on the girl. Grinding his teeth, he fought the urge to berate her. He had done his share of hiding the truth, and in the end, he could not blame her for guarding this secret. "You have put us in a dangerous position," he said instead. "This dragon could be the very reason they are upset."

"The dragons rule all of Eriden," Meena reminded him, wiping at her drops of sorrow. "Not even the trolls would question their presence. It is ours that offends."

"Then we will set things straight and gain their permission to be here," he vowed. "Rey, get your sword and walk with me. We know the direction of their dwellings based on the tracks we've seen. We'll follow them and return as soon as we have their blessing," he informed the rest, picking up his own blade and waiting for Reynard to join him on the porch.

Clomping down the steps, the younger man followed a few paces behind until they reached the line of trees at the back of their cottage. Running to catch up, he could see the Mate's rage by the way he carried himself. "I don't think this is a good move," he challenged.

"You agree with the women then," Piers snarled, never breaking his stride. "Perhaps you should turn tail and join them, cowering in the cabin."

"I'm not afraid," Rey snapped, "I'm simply concerned about your state of mind. You seem tense; if I were the king of the trolls and you presented yourself before me, I would doubt you were looking for peace."

"Shut up. You're only a boy –"

"I am not a boy!" Rey cut him off. "I'm a man, same as you. Maybe not as old, and I certainly haven't seen as much as you, but my opinion is as valid as yours."

Pushing limbs out of the way as they moved, the Mate held one for a moment, allowing his comrade to step forward before he released it, smacking him square in the face. "Man, hmm?"

"That's a dirty trick," Rey growled, wiping at his bloodied nose as the other man left him where he stood.

Ignoring him, the Mate marched on, his fever cooling. Regaining his head as they reached the large clearing that lay northeast of their cabin, he waited for him, then said in a calmer tone, "Aye, a dirty trick indeed. You're a good man, Reynard Daye. One of the finest I've ever served with."

Instantly on edge as they walked across the mud-covered field, he replied, "Thank you. I'm glad you think so, but why are you telling me this now?" His eyes darting around, he searched the sky for any sign of Amicia's new friend, then the far side of the clearing, where the forest closed in and carried up the side of the mountain. "I don't like this," he said more quietly.

"Aye, I gathered that," Piers chuckled, pausing to stand for a moment. "I was thinking we should plant those crops we spoke about here. The soil appears dark and rich," he observed, lifting a boot to expose the ebony mud-coated soles.

Frowning, Rey studied him. "You really think the trolls will allow us to stay here?"

"Of course. Why wouldn't they?" He clapped him on the back. "We haven't done anything to harm them." He smiled, his mood greatly improved at thinking about their future.

"Well, you'll have to ask Bally about the crops. We raised cattle and ran a dairy, remember?"

"I do," Piers laughed, his voice carrying across the open field. Catching movement among the trees, he raised his chin in their direction as he said more quietly, "It would appear the trolls have come out to greet us."

Continuing to meet them, but at a much slower pace, the pair tromped over the wet earth. Gripping his sword anxiously, Rey again wondered what the hell they were doing. "There are so many of them," he observed as more of the creatures cleared the shadows and grouped together, waiting for them.

"Just don't make any sudden movements and leave the talking to me."

"Aye."

"Hello!" Piers called when they were only twenty feet away from the gathering.

Holding a smile and hoping to appear amicable despite his weapon, the Mate inspected the group of males before him, or at least he assumed that they were male. Most wore no covering across their chest, exposing a large amount of grey or blue flesh. A few appeared to be heavy set, but most were on the thin side to the point of being boney.

Their hair was another matter, as it ranged in color from ghost white to a pale grey or silver, and their eyes practically glowed they were so faint. The last thing he observed as they drew closer was their height. He had thought the elves, or at least the reigning ones, were oversized, but the trolls held at least another foot on top of them, making their average height eight foot from what he could see.

"These guys look so different," Rey whispered, drawing the same conclusions.

"Shh, don't be rude," Piers instructed, holding his grin.

"Far enough, mortal of the rim," a decorated male called when only ten feet lay between them.

"I'm Piers Massheby," the Mate announced, wearing his wide fake smile. "My friends call me The Mate."

"I am aware of you and your friends," a large troll in front replied, scowling at his use of their tongue. "I am Yaodus, king of these lands, and your words are of no use to me."

"Oh," Piers clipped. "We've come to speak to you. We found your..." His voice trailed away, unsure what to call the sacrificed animals.

"They were a warning, one you do not heed," Yaodus groaned. "Now you die."

"No, wait!" the Mate shouted, dropping his sword to hold up his palms. The blade landed, tip first, so that the handle rocked back and forth in the air. His eyes drawn to the shiny metal, he stared at it for a moment, his mind trapped in the night he had faced the dragon on the Sea Serpent before he swam to the raft and escaped with the others.

"Please," he said more calmly, returning to the present. "We are here in peace, as we mean you no harm."

"Harm is of no meaning," came the burly reply.

Perplexed, Rey stepped forward, stabbing his weapon into the ground to his left. "No meaning," he repeated. "Sure, it has meaning. You recognize that we are men, you know we are trapped here. All we want is to leave."

"Then leave," Yaodus bellowed, "back the way you came."

"We can't go back," Piers replied weakly, his brow furrowed. "We came here to build a ship, that we may sail from these shores and return to the rim."

Laughter rippled through the forty or so trolls who had joined their sovereign. "Such fools," he informed them, hoisting his spear and throwing it across the narrow gap between them.

Caught in the chest, on the right side, Piers gasped. The blade cut cleanly between his ribs, and shoots of pain took him to his knees as he grasped at the handle. Falling onto his back, he lay flat, staring at the sky above him.

"No!" Rey screamed, grabbing his sword and waving it at them wildly. Laughter rumbled again, louder this time.

Realizing he could not take them all, he dropped to his knees next to his friend. Tossing the weapon aside, his hands hung in the air as he considered his options. Seizing the wooden shaft, he huffed, "Should I pull it out?"

"No," Piers grunted, rocking his skull side to side against the wet earth. Reaching up, his fingers wormed through the dark ringlets to find the back of his comrade's neck. Pulling him down, closer, his lips whispered, "Tell Meena I'm sorry and that I have loved her as no other."

"Shit," Reynard spat, his eyes filled with tears. "This isn't happening," he gasped.

"Please," the Mate begged, knowing his end was near. "Tell Amicia that I did my best to be the man she needed me to be… " His voice trailed away, and his eyes stared at the sky above. In the distance, to the east, he could see three shapes, like small points in the sky. "The dragons," he gasped.

"Piers," Rey sobbed. "Don't talk, ok. Let me think. There has to be a way to stop this."

Standing behind them, the trolls seemed to be enjoying the display. "The weakness of mortals," the king spat.

"You've just stabbed my best friend in the chest," Rey declared through gritted teeth. "You are savages. Let us build our vessel and be gone from this wretched place. You could have allowed us that!" he screamed, getting to his feet to face them. "He didn't have to die!"

"You wish to be shown sympathy?" Yaodus snarled.

"We wish to be shown something! Decency would have sufficed. We've done nothing to you. Given you no cause to be treated as such. Is there no healer among you?"

"A healer," the decorated troll to the king's left chortled. "I am all the healer we have need of; I see the dead to the next life. Shall I escort your friend?" he offered, a crooked grin on his pale lips.

His vision swimming, Rey wiped his snot on his arm, below his sleeve, tears of anguish and rage filling his eyes. "You bastards," he said quietly, settling to his knees once again and laying his head next to Piers's as he cried.

Stepping forwards, the king reached his victim to reclaim his spear. "Return to your women," he commanded. "We come for the rest in three days. You should be gone before we get there."

The blade yanked from his chest, scorching pain filled the Mate's lungs, as the blood poured into the cavity of his chest. He knew he only had a few minutes and that no medicine could save him. *"Ami,"* he reached out, searching for the girl he would never hold.

"Piers," she replied, her voice trembling.

"I was wrong, love," he informed her. *"Prepare what you can and be ready to leave. Rey will be there in a few minutes, and you must flee this very night. The trolls are coming for you... They will kill you all if you cannot get away."*

Aloud, he gasped, "Go, my friend. Return to the others and lead them from this place."

"I'm not leaving you here," Rey cried, his hand covering the gurgling wound. "Dear God, please help us. Please don't let it end like this."

THIRTY

No Long Goodbyes

"NO!" Amicia screamed, flying out the door and tearing into the woods.

Limbs of trees smacked her in the face as she ran. Ignoring the sting of the cuts and scrapes, she pushed on, sliding and falling over the rocks and remaining snow that spotted the forest floor.

Hot tears burned her cheeks as she called, "You can't have him!" as loudly as she could. In that moment, she wished she were a dragon, able to fly, able to reach him in time.

Her lungs on fire, her side ached, but she pushed for every step, oblivious to any other thing around her. *I must reach him. They cannot take him from me.* The realization that she was not his tickled the back of her mind. *They cannot take him from HER.* It would destroy Meena to lose him.

Panting, fresh drops of sadness formed. *Meena.* This woman had known great sorrow. Suffered great loss. *No, they cannot have our Piers*, she inwardly fumed, her teeth grinding as she seethed.

Behind her, staff in hand, the wan ran hard to keep up, watching the flaxen waves flying behind the girl as she ran. Slipping a few times, her skirt snagging on some of the spring sprouts, she wanted desperately to catch her. She didn't know what the girl had seen; Amicia had neglected to tell her before she ran from the cabin. Whatever it was, she had to get there.

Her arms pumping, Amicia reached an open field. Across on the other side, she could see Rey hunched over, the Mate lying flat upon the ground. Nearby stood a gathering of large pitiful creatures. Their blue-tinted bodies grotesque, she knew who they were; *the trolls.*

Instantly, anger replaced her tears. She wanted to kill them. To hurt them and torture them for what they had done. "No!" she shouted, alerting them to her approach, and a ripple of murmurs passed through the collection of onlookers.

Arriving next to Piers, she sank to her knees, digging them into the soft soil.

"Ami," he breathed, coughing slightly, with blood oozing from his mouth.

"Stop it," she spat. "You aren't going to die here. You can't die here!" she declared. Fury coursed through her, and she fought to control the rage. Pulling her hamar gem from her pocket, it glowed brightly as she closed her eyes, imagining the wound beneath her hand as his thick blood coated her fingers.

She watched it through her spirit, the layers of his flesh, and the wound within, focusing all that she was upon it. She willed it to close. To be healed. *To be gone, as if the blade had never pierced his flesh*, she panted. The light from the magical stone spread, glowing around them, intensely white and pure.

His eyes wide, Rey got to his feet, backing away, as did the gathering of trolls. Wiping his mouth with the back of his hand, the blood on his fingers caked with dirt smeared mud upon his cheek.

Reaching them, Meena's staff fell from her trembling fingers and landed with a thud. Collapsing next to the couple as Ami worked to close his wounds. Tears streaming in an instant, she waited. "Please, no!" she wailed. He drew no breath, and she could see no life in his wide, empty eyes.

Anger seized her, and she grabbed the wooden shaft, fighting the material around her legs to stand in the thick mud of the field. Facing the trolls, she stomped towards them. "You animals!" she screamed, knocking them back with a wave of energy, sending them reeling, many of them to the ground.

Their king raised his arm against the blast, laughing at her attempt to shake him. "Puny wizard," he mocked.

Rising abruptly, Amicia faced them as well. "What of me? Am I puny as well?"

Raising her stone, the light glowed brightly, and Yaodus glared at it, then dropped his gaze to stare at her, as if seeing her for the first time.

"Death cannot have him!" she screamed. "You will leave this place. We have as much right to be here as you do; any of you!"

Above them, Lamwen screamed, as Jarrowan and Putwyn joined him, slowly circling the gathering at only a few hundred feet. Staring up at them Yaodus gasped. "Dragon's fire," he challenged.

"That's right!" the girl bellowed, her fist clenched around the stone. "I bring the dragon's fire," she snapped, shaking her stone at him. "All I have to do is say the word, and they will burn your forest to the ground."

Staring at her, the troll did not doubt, as he could see the flame within her. Taking a step forward, he dropped the spear that he carried, Piers's blood still coating the tip. "Forgive us, my queen," he begged, kneeling on one knee before her. "We did not know," he whispered.

Shaken, Ami stared at him, dimly aware that the rest of their group had joined them and stood on the far side of the field, watching from the edge of the woods. The wind catching her wild hair, blowing it around her, the magnitude of their loss slammed into her.

"NO!" she screamed at the top of her lungs, her fists clenched. Spinning, she fell across his lifeless body. Slamming him in the chest with the side of her fist, she cried, "You can't leave us. You can't!"

Her jaw clamped shut, she sucked and pushed the air over her teeth, which bubbled with her saliva. Forcing herself up, she focused once more, cupping the stone and exhaling a deep breath slowly. From within, she willed the life force to be returned to him. "Come back to us," she whispered. "Come and take Meena to be your wife. Lead us and protect us on our journey of darkness, through this wretched land that knows no humanity," she begged.

The light in her hands grew dim, and she stared at it, focusing. "It's coming," she whispered. "I feel it!"

"Ami," Meena called to her softly, fear twisting her gut. Stepping towards her, she laid a hand upon her shoulder, but the moment she did so, the gem lit up brightly, as if it were a flash from the sun.

Blasted away, Amicia and Meena both sprawled upon the ground. Piers inhaled a deep breath, his chest expanding and his back arching as his life returned to him within the burst of illumination. Coughing, he rolled over onto his knees, bent over on all fours, sputtering. His hair pulled loose, it hung down, wild around his head and face as the wind swept against them.

The dragons above them squawked, their screams echoing through the valley. Sitting back on his haunches, he looked up at the creatures, then lowered his gaze to find the two women had regained their feet before him.

"I'm not dead," he croaked, taking in their muddy appearance, as if they had rolled in it.

"No," Meena sniffed, on her knees once more beside him, her hand holding his face as the other dropped over his back and pulled him against her.

Spinning, Amicia faced the trolls, glaring at the king. "You will not harm one of us again." Cutting her eyes over, she glared at the decorated version next to him. "Which of you officiates?"

"Officiates?" Yaodus asked, perplexed.

"Yes. Surely you have weddings. Husbands, wives... families?" she probed.

"Me," his decorated comrade professed. "You wish to be married?"

"Not me, them. You will marry them in three days. You will come to our cabin and bless their union. You," she turned to their leader, pointing a stiff digit in his face as he still knelt before her. "You will attend and extend to us your welcome to the forest of Yilaric. If you fail to do this, or if any of your kind brings harm to one of us again, I will see to it that no troll draws breath in the Kingdom of Eriden again."

Her threat could have been empty, but it could have been exactly as she promised. Getting to his feet, the man before them bore testament to her strength, the sheer depths of her power, and the old troll king knew which he would believe.

Making a final circle, the dragons flew south, landing within the same valley but well away from the proceedings. His friends gathered near, Lamwen growled, "She has yet again demonstrated her talent. No wonder it took our twisted king so many to bind her into human form."

"Tis true," Jarrowan replied. "Mine eyes have seen, and my heart believes. But we are yet three, how shall we stand against our king when so many has he?" The dragon had been a witness, a hidden shadow as he watched the dreadful event the night the Supreme Dragon had been caged and his heiress imprisoned in her flimsy human form. "I can bear testament, but few would listen," he moaned.

"For now, we walk in the shadow, as we are not ready for the light," the third beast observed, his massive chin raised as he peered into the sky.

"Yes," Lamwen agreed. "Go. Return to the cliffs and search for others. Do it quietly, like a whisper upon the wind. Not all of Adiarwen is happy with our new sovereign. Some see the lacking he has and are displeased with his reign. Seek them out and woo them to our cause."

"We shall not speak of the girl. Should any hear, they should not know the source of his undoing. She is strong, but she could be taken if they were to find her," Jarrowan warned.

"Yes," Lamwen hissed. "Keep her name guarded, do not let it fall from your tongues. Our princess we will protect as we champion her cause."

THIRTY-ONE

Wedding Trolls

PIERS AWOKE to bright light on the third day. A smile on his lips, he laid his arm across the bed, where he had slept alone. Meena's people bore superstitions about such things, and he was not allowed to see her since the sun set the night before. No, he would not lay eyes on her again until he stood before their friends and took her as his bride.

"Good morning," Amicia sang, giving the door a firm knock before she sauntered inside, carrying a bowl of water for him. "And how is our groom?"

"Alive," he chuckled, running his hand over the healed wound on his chest. Catching her hand, he stood and pulled her to face him. "You know, at some point, we are going to talk about this."

He didn't specify what, only placing his palm over the place a troll's spear had formed a hole in his lung.

"Aye," she agreed. "Someday I want to hear all about it," she grinned, pulling away as if to leave it at that.

"That's not what I'm talking about, Ami," he replied, refusing to release her as she pulled as if to get away from him. Raising her arm, she struggled for a moment, then let the appendage fall limp.

"We both did some things that day," she sighed. "Yours was pretty stupid," she spat turning to face him. "Let us not ruin your wedding day, shall we?"

"You knew I never wanted to be married," he quipped, raising his brow. "Why would you arrange for a troll, of all people, to marry us?"

233

"Seemed like a good idea at the time," she shrugged. "Besides, if you really wanted to get out of it, I gave you three days to say so."

"Aye," he growled, studying her cool collected self. "And you're not going to tell me anything. How you managed this?" He brushed the spot again, as if he could flick it away with the tips of his fingers.

Staring at the scar, the crooked edges pink and puckered, she sighed. "I didn't know I could do it. I only knew I had to try."

"And what about the dragon. Tell me about him."

"I'm not ready to talk about Lamwen," she spat, taking a step back.

"Oh, you're not ready, are you?" Piers observed, his expression tense. "I thought I knew you, Amicia."

"I told you that you didn't," she laughed, shaking her golden hair at him. "When I said that I would stop harassing you to marry me."

"So, you arranged for it to be someone else," he smirked, finally losing the scowl.

"I didn't pick her. You did. All I did was arrange the wedding. Wash and get outside so we can get her dressed and ready," she commanded.

"Is she really going through with this?" he asked, sounding skeptical as he dipped his digits in the liquid.

"Of course she is. She's in love with you. More than I ever have been," she replied with a crooked grin as she made for the door, closing it behind her.

Alone, the Mate washed his face and then more of his body, still thinking about what had happened the day he and Rey had stood up to the trolls. *She's right about that,* he berated himself. *It was a damn fool thing to do.*

Staring at the clothing Meena had sewn for him, he thought about their stop at the northern village, then sighed. Never had a woman loved him so much, and never had he felt less like he deserved it. Meena always saw the best in him and yet loved him as he was; every pitiful flaw.

"I swear to you," he whispered to himself, brushing the sleeve. "I'm going to live each day, from today to the end, doing my best to be the man you believe me to be."

Donning the clothes, he tied his hair up, then opened the door to have a peek. The rest of the house quiet, he assumed the girls were waiting for his exit. "Guess I shouldn't disappoint them," he chuckled, his step light when he passed through the front door. On the porch, the other men of the house were waiting for him. "What's the plan?"

"Well, we've been instructed not to get dirty and to let them know when the trolls arrive," Rey informed him, getting to his feet. "How do I look?"

Laughing, the Mate only shook his head. "These girls. It was bad enough when it was just Amicia trying to take care of us. Now it's her and Meena and even Zaendra from time to time."

Grinning, Animir held up his arms, showing off his new robe. "You have to admit it's pleasant that they are giving us such niceties."

"Aye," the Mate agreed, glancing at the chairs lining their small porch. "Ok, we sit and wait, I suppose."

They didn't have to wait long, as the trolls were punctual; a group of six made the trip. Rising to meet the king, Piers hesitated, unsure how to act on such an occasion. Standing at the top step, he looked at Yaodus eye to eye. "I'd bid you welcome, but that didn't work out so well for me last time," he growled, glaring into the dark, almost perfectly round eyes of the man who had killed him.

Bowing before him, the king observed, "It wasn't a good day for any of us. Thankfully, we have this second chance. My high priest is here to see to your vows," he informed him, offering the other troll. "And I have brought my wife, my daughter, and our two sons to bear witness."

"Your family," the Mate observed, puckering his lips at the lavender skin of the woman and the soft pink hue of their girl. "No one believes trolls have families," he observed, feeling overdressed with the ragged coverings of their guests. *At least they aren't naked,* he mused.

"No one really knows much about us. We keep to ourselves; we like it this way," Yaodus agreed. "Perhaps it is time for a change," he offered, holding his hand out towards the shore. "Where shall we stand?"

"It's all over here," Bally informed them, scurrying down the steps and leading the way to the place the girls had specified for the ceremony.

Watching them go, Rey knocked on the door. "The trolls are here," he informed Lin when she cracked it to peer up at him.

"Very good, Rey Daye," she grinned. "Five minutes, we be ready," she informed him with a shooing motion.

Leaving the porch, he joined the others, standing in the spot Ami had decided was to be his. "We have about five minutes," he said with a grin, suspecting that all the girls had new dresses as well.

It didn't really surprise Piers that it was closer to half an hour before the four women arrived, but when they did, the rest became a blur. Walking in a line, Lin led the way, her appearance odd, covered in her new black gown and not her magical garb. Following, Zaendra also wore a new yellow dress, one that accented her dark flawless skin. Arriving at her position, she stood next to Baldwin, who had awaited behind him.

Turning his attention back to the procession, Piers's eyes grew wide as Amicia strutted along in a slow, even gait. Her dress simple, it suited her, and he smiled at the look of awe on Rey's features as she stood next to him behind his bride's spot before their officiant.

Meena came last, in the simplest, most beautiful gown he had ever seen. A straight cut, the hem encircled her calves, shimmering as it hung around her. On her feet, she wore satin slippers, with her hair tied up and bound with ringlets escaping to tease her neck. "God help me," Piers breathed, looking at her from head to toe.

"It's a bit late for that," she laughed, taking her place next to him and turning to face their priest, who towered above them. Behind the priest, the family of trolls formed a line so that a circle of friends enclosed them.

A few minutes later, after a brief speech, the troll gave them both a grin, instructing them to kneel before him. Lifting a bowl of water, he sprinkled it over them, then announced, "You may congratulate the happy couple."

Lifting her chin with trembling fingers to give her a gentle kiss, the Mate knew he would keep his promise, spending each day to come doing his best to deserve her.

"Ah ha!" the king shouted, clapping thrice when their lips met. "And now we shall celebrate!" Bending over, he whispered to his eldest son, who broke into a wide grin as he left the group and ran up the beach, his bare feet kicking up the rough sand as he went.

Turning into the trees about fifty feet to the north, Amicia scowled as she observed, "Is he going home without you?"

"No. He is summoning the wedding party," the queen informed her with a smile. Shorter than her mate, the woman still held almost two feet over the girl when she sidled up to stand beside her. Her eyes large and round, like dark plums beneath her light brown hair, they glistened in the spring sun. Her pale purple flesh smooth, she held an air of regality, despite the shabbiness of their attire.

"Wedding party," Meena repeated, confused. "But we are the wedding party," she contradicted while indicating her friends.

"Not today," Yaodus laughed. "Today you are trolls, welcome within our kingdom. This is what you wanted, yes?" he asked, turning to face Ami. "To be given a place among us?"

"I did," she stammered, watching as pale bodies began to pour out of the line of trees, "I guess."

The first few trolls carried long sections of wood, which they laid out in five pyres about thirty feet apart so that they covered their entire beach end to end with dancing flames once they were lit. The trolls behind them brought large dead animals that appeared to be elk; these had been cleaned and prepared for roasting on spits which were assembled over the flames.

"What the devil is this?" Piers demanded, as smaller trolls came along, some bearing drums and stringed instruments, which they plucked.

"It's a wedding party," the king's youngest repeated with a smile on his blue lips, hopping around to the beat of their play.

"It's a celebration," Meena whispered in awe. "They are actually going to hold a feast for us."

"Of course," the king laughed, his arms wide. "We will make merriment with our new friends, and you will remain in the forest for as long as our queen desires it," he declared, giving Amicia a full bow.

When Ami glanced at his wife, she grinned, but lowered her face at her, which gave the girl an odd twist in the pit of her gut. People called her princess so often, she hardly noticed, but she had been referred to as queen twice by the troll before her. Inhaling deeply, she prepared to demand why, but as she looked around at the festival, she realized it was not the time or place for a detailed explanation.

As soon as the musicians had warmed up and the meal set to cook, the crowd began to gyrate to their rhythms. "This is incredible," Rey called into her ear as he offered her his hand. "Dance with me," he chortled.

Writhing next to him, the couple did their best to imitate the movements of their benefactors, then fell into fits of laughter when they couldn't keep up. Helping to serve the meat as the sun sank low in the sky, they ate and drank from large casks that had been hauled out on odd, two-wheeled carts.

"What's in the kegs?" Bally asked, eyeing them suspiciously as large cups were served.

"It's a special beer," Yaodus explained, giving Piers a nod as he handed him a portion of the brew. "A tradition among our people, made from the roots of a jusue tree. We make it in the fall and store it to keep us through the winter. This is the last of last year's supply."

"You are so different from what we had always heard," Meena observed, her happiness radiating from her.

"Yes," Amicia agreed. "I'm so glad you have given us your welcome. Although I must admit this is far more than I expected."

"True friends should only be given the best," the king replied, raising his cup in a toast. "One day, you will come and visit us in our caves, and we will teach you all there is to know about the trolls."

Up the mountain, a large form rested between the trees, his eyes trained on the girl. As the sun disappeared, a second dragon arrived and landed to share his clearing. "What news have you?" Lamwen asked, not bothering to move.

"We have only just begun, but I fear there may be a problem," Jarrowan replied, also watching the proceedings below.

"Then give me the details," the captain sighed.

"A few of the dragons we have spoken to seem to think this is a game. A trick of some kind. We have discussed it, and we thought you should know."

Lifting his giant head, Lamwen faced him. "Should know what?"

"There are those on the council who are plotting against Gwirwen and not for the benefit of Ziradon or his heir, which they claim was murdered the night of Gwirwen's rise. I'm afraid she may be in danger, and not from the king or his followers; if they wish to hold to their version of events, she would need to be eliminated."

"Perhaps that is why he met with me alone last time," the great green dragon mused. "He may be aware of a plot against him."

"More than one, from the looks of things," his companion growled. "What should we do? I'm not telepathic, so even if I hear of anything, I can't reach out to you. I would have to pay another visit."

"Alas, so few dragons are."

"You speak to the girl, though," Jarrowan insisted.

"Yes, she is exceptionally talented. Look how the trolls fawn over her. You would think she was one of them. They have never brought in strangers so." Gazing down at the group, a dark thought formed in the back of his mind, one that he didn't dare to put into words. Instead, he reassured his visitor, "We will be fine. Keep to the plan, only speak to those you know harbor a desire to seek our new king's demise. We will build our army slow but sure."

"Yes, my captain," the other dragon agreed before leaping into the air to make his return to the cliffs.

Curling his long tail, Lamwen watched until the flames died away and the trolls made their way back into the woods. Considering their behavior, he couldn't help but wonder if the old troll had guessed who the girl was, and if he had, what it might cost them in the end.

Books in the Dragon of Eriden Series

.

Whisper of Suffering
Journey of Darkness
Betrayal of Honor
Kingdom of Ruin

Maps of Eriden & The Rim of Mortals

Kingdom of Eriden

New Aboolia
Crimson Caves
Aboolia
Heewan
Peaswan Desert
Whitefair
Western Coast
Forboding Forest
Esterbrook

Northern Woods
Rhong
Asomanee
Central Mountains
Shadowlands
Jerranyth

Adiarwen
Dragon Cliffs
Dragon Rock
Falconmarsh
Rocky Coast
Elflands
Biron

Characters by Race

Humans

Amicia Spicer is a young woman from Nalen discovering her true identity as the story unfolds. Her mother has revealed a secret about her origins upon her deathbed, and Ami is looking for the place she belongs in the world.

Reynard Daye is a young crewman aboard the Sea Serpent. He survives the destruction of the ship and joins the unlucky group of mortals as they crash upon the shores of Eriden.

Piers Massheby is the first mate aboard the Sea Serpent. He is a strong leader and guides the group through their perilous journey in search of a way home.

Baldwin Carter is the cabin boy on board the ship. He is mostly along for the ride, being young and inexperienced at handling the hardships that the group faces along the way.

Minor Human Characters:
    Rupert Miller – Amicia Spicer's friend from Nalen, he expects that she will become his betrothed when her parents no longer need her.
    Gus Spicer – Amicia's father.

Arely Spicer – Amicia's mother.
Shamus Smith – blacksmith in the desert city of Whitefair.
Geoffrey Tabard – trader from Whitefair.
Humphray Heron – trader from Whitefair.

Sirens

Olirassa is queen of the mermaids. She is the sovereign and protector of the city of Riran.

Oldrilin is Reynard Daye's caretaker in Riran. She becomes caught up in their escape and is swept away onto their adventure through Eriden. Her devotion to Rey is sincere, and she proves to be a valuable member of their group. She seems to have little magical ability but is able to transform into a large black fish.

Elves

Cilithrand is the queen of the elves. She resides in a magnificent palace in Jerranyth, located on the southern end of the elf lands, which consists of the lower end of the central mountains of Eriden.

Animir is an elf of higher class that has been outcast from his station. He no longer feels a part of his elf kin, and helps the group to escape Jerranyth, thereby joining them on their quest to find a way home. He had been banned from using his innate magical abilities, but with the freedom of the group, he explores his talents and regains his ability as a strong wielder of magic. A resourceful member of the group, they value his friendship and utility.

Minor Elf Characters:
    Sadrir – serves the group while they are in Jerranyth.
    Anerion – lead huntsman to Lady Cilithrand.
    Galiodien – Cilithrand's father and former king of the elves.
    Cothiel – female companion to Piers in Jerranyth.

Nymphs

Preivia is queen of the nymphs. She is the sovereign and protector of the city of Esterbrook and the surrounding areas known as the glen and the meadows.

Zaendra is an earth nymph. She is pleased to meet the group when they come into the glen and attaches herself to their company. Spending time with them while they reside in their cabin, she packs her things to leave with them at their departure, as she has always wanted to explore more of Eriden and sees this as her chance. She has some magical abilities and proves to be a valuable member of the group.

Wolves

Uscan is the alpha of the southern pack of grey wolves. His loyalties are often murky, but he holds an affinity for Amicia Spicer. He acts in her best interest both as a friend and advisor. As for the southern pack, they protect the Shadowlands, a cursed area of woods that acts as a natural barrier between the glen and the mountains of the elf lands.

Edeill is the alpha of the northern pack. His loyalties are also in question. His pack of great white wolves are the protectors of the northern woods, and they patrol a much larger area than their southern kin.

Minor Wolf Characters:
    Mirean – scout sent to Esterbrook for the southern pack.
    Aelalle – beta of the northern pack.

Wizards

Meena Gavaan is a wan, a female wizard, but unlike most, she was born with the ability to use magic, which is forbidden within their people. She has led a difficult life and faces tough choices throughout the story. She meets the group upon their arrival in the desert community of Whitefair and agrees to help them for a price. She leaves with them when they flee the oasis and travels with them on their journey, earning her place within the group with her special magical skill set and talent for using her powers in practical ways.

Minor Wizard Characters:

Jaco Gavaan – Meena's deceased husband.

Gradien Silversmith – magistrate of the wizard city of Whitefair, he is a powerful wizard, but also a bit of a scoundrel.

Corvack – head of the security force in Whitefair.

Trolls

Yaodus is the king of the trolls. He is a powerful wielder of magic, which is rare but not unheard of among the trolls. He is distrustful of everyone outside of their community and takes his role of protector of his kind with the utmost of dedication. He is an unlikely ally of the group after Amicia convinces him of her worth, and his help is often the difference between life and death for the mortals and their friends.

Traok is Yaodus's eldest son. He is met several times, as he acts as the liaison between the group and the troll community on several occasions.

Dwarves

Baeweth is the king of the city of Rhong. As their sovereign, he is the protector of the growing city beneath the mountain. However, his family and people have endured a great deal in the last few hundred years. They have denounced the use of magic and are rebuilding after a daemon drove them from their previous home of Asomanee.

Hayt is the king's great nephew and heir to the throne. He holds no desire to ever be king and devises a way to win the trust of the group, then helps them escape rather than see them handed over to the dragons. He is a skilled engineer, and his abilities and knowledge prove useful to the group on their quest.

Minor Dwarf Characters:

Asyng – the king's sister and Hayt's grandmother, she is Baeweth's advisor.

Firen – Hayt's good friend and fellow engineer.

Vael – Another acquaintance of Hayt's, he is the guard on duty when the group prepares to escape.

Daemons

Kedoria is the queen of the daemons. Her loyalties to the elves are shaken when she is captured by Animir and recruited by Amicia. She commands the daemon forces, but they are only able to live in total darkness, which severely limits her utility within the group. She has a few named minions, but they are only briefly mentioned in the events of the story.

Gnomes

Thirac is the sovereign or king of the gnomes, also called the head of the elders. He is untrustworthy and holds little concern for the Kingdom of Eriden. Their people watch events unfold and record them in their tomes, which are stored in their great libraries hidden inside of the old trees of the marsh lands.

Sevoassi is the gnome the group encounters in the northern woods. He is a trickster who helps them escape the northern pack and gives Amicia a special red orb of unknown origin or purpose.

Minor Gnome Characters:
   Ziyath (grumpy) – member of the order of the ossci, the highest and most powerful of the gnomes.
   Mizath (happy) – member of the order of the ossci, the highest and most powerful of the gnomes.
   Yimath – member of the order of the ossci, the highest and most powerful of the gnomes.

Dragons

Ziradon is Kaliwyn's father and rightful Supreme Dragon of Eriden. He is overthrown at the beginning of the story by Gwirwen, who imprisons him that he may suffer for the rest of his days. A powerful wielder of magic, he is seven hundred years of age. During his life, he has lost two wives and all of his sons. Princess Kaliwyn, his dragoness and heir to the throne, is all he has in the world.

Gwirwen is the current King of Eriden, but only because he was successful in taking over the throne. He is not as strong as Ziradon, and certainly not as wise. His poor choices lead to certain destruction, as the prophecy of the destroyer appears to be fulfilled by his doing.

Kaliwyn is the daughter of Ziradon and rightful heir to the throne of the Supreme Dragon of Eriden. Forced into the form of a mortal as a young dragoness, she is taken away to Nalen, where she is found and raised by human parents. She is not aware of her true self and must discover her dragon heart before it's too late.

Lamwen is the captain of the king's guard. He is assigned to protect the coast of the continent and leads the guard in that role. When the group makes it ashore, it is the guard's job to eliminate them. When their attempts prove unsuccessful, he is reassigned to spy on the group, where he learns of Amicia's identity. Becoming her friend and guardian, he is eventually welcomed by the travelers and becomes vital in their success.

Minor Dragon Characters:

Ziewen – female dragon, loyal to and eventually mated with Gwirwen.

Pardodan – loyal to Gwirwen, he longs to improve his rank in the king's guard.

Vaudien – loyal to Gwirwen, he takes Lamwen's place as captain of the king's guard when he is removed.

Kilawon – Kaliwyn's mother and Ziradon's late mate, who was murdered by Gwirwen.

Jarrowan – Lamwen's friend and supporter, he spends time with the group and even experiences human form for a few days.

Putwyn – a less than decisive member of Lamwen's followers who betrays him, then wishes to rejoin them. Most noted for helping the group escape the dragons by arranging for Baeweth to help them.

Onothwyn – a lesser member of the king's guard who helps to hunt the group.

About the Author

Anyone who knows me could tell you, I am a friendly kind of person, never met a stranger and take up conversations anywhere at any time. I work hard, and my mind never seems to shut down, as I wake up often in the middle of the night with ideas pouring out and demanding to be dealt with. Of course that means much of my books were written in the middle of the night.

I grew up and still live in the great state of Texas where everything is bigger, where we have warm weather and a central location. I love my state, my town, and my family, which includes my four sons, my significant other, and many friends as well.

I have thoroughly enjoyed writing this story and hope that you will love reading it just as much. And of course, there will be many more adventures to come.

You can follow Samantha Jacobey at:
Website: www.SamJacobey.com
Facebook: https://www.facebook.com/SamJacobey
Twitter: https://twitter.com/SamJacobey

Also by SAMANTHA JACOBEY

A New Life Series

http://myBook.to/ANewLifeSeries

An epic adventure, TORI FARRELL's life IS one wild story... escaped from a biker gang and running from drug lords... used by the FBI and hoping to protect her present from her past... IT'S DARK - IT'S BRUTAL, and it's WORTH EVERY MINUTE OF IT!! (Mature Adult, 18+)

Summer Spirit Novella Series

http://myBook.to/SummerSpiritSeries

No one EVER had a summer romance like this... Charlie visits another plane, parallel to our own, where Summer Angels and Dark Angels battle over the fate of man. A unique twist on an old idea that will keep you guessing; will Charlie and Clarisse ever find their HEA? (New adult)

Irrevocable Series

http://mybook.to/IrrevocableBoxedSet

From affluent beginnings, BAILEY DEWITT's life has become a broken mess... after her parents died unexpectedly, she didn't think it could get any worse. But when the arrogance of man catches up and puts the entire world into a dooms-day spiral, there will be only ONE PLACE she can run to - the ONE PLACE she wanted desperately to escape. (New Adult)

Teach Me to Prey

http://hyperurl.co/e9qs9f

In this standalone thriller, JASON TRUITT and his friends have gotten their way for years. Deceit, sex, and foul play aren't normally covered in the curriculum, but they're doing whatever it takes to get under BECKY STEWART's skin. When one of the boys turns up dead, it's a race against time to save the others; a STUNNING STORY that will get your heart racing and leave you breathless by the end... (New Adult)

The Wicked Awakened

http://hyperurl.co/2qsgl6

A Halloween novel; a five-hundred-year-old witch wants to turn SARAH MATTHEWS' body into her new home… A twisted tale involving a coven hell bent on seeing that she succeeds. Who will come out on top in this epic battle of wills? (Mature Adult, 18+)

The Binding

http://myBook.to/TheBinding

One cursed diary will change two strangers forever...Can Meri and Rider use her mother's old book to figure out why someone is after them? Or will the guilty party succeed, ripping the tome away before killing them and then slithering back into the darkness…

Also From Our Lavish Family

The Norn Novellas
A. Nicky Hjort
https://www.lavishpublishing.com/authors/nicky-hjort-1/

The Norn Novellas are all chapters in the epic saga of the youngest and most fickle of the four Norn Sisters. The same feisty immortal creature who must escape her inherent inner darkness to learn the meaning of life.

Each story takes a classic fairytale and spins it on its head, as we learn that maybe Norse Mythology was so much more than legend. And to think, you thought you knew those old tales so well.

Meet Za and find out what really happened...

When Tundra Turns to Ardnyt - Book 1: In the center of a magical world there grows a beautiful and terrible chasm of climbing plants. On one side of the Ivy Wall we find the hell-of-Tyndra, on the other, the heaven-of-Ardnyt. But legend has it that in the middle...lives a preternatural beast that imprisons and tortures the children from both sides.

When the war against time begins, Azza will have to cross over the Ivy Wall, something that has never been done before by a living being. But if she does make it through, she just might discover who she really is and how she became trapped in this alternate reality.

A fairytale at heart, this is the first chapter in the epic saga of the youngest and most fickle of the four Norn Sisters. The same feisty immortal creature who must escape her inherent inner darkness to learn the meaning of love.

A veritable palindrome from start to finish, the narrative of Where Tyndra Turns to Ardnyt journeys through duality to discover what shocking truths emerge when up becomes down, life becomes death, suffering becomes release, and the most unexpected endings become the most surprising beginnings.

Welcome to a place where forwards and backwards are exactly the same direction. Here Where Tyndra Turns to Ardnyt.

Where Ebon Sounds Like Ivory – book 2: Norse legend has it that the arms of the Yggdrasil tree—a sacred instrument of Odin—are ever-reaching, and its survival is necessary for life itself to continue.

During Winter's Solstice, when the search for her mortal mother begins, Za will have to cross over the Ebon Branch of the Dead—a feat that has supposedly never been survived intact. But if she does make it across and back home, she just might discover why she and the other three Norn Sisters of Fate came to be.

A fairytale at heart, this is the second chapter in the epic saga of the youngest and most fickle of the four Norn Sisters. The same feisty immortal creature who must discover her true origins to understand her inherent inner darkness. Only this way can she learn the meaning of unconditional sacrifice in the name of impenetrable love…when, as her destiny would have it, all the branches of such a powerful tree tremble treacherously in her tiny little hands.

A veritable unraveling of Snow White, the narrative of Where Ebon Sounds Like Ivory journeys through the most horrible of realms where shocking truths emerge. Here where death mimics life, obsession masquerades as devotion, and the most unexpected endings become the most surprising beginnings of a classic tale. One…you thought you knew so well.

Welcome to a place where the darkest of melodies births a miraculous tune of surrenderance. Here Where Ebon Sounds Like Ivory and Christmas, as we know it, begins.

Behind Blue Eyes Series
Sara J. Bernhardt
https://books2read.com/BlueEyesBeginner

A father's desire to save his child presents him with an unthinkable choice that leaves him darker than human, forced to roam through time alone as he searches for the place he belongs.

Adam Gold – Book 1: Fleeing the French invasion of Geneva Switzerland in the 1700s, Adam Gold books passage to America with his family. On the ship, Adam's daughter falls fatally ill. A mysterious man comes to Adam with a way to save his child by turning Adam into something darker than human.

The Medallion – Book 2: Adam Gold, an immortal with sweet eyes of blue, rushes through the centuries on a quest for reason and a thirst for revenge. To cope with his pain and regret, he sleeps away the years and awakes in a new era with a powerful, ancient vampire who sets her sights on him.

Golden Shackles – Book 3: When the ancient queen, Sekhmet snatches up Adam, he is faced with a terrifying decision. To help aid her in her vile plans or dare to stand against her.

Plus 3 more segments!